STAR NOMAD

STAR NOMAD

(Fallen Empire, Book 1)

LINDSAY BUROKER

ISBN: 153463455X
ISBN-13: 9781534634558

ACKNOWLEDGMENTS

As an author, it's super exciting to launch an all-new series. Regular readers may know me for my fantasy novels, but long before I found out about *The Hobbit* or Dungeons and Dragons, I watched *Buck Rogers* and the original *Star Trek* with my mom as a kid.

So far, I'm having a lot of fun writing this series, so I definitely hope you enjoy it. Before you jump in, let me thank Shelley Holloway, my editor, and Sarah Engelke, my steadfast beta reader who zipped through this in a week so I could make an ambitious publication date. I would also like to thank Tom Edwards for the great cover art.

CHAPTER ONE

A dark shape scurried through the shadows ahead, disappearing under the belly of a rusted spaceship. Alisa Marchenko halted, tightening her grip on her old Etcher 50. Rustling sounds came from beneath the ship, along with a low growl. Alisa hoped it was just another of the big rodents she'd seen earlier. Those weren't exactly friendly, but at least they didn't endanger anything higher up than her calves—so long as she remained standing.

Mica, her fellow scavenger on this self-appointed mission, bumped into her back, jostling her. Alisa caught herself on the hull of the rusty derelict and grimaced when her palm smacked against something moist and sticky. She wiped it on her trousers, glad for the dim lighting in the cavern.

"Sorry," Mica whispered, the shadows hiding her face, but not the fact that she carried a toolbox almost as big as she was. Alisa ought to have *her* leading the way—she could sling that box around with the authority of an assault rifle. "Can't we risk a light?" Mica added. "We might trip over some unexploded ordnance down here and blow ourselves up."

"I see your pessimism hasn't faded in the years since we served together."

"Pessimism is an admirable quality in an engineer. Pessimistic people check their work three times, because they're sure something won't be right. Optimistic people check once, trust in Solis-de to keep the ship safe, then blow everyone up."

"I think you're mistaking the word optimistic for inept."

"They've got a similar ring to my ear."

Alisa looked past Mica's short, tousled hair and toward the mouth of the massive cavern. The skeletons of dozens of junked ships stood between

1

them and the harsh red daylight of the desert outside. She was tempted to say yes to Mica's suggestion of light, but the sounds of punches and grunts arose less than fifty meters away. A guttural male voice cursed in one of the Old Earth languages, and someone cried out in pain. A juicy and final thump followed, making Alisa think of a star melon splatting open after falling from a rooftop. Men laughed, their voices rough and cruel.

"No light," Alisa whispered.

Mica shrugged, tools clinking faintly in her box. "You're the captain."

"Not unless this works, I'm not."

"I thought you got promoted at the end of the war."

"I did, but the war's over," Alisa said.

The war was over, and the Alliance had forgotten about her in the aftermath, leaving her in the hands of the dubious medical care available from the local facilities. Alisa had eventually recovered after spending a month in a dilapidated turn-of-the-century regeneration tank and two months learning to walk again, but she had little more than the clothes on her back. Worse, she was stranded on this dustball of a planet, billions of miles from her home—from her daughter.

Her fingers strayed toward a pocket with an envelope in it, one of her few possessions. It contained a letter from her sister-in-law Sylvia, a letter written by hand in a time when most communications were electronic, a letter that had taken weeks to find her in the hospital, a letter that explained that her husband had died in the final bombings of Perun Central. Only knowing that her eight-year-old daughter still lived and was staying with Sylvia on Perun had given Alisa the strength to endure the months of rehabilitation and the weeks of scrounging and planning to reach this place, to come up with a way to get back home.

Mica started to respond to her comment, but Alisa turned her back to end the conversation and continued picking her way through the junk piles. Talking was not wise, not down here.

More noises came from the wreckage all around them, including a chewing sound that Alisa found unnerving. A few more steps, and she heard something being dragged through the fine dust on the cavern floor, dust that drifted upward with her steps, teasing her nostrils, making her want to sneeze. She pinched her nose, having no delusions that the men hiding in here were anything but criminals, criminals who wouldn't care that she had helped free them from the oppression and tyranny of the empire.

As they drew farther from the entrance, the smell of the junk cavern grew stronger, scents of rust and oil and burned wires, but also of butchered meat and carcasses left to the animal scavengers. Alisa was tempted to keep pinching her nostrils shut.

"Are you sure you know where you're going?" Mica whispered.

"I know where I left the ship six years ago."

"That's a no, right?"

"The engine was smoking by the time I made it in here. I doubt anyone fixed it up to move her." Another clunk came from the darkness, and Alisa added, "Talk later."

Soft growls and snarls came from the path ahead. Alisa made herself continue onward. The creatures making the noises did not sound large.

She caught herself reaching toward the side of her head, to tap on the earstar that had hung there like jewelry for so much of her life. Assuming the satellites were still in orbit on Dustor, she could have used it to call up a map of their surroundings, but she had lost it in the crash. Mica did not wear one, either—she'd said she sold hers for food. Apparently, computer and communications tech was easier for her to give up than her tools.

Alisa's toe bumped into something on the narrow path. It did not feel like a rock or piece of debris. She started to step over it, not wanting to know the details.

A beam of light flashed up ahead, someone heading down the path toward them. Alisa stepped back and grabbed Mica's shoulder, pushing her toward wreckage to the side of them.

"Hide," she breathed.

The light was definitely coming in their direction.

Mica found something to crawl under. On the opposite side of the path, Alisa patted around a pile of dusty reels of cable of all different sizes, the mound rising well above her head. She squeezed between it and something large, poky, and metal. There wasn't room to get more than a couple of feet off the path. She hoped that whoever had the light did not look around.

The beam of light approached, angled down toward the ground from someone's earstar. The footfalls of several people accompanied it.

Alisa squeezed more tightly into her spot, turning her head from the path, not wanting her eyes to reflect the light. A few male grumbles and curses reached her ears as the men navigated the route, bumping into things, kicking dented cans out of the way.

Before the group reached her, their light played across the thing she had bumped into on the path. A human body, that of a woman. The clothing was ripped, flesh torn away by some hungry animal, but the sightless eyes remained open, an expression of utter terror frozen in them.

Alisa closed her own eyes, not wanting to see, not wanting to wonder if she, too, had been driven down here by desperation, searching for a way off this world.

The men with the light continued down the path without slowing. A faint *tink* came from the other side, and Alisa winced. She didn't think Mica had been foolish enough to make noise—there was probably another rat poking around behind her—but the sound might cause someone to look in that direction.

The men stepped over the body without slowing. Alisa watched them out of her peripheral vision, noting the scarred, bearded faces, the greasy hair, the tattoos, and the weapons they carried, a mishmash of daggers, shotguns, BlazTeck energy particle weapons, and rifles collected from who knew where. One carried an e-cannon that looked like it had been torn off one of the ships and modified for hand use. Alisa reminded herself that she, too, was armed, with the Etcher she had traded for, but it carried bullets rather than battery packs, and if she fired it, everyone in the cavern would hear.

The greasy men continued down the path, and she allowed herself to relax an iota. She waited until the light had disappeared and the sounds of footfalls had faded before easing out of hiding. Her long braid of dark brown hair got caught on a protruding piece of scrap, and she resolved to have it cut as soon as she had money. Whenever that would be.

"Blessing of the Suns Trinity," she whispered for the fallen woman's soul, then stepped past the corpse. "Mica?"

"I'm here." Her voice sounded subdued, perhaps because she, too, had seen the body.

The path opened up as they continued down it, hurrying in the opposite direction from the men. An old conveyer belt stretched across a cleared area, with the skeletal shape of a crane rising up from the shadows. Alisa's heart sped up with anticipation. She remembered walking past this spot on her way out of the cavern years ago.

A gasp came from behind her, followed by the sound of something clunking to the ground.

Alisa whirled around, raising her gun. The darkness lay thick along the path, towers of junk stacked high to either side, and she couldn't see much.

"Mica?" Alisa risked whispering. That had sounded like her gasp.

A flash came from the side, followed by the scent of burning tar. A homemade fire starter had been thrown to the ground, and flames leaped up, bright enough to reveal Mica—and the big man holding her with his hand around her neck. A wiry man stood at his side, his hand blazer pointed at Alisa. Mica's toolbox lay on its side in the dust at her feet. She struggled briefly, then grew still as her captor's grip tightened. An utterly pissed expression contorted the angular features of her face.

Alisa admired her lack of fear, but felt a twinge of disappointment that her comrade had let herself be captured so easily. As a pilot, Alisa had fast reflexes in the sky, but she doubted she could shoot both men before the one with the blazer shot her.

"Thought I heard something," the big man holding her crooned. He was one of the ones who had walked past them, with so many scars on his bare arms and face that they must have been self-inflicted. Despite his height, his features were gaunt, with no fat under the stringy flesh of those arms. "Got some pretties to add to our collection. This one feels good. Be fun to cut on her a little." He leered and shifted his grip so he could grope Mica's breast. "Spider, get that one's gun. Can't be having some girl shooting at us while we're working our art."

Mica radiated fury, and she tried to bash her head back and hit her captor in the face, but he was too tall. She stomped on his foot, but he wore hard boots and didn't seem to feel it.

The wiry man grinned, displaying a mouth of missing teeth, and bounced up and down. He did not speak but took a step forward, holding out his free hand as he kept his blazer pointed at Alisa's chest. She kept her Etcher pointed at his chest, too, assessing him in the dancing firelight. His chest looked stockier than his narrow frame would have suggested.

Was he wearing body armor under his clothes? On the chance that it might deflect bullets, she shifted her aim to his eye. He halted, squinting at her, and twitched his free hand toward his big comrade.

"Why don't you release my engineer and let us go about our business?" Alisa asked, trying to sound calm and reasonable. "We fought for the Alliance. We're not your enemies." Or your playthings, she added silently, horrified at the idea. She doubted talking would do any good, but maybe it would buy her a moment to think of something better to do.

"Alliance doesn't mean worm suck down here," the big man said. "Empire, Alliance, it doesn't matter who's in charge. None of them make it easier to find food around here. Spider, a girl's not going to shoot you. Get her damned gun."

Alisa *didn't* want to shoot them, not when it would alert everyone in the cavern to their presence. She was also well aware that she wasn't wearing body armor or anything else that would deflect attacks.

"Oh, she'll shoot you," Mica wheezed, not as daunted as one might expect by the hand around her throat. The big man had her arms pinned, but she eased her fingers toward her shirt pocket so she could reach it. "She *likes* shooting people. Mostly imperial asteroid kissers, but I bet she'll make exceptions for greasy troglodytes whose only memories of bathtubs come from their ancestors who colonized this hole."

Spider had started toward Alisa, but he paused at Mica's words. More the part about Alisa's willingness to shoot him, rather than that bathtub insult, she wagered.

"Enh, just blow her away, Spider," the big man said. "Ain't worth getting killed trying to steal a *veruska's* stinger."

The wiry man nodded firmly, his hand tightening on his trigger. Seeing the determination in his eyes, Alisa fired first, then flung herself to the side. She rolled under the conveyer belt as a crimson blazer bolt streaked through the air where her head had been. Spider shouted in pain, but Alisa knew she'd only struck a glancing blow, if that. She prayed the hulking man wouldn't break Mica's neck as she scrambled into the shadows, expecting Spider to fire again.

Instead, a boom erupted from nearby, the noise hammering at Alisa's eardrums. One of the men yowled, the sound a mingle of frustration and agony.

Alisa couldn't tell which one it had been. She rose to a crouch behind a support under the conveyer belt, using it for cover as she sought a target. Acrid blue smoke filled the air from whatever explosive had been detonated.

Spider rolled about on the ground, almost smothering the flames from the fire starter. He clutched his ear, blood streaming between his fingers, his mouth open as if he were screaming, but nothing came out. Alisa had landed a better shot than she'd thought.

Despite his pain, Spider hadn't dropped his gun, and even as Alisa lined up her aim for another shot, he glimpsed her through smoky air. He fired wildly in her direction.

She ducked back and targeted him through the support legs. Though a blazer bolt slammed into the belt a few feet away, sending shards of the machinery flying, she forced herself to find the calm in the chaos, to take a careful second to ensure her aim was true. She fired once.

Her bullet slammed into Spider's forehead, and his head flew back, striking the earth and sending a puff of dust into the air. His arm fell limp, landing in the flames. He didn't move it, and the smell of burning clothing and flesh soon scented the air along with the acrid taint of the smoke. Alisa grimaced. The war had taught her to kill, but she would never find it anything but horrifying.

Mica and the big man had disappeared, only her toolbox remaining, along with a dark smudge in the dust next to it. Alisa hopped over the conveyer belt to investigate, aware of shouts coming from all parts of the cavern. Most were inarticulate, a few in languages she couldn't understand, but an enthusiastic call of, "Fresh meat!" made her shudder.

She couldn't stay around here, but she couldn't leave Mica, either. She was cursing herself for not seeing which direction they had gone when she glimpsed the remains of a warped casing on the ground. She picked it up, sniffed it, and dropped it immediately, the pungent scent familiar. Her fingers tingled from the brief contact.

A shuffling came from piles of scrap, and Mica walked into view, rubbing her neck and grimacing. "Animal."

"Was that a rust bang?" Alisa asked, remembering the explosives the ground troops had often led with when assaulting imperial ships and fortifications. The acidic smoke could corrode even state-of-the-art combat armor. It was not as deadly to skin, but she'd seen people horribly disfigured and even killed from close contact.

"Sort of a homemade version."

"That you kept in your pocket?"

"I keep lots of useful things in my pockets." Mica picked up her tool-box, and they moved away from the body and the still-burning fire starter. "Don't you?"

"I have half a chocolate bar and three tindarks in mine."

"How'd you get chocolate in this hole?"

"I traded the painkillers the hospital gave me before kicking me out." The medicine was highly coveted out in the lawless streets of the backwater planet, and Alisa had gotten her Etcher and a multitool out of the deal too.

"You didn't need the painkillers?" Mica asked.

"Not as much as I needed the chocolate."

"You're an odd woman."

"Says the engineer who carries rust bangs in her pockets. How did you manage to use one of those on that big brute without being hurt yourself?" As they walked, Alisa waved at Mica's rumpled overalls, as faded and stained as hers—it hadn't been an easy five months for either of them. Those over-alls weren't any more damaged, however, than they had been when they'd headed into the cavern. "You appear remarkably un-corroded."

"The rust bang was insulated."

"How?"

"It went off in his pants."

"Ah. How did it get in there?"

"Must have fallen in." Mica's typically dour expression faded for a moment as she winked. "You rolling around in the dust and shooting people was a suitable distraction for it to do so."

"Glad to hear it."

Alisa managed a brief smile, amused that she had been worried her ally couldn't take care of herself.

Lights flashed on the rocky ceiling far overhead, and the sounds of excited shouts grew closer. Shoes pounded in the dust nearby, reminding Alisa that they had made a lot of noise.

She turned her walk into a run, veering toward an aisle choked with piles of parts and some kind of vine that had no trouble growing in the dark. Though she worried that the half-starved brutes who called this place home would catch up with them, she felt more sure of her route now. The aisle had been a road the last time she'd been in here, with the place slightly more organized back then, and with fewer corpses along the way.

A gun fired behind them, and the sounds of a squabble broke out. Alisa hoped the scavengers would be satisfied that they could search—or eat—Spider's corpse and wouldn't look further, but she didn't slow down. She couldn't count on that, nor could she count on safety once she reached the *Star Nomad*. It had been inches from derelict status when she'd seen it last; the Suns Trinity only knew what condition it was in now. She was probably delusional to believe that Mica and her toolbox could fix it.

As they neared the back of the massive cavern, the shouts growing distant behind them, Alisa finally slowed down. Her lungs forced her to, even if her brain didn't want to acknowledge the need. It was just as well. They ought to return to proceeding with caution.

"Is that it?" Mica whispered, pointing past Alisa's shoulder.

They had reached another clearing, this one with a slender beam of daylight slashing down from a hole in the cavern ceiling. It provided just enough illumination to make out the hulls of four ships parked around the area. Grease and oil stains smeared the dusty ground in the open space, suggesting a fifth ship had rested there once. If one craft had flown out of here, Alisa hoped that meant another one could.

She stopped to stare at the familiar shape on the far side of the clearing, a tangle of emotions and memories washing over her. This ship had been responsible for her mother's death, and six years hadn't changed Alisa's feeling of aversion toward it. Aversion and resentment. The clunky old freighter was even less impressive than she'd remembered.

The *Nomad* hadn't been a beauty even in her heyday, and now dust dulled it further, coating every inch of the boxy hull while cobwebs draped the twin thrusters. Shadows hid the top and the front of the craft from her view, but she knew they would be equally neglected. She and Mica would have to assess the hull carefully, see if it was possible to make the craft spaceworthy again. Alisa ought to be able to advise her engineer on that. She certainly knew the *Nomad* well enough. Long before her mother's death, Alisa had grown up on the ship, learning to fly and helping her mother run cargo from planet to moon to space station throughout the system. Under the empire's rule, her mother had been forced to pay taxes and tolls at each port and had barely eked out enough of a profit to keep her ship in the sky and her daughter fed. But through sheer determination, she *had* kept Alisa fed. She had been a good mother—a good person—and emotion thickened Alisa's throat as the years seemed to slip away, and she missed her anew. And she once again resented that the old ship had given out without warning, life support disappearing, her mother unable to—

"Captain?" Mica asked.

Alisa stirred, pushing aside the memories. "Yes. That's it."

She took a deep breath and walked through the dust toward the craft. She went slowly, looking left and right as she crossed near the light of the sunbeam. Just because they had left the other scavengers behind didn't mean there couldn't be more back here. The hatch was closed on the old freighter, the wide cargo-loading ramp folded away inside.

A bronze plaque had been bolted to the hull next to the hatch. It was too dusty to read, but she knew what it said: *Property of Finnegan's Scrap and Holding Company.*

She had been there the day old Finnegan had affixed it, the day she sold the ship to him. Even if she had been grossly underpaid by the unscrupulous businessman, Alisa hadn't been in the mood to argue back then, not with her mother's death fresh in her mind. Still, she knew she couldn't use that for justification of what she meant to do now. Steal it.

But Finnegan had died in the bombings of Dustor's nearby capital— she'd researched that when formulating this plan—and nobody had come out to claim this junkyard in the year that had passed since then. People had likely been stealing from it for months, ever since the security guards had quit patrolling and the lowlifes had moved in.

As she neared the hatch, a growl came from under one of the other ships. As she turned to look, something furry with a spiky ridge along its back burst out of the shadows. A sand badger. Forty pounds of fangs, fur, and bad temperament. It sprinted straight at her, snarling.

Alisa whipped her Etcher toward it and was an instant from shooting when she remembered the need to be quiet. If she fired, the noise would only draw more scavengers, and she couldn't simply run and hide now. They had to stay here long enough to fix the *Nomad* and get it flying.

Jerking the gun up, Alisa met the giant badger's charge with a side kick instead of a bullet. She pivoted on her left foot, launching her right toward the thing's bristly snout, glad the hospital had returned her sturdy boots to her upon release. The sole crunched into the badger's face, halting its charge but not its ferocity. It twisted its neck, snapping at her leg as she retracted it. She launched a second kick without setting down her foot. This time, it saw the attack coming and scuttled to the side more quickly than something with such short legs should have been able to.

As she danced away from another charge, Alisa yanked her multitool off her belt, flicking it to extend the laser knife. Mica ran in behind the creature, an oversized wrench in hand. When Alisa kicked the badger in the snout again, Mica lunged in and clubbed it in the back. The blow probably didn't do much harm, but it made the sand badger spin around, its spiked tail nearly whipping Alisa in the leg. The creature snarled and charged toward Mica, who scrambled back as she waved the wrench back and forth like a fencer's foil.

Alisa sprang after the badger, slashing with the laser knife. It cut through the spiked tail, lopping it off and eliciting a squeal of pain from the animal.

She winced at the noise and darted in, hoping to finish it off, but the badger was done fighting. It scurried back into the shadows, leaving a trail of blood in the dust.

Alisa let it go, doubting she could have caught it anyway. As she stood, gun in one hand and multitool in the other, she tried to slow her breathing so she could listen and hear if anyone was coming. All that filled her ears was the sound of her own ragged breaths. She hadn't recovered her stamina yet, and it annoyed her how long it took for her breathing to return to normal.

Mica returned her wrench to her toolbox and joined her. "Remember how skeptical I was when you told me that if I joined you, we'd find a ship that could take us back to civilization?"

"Yes." Alisa flicked the multitool again, retracting the laser blade and sticking it back in her belt sheath.

"I wasn't skeptical enough." Mica curled a lip at the bloody stump of badger tail lying in the dust, then looked at the freighter and curled her lip even further. "A Nebula Rambler 880? They stopped making those fifty *years* ago."

"That just means it's a classic," Alisa said, though she couldn't help but remember how her mother had died and shudder. The ship had gone from feeling like home to a cemetery overnight for her.

But it was the only ship she was going to find that nobody else had a claim on and that might still be spaceworthy. Assuming they could fix it. And assuming it had enough juice left in the battery to open the hatch so they could get in. She wondered if it would still recognize her as an authorized entrant.

"Yeah?" Mica asked. "Does it have shag carpet?"

"Just in the rec room."

Mica snorted.

Alisa reached for the sensor panel beside the hatch.

A shadow dropped from the sky.

She sprang back, jerking her gun toward the figure that landed beside her. A hand, an impossibly strong hand, clamped onto her wrist, squeezing until she gasped, her fingers loosening. Her gun was torn from her grip, and she was thrust backward before she could contemplate a kick or a punch.

The force of the thrust stole her balance, and she tumbled to the ground. Though she managed to turn the fall into a roll and come up in a crouch a few feet away, it didn't matter. She'd lost her Etcher, and she was too far away to use the laser knife. Not that it would have mattered. Dread filled her as she recognized her opponent—and the fact that he was pointing her own gun at her.

CHAPTER TWO

He was a cyborg.

Oh, he looked fully human, with icy blue eyes, a strong jaw in need of shaving, and black hair even more in need of cutting, but humans didn't jump thirty feet from the top of a spaceship, land on their feet next to a person, and proceed to attack so quickly that an Alliance officer with combat training didn't have time to react. If there had been any question about his enhanced capabilities, the dusty black imperial fleet uniform jacket that he wore would have eliminated them. The rank pins had been removed from the collar, but the front of it was covered with patches that denoted a deluge of training, everything from atmo-parachuting to weapons and demolitions expertise. There was also a round patch with a fist over a sword and a shield. The symbol for the Cyborg Corps.

Alisa had lost colleagues to the Cyborg Corps during the war, and like all Alliance soldiers, she had heard the rumors that they had been responsible for the assassinations of many of their top brass and several political leaders. This cyborg wasn't young—he had a few gray hairs at his temples—so he had probably been a senior sergeant. He might even have led some of those assassination teams.

There was no warmth in the eyes that stared relentlessly into hers, and they were uncomfortably knowing, as if he could read her mind. Not likely—she had never heard of a cyborg with Starseer capabilities—but that didn't make her feel any better.

"You'll have to get him to turn around," Mica said.

She stood several feet away, her toolbox still in hand. The cyborg hadn't pointed a weapon at her. Yet.

"What?" Alisa asked, never taking her gaze from her enemy.

She didn't know what she could do if he decided to shoot—his reflexes and aim would be a lot better than those of the wiry thug they had left burning—but she would face him, regardless, keep her chin high. Whatever skills and abilities he possessed, his side had lost the war. Her people, comprised only of full-blooded humans, had won.

"You know," Mica said, "so I can club him in the back like I did the badger."

"Ah," Alisa said, watching the cyborg's face, looking for some hint that he might appreciate their humor—or at least that he wasn't contemplating killing them.

She rose slowly from her crouch, not liking the way he could look down at her. Unfortunately, he still looked down at her. She wasn't a short woman, standing a couple of inches shy of six feet, but he still had six or eight inches on her. The breadth of his shoulders and solidness of his limbs made her sure he would have been an intimidating man even without the cyborg implants. The imperial fleet doctors had probably loved getting their hands on him.

He tracked her movement, his gaze flicking downward briefly, taking in her uniform jacket, she suspected, not checking out her boobs. He wasn't the only one wearing signs of his last career. Though her worn trousers and shirt weren't anything remarkable, she wore the same jacket she had worn throughout the war, a mottled blue and gray Alliance military jacket. She didn't have as many patches as he did, but the one on her left breast proclaimed her a combat pilot. He might even now be wondering if she'd blown up some of his buddies. She wouldn't be surprised if she had, but it would have been from the cockpit of her Striker-18, not from the ground.

"Go away," the cyborg said, his voice as hard as his eyes.

Mica looked at her, her brows rising in surprise. She wore civilian clothes, and the cyborg had barely glanced at her, but she must have noticed him checking out Alisa's uniform jacket. Maybe she'd expected him to shoot her.

Honestly, Alisa had expected it too. In the brief weeks she had been out of the hospital, she'd noticed that the end of the war hadn't meant an end in hostilities, not here on a planet that housed both former Alliance and former imperial soldiers, many squabbling over what was no longer claimed or defendable by law.

"Go away?" Alisa asked, not because she hadn't understood him but because she *couldn't* go away. She had come for the ship he was standing in front of, and she wouldn't leave without it. Would it be better to admit that and try to bargain with him, or to hide in the shadows and watch from a distance, hoping *he* would leave eventually? "We just got here. We're interested in…"

She trailed off because the cyborg had turned away from her. He waved his hand at the sensor she had been angling toward earlier, and a *hiss-clunk* sounded as the hatch opened, and the ramp inside unfolded in three stages, the end coming to rest on the ground.

She didn't know whether she was more indignant that he'd dismissed her as a non-threat by turning his back or because he'd somehow gained access to the ship. The latter wasn't all *that* hard, but it did suggest computer knowledge she wouldn't have expected from a ground soldier, cyborg or not. They were usually combat specialists and not much more.

He tossed her gun at her feet and stepped onto the ramp, clearly intending to go inside and shut the hatch on them.

"Wait," Alisa blurted. She ran and picked up her gun and started toward the ramp. "We came to—"

She halted mid-sentence again, this time because he'd paused, turning back toward her, another weapon in hand. *His* weapon, this time. A single-barreled destroyer, a handgun that had the nickname "hand cannon" for a reason. It was the first thing in the cavern she had seen that wasn't dusty and neglected, and it was pointing between her eyes.

"I said, *go away*," the cyborg said, his tone and his narrowed eyes promising that he would shoot if she lifted her gun toward him or tried to follow him.

"I can't," Alisa said, though she probably should have opted for her earlier thought of hiding and simply waiting for him to leave. But it would take days for Mica to fix the ship, if not weeks, and if he was squatting here, they would have to deal with him one way or another. "We need this ship." She waved to the *Star Nomad*, careful to use the hand that wasn't holding the Etcher. That she kept pointed toward the ground.

"It's mine," he said.

"Technically, it's Finnegan's," Alisa said, wondering if he knew anything about the junkyard or the history of the place.

"He's not here. I am."

"Look, we plan to fix it." Alisa didn't know how wise it was to share their plans, but she waved at Mica and her toolbox anyway. "I'll happily trade you that lovely ship over there for this one. It's *bigger*. I happen to know the living quarters are cramped on this freighter. All of the extra space went to the cargo hold. You'll find that ship over there much more palatial. You're a tall fellow, right? Surely a little more headroom would be desirable. My friend there could even fix it up for you, perhaps put in some sparkly lights and heated bunks. You can bring back the ladies and impress them with your fancy lodgings."

She thought a little humor might draw the cyborg into a conversation— or at least a negotiation—but if anything, his eyes grew even harder at the talk of ladies and lodgings.

"You make me sound like a contractor that builds brothels," Mica muttered.

"You're versatile. I've seen your work."

The cyborg turned his back and started up the ramp again, but some new thought must have occurred to him because he paused and pinned Mica with his cool stare. "You're a mechanic?"

"An engineer. I served in—"

Alisa made a shushing motion. The cyborg already knew what she was, but it would be better not to increase his ire by letting him know Mica had been an Alliance officer too. If he was unaware of that, maybe he would be open to working a deal with *her*, if not Alisa.

"She's a mechanic *and* an engineer," Alisa said. "She can fix anything. Got a creak in any of your mechanical parts? I bet she can even fix you."

The cyborg's eyes narrowed again.

"Your jokes aren't helping as much as you seem to think they are," Mica whispered to her. "I believe he's going to shoot you."

Alisa thought about mentioning how charming Mica's pessimism was, but was afraid she was right. Instead of trying to be funny, Alisa met the cyborg's eyes and decided to make a plea toward his humanity, if he had any.

"Please listen to me for a moment, Sergeant, is it?" she guessed. He definitely had the look of a no-nonsense veteran, and she hadn't run into many officers among the Cyborg Corps—despite being willing to use cyborgs, the imperial fleet had always seemed to prefer fully human officers in leadership positions. When he didn't respond to her guess, Alisa pressed on. "This ship used to belong to me. I know it from nose to tail, because I grew up on it. I brought Mica here to see if we can get it fixed up and into the air. As you might have noticed, rides off this planet are scarce right now."

Alisa figured he had been stranded here after the war, too, left behind because of an injury or perhaps just left behind because there had been nobody left to look after—and pay—the soldiers in the imperial fleet.

"I know exactly what's wrong with the ship," Alisa said, pressing on when he once again did not respond, "and I believe fixing it is possible." If nothing else had been done to it in the last six years. Seeing that the cyborg had access made her worry that others had found access and might have been inside, scavenging every last piece of the ship's innards. "We want to fix it and take it off this planet. If you're just making a home inside there, then I was serious in my offer. We'll help you fix up another place to live, any ship here that you want."

"To where?" he asked.

It took Alisa a moment to realize he was asking where they intended to go.

"Teravia," she said, lying. There was no way she was giving him her flight plan.

Those already narrowed eyes closed to slits, and she was reminded that he was pointing his gun at her chest. She expected him to accuse her of lying, but instead, he asked, "You willing to stop in the Trajean Asteroid Belt on the way?"

"On the way? The T-Belt isn't on the way to anything except the Dark Reaches."

"You want to get on this ship, you'll *make* it on the way. To *Teravia*," he added, putting emphasis on the name. Yeah, he knew she was lying.

It didn't matter if she was lying. The T-Belt wasn't on the way to her real destination of Perun, either. Taking that diversion would add a minimum of ten days to her trip.

Alisa closed her eyes, seeing her daughter's face in her mind. Even though it had already been well over a year since she'd been able to get home to see Jelena, she hated the idea of extending that absence any longer than necessary now that the war was over and her service to the Alliance was fulfilled. Especially now that she knew Jonah was gone and that their daughter was staying with an aunt whose inner-city artist's loft wouldn't be an ideal place for raising a child.

"Ah, Cap—Alisa," Mica whispered. "Mind if I have a word with you?" She eyed the cyborg, then jerked her chin toward one of the other ships.

"Give us a moment to discuss our flight plans," Alisa told the cyborg, then added a, "Please," remembering that she'd decided to be reasonable with him. Reasonable people said please and thank you, even when dealing with the enemy.

The cyborg said nothing, merely leaned against one of the support posts that lowered the ramp from the side of the ship. He folded his arms, his destroyer still in one hand, his expression one of indifference. Alisa didn't know if it was a mask or not. He had seemed vaguely interested when he'd learned Mica was an engineer, and it sounded like he wanted a ride. Interestingly, he wanted a ride somewhere specific and remote. Most other people just wanted to get the hells off this dustball.

"You don't want to go asteroid hopping?" Alisa asked when she and Mica were out of earshot. She didn't think her colleague would mind the delay since she didn't have a pressing need to return to Perun the way Alisa did.

"With a cyborg? Are you spaced? What if he decides to shoot us once we get to wherever he wants to go? Or what if he gets an itch and rapes one of us? Both of us. Hells, we can't outfight him. Did you see how fast he took your gun away?"

"I'm trying to forget, thank you."

"If we were stuck on the ship with him, we'd have no place to escape. There's nowhere to run, not like here." Mica waved toward the shadows.

"On the ship, off the ship, if he didn't want us to escape, nothing would keep him from running us down," Alisa pointed out, aware of how fast cyborgs were on foot.

But, even though she made the argument, she had to concede to Mica's point. There wouldn't be anything to keep him from taking over once the ship was fixed and they were in the air. And what kind of loon wanted to go to the T-Belt, anyway? There was nothing out there except automated drilling stations and smuggler and pirate hideouts. Showing up there in a clunky freighter without a weapons system wouldn't be wise. From what she'd heard, even heading to Perun would be a risk these days.

"He's probably fantasizing about shooting you right now," Mica whispered, glancing at the cyborg. He hadn't changed position. He was looking out into the cavern rather than at them. "Whatever he was in the imperial fleet, I bet it wasn't a homeless vagabond forced to squat in a junkyard full of cannibalistic maniacs. We were on the side that drove him to this. Don't think he won't resent us."

Alisa couldn't accuse Mica of being overly pessimistic this time. In all likelihood, she was right.

Still…

"I don't see what choice we have," Alisa said. "He doesn't look like he's moving."

"We'll take another ship then."

"*What* ship?" Alisa waved at the sea of dust, rust, and shadows surrounding them. "These are all derelicts in here—they probably didn't fly when they were brought in, and they've surely been scavenged to the core and back since then. The *Nomad* is—was…The engine was still working and the hull was intact. I didn't sell her because she was in poor condition."

Mica sighed. "I know. You told me. But that was then. We don't know what condition she's in now."

"She's the most likely ship in here to ever fly again. Listen, I'd actually been thinking of taking on some passengers, anyway, if we can get her working. We need money for supplies, and people would line up for miles at a chance to get off this world and back to one of the core planets."

"Oh, I know *that*, but how many of those people could actually pay? You may not have noticed, but Flint Face over there didn't offer to drop any tindarks in your purse."

"I know, but others might, and if we have paying passengers, we could use their money to hire a couple of security men, too. Some beefy brutes who could stand between him and us." Alisa pointed her thumb toward the cyborg.

"You really think a rent-a-guard is going to be a match for an imperial cyborg?"

"Maybe not, but if we had a crew and passengers, he might be less likely to try something…untoward."

Alisa couldn't help but think of Mica's earlier words of rape and killing. Was she being naive in contemplating this? Did they have any other choice? It wasn't as if she had the money to *buy* a ship, even if there had been any available on Dustor. What little she had received from Finnegan all those years ago had gone toward the down payment on the apartment that she and Jonah had purchased, an apartment that had apparently been incinerated by bombs. The virtual financial system was a mess these days, with accounts no longer being accessible across the sys-net, so the three coins in her pocket were all she had to her name. Technically, she ought to still have some money in her bank account on Perun, but what remained of the empire had settled in there, and as an Alliance soldier, she wouldn't be welcome. She had no idea how she was going to get in to find her daughter, but she had a week's voyage to figure it out. Now, she would have a week and ten days.

"Untoward." Mica curled her lip. "You know what's worse than an optimistic engineer?"

"An optimistic captain?"

"Exactly."

Alisa left Mica grumbling to her toolbox and approached the cyborg again. "You'll be pleased to know that we've decided that we would be fools not to visit the magnificent wonders of the Trajean Asteroid Belt before heading to our final destination."

She expected the cyborg to say, "Good," or something of that ilk. Instead, he grunted and walked inside.

"Oh, yes. It's going to be fun playing Carts and Chutes with him in the rec room during the evenings."

CHAPTER THREE

The cyborg never left the ship.

It had crossed Alisa's mind that if he ever did, she and Mica could maroon him here, assuming they got the *Star Nomad* working. After all, she hadn't given her word that she would take him, and it wasn't as if he had done her any favors. Letting her onto a ship that she had as much right to be on as he did not qualify. But he never left.

He had claimed one of the small crew cabins for himself, and Alisa hadn't presumed to open the hatch to peek inside. He didn't speak to them unless asked a question, and it wasn't guaranteed even then. After three days, Alisa still did not know his name, though she had asked once, figuring he would be less likely to shoot them later on if he came to know them. So far, he hadn't shown any interest in knowing them.

Alisa assumed he had a box of ration bars or ready-meals in his cabin, because he never visited the mess hall, not that there was much reason to. To save power until they could get the main engine online and fueled up, Mica hadn't turned on electricity to the non-essential parts of the ship, and there wasn't any food in the refrigerator. All Alisa and Mica had were ration bars and pouches of dehydrated vegetable patties with the texture of sawdust. If they managed to fly the ship into town and find some paying passengers, they could buy better supplies for the trip.

"Captain?" Mica asked one afternoon when Alisa's determination to clean all of the dust, cobwebs, and rat droppings out of the ship took her through engineering with a mop. Mica slid out from under a console, her short hair even more tousled than usual, though her worried expression was probably a result of more than hair woes.

"How're we doing?" Alisa crouched beside her, a tendril of unease worming through her stomach.

Even though Mica had done a thorough analysis of the ship on the first day, Alisa kept expecting her engineer to stumble across something that would keep the *Nomad* grounded indefinitely. Finding parts for the craft hadn't been easy even before the war, and if it turned out they needed something proprietary that couldn't be made in the little machine shop in the back of the engineering room, well…the odds of finding it on Dustor were not good. Further, from what she had heard, mail-order was out of the question these days. She was lucky her sister-in-law's letter had reached her.

"There are peculiarities," Mica said, glancing toward the hatchway, as if she expected the cyborg to be lurking there.

He wasn't. Alisa had stumbled across him doing pull-ups from a bar in the cargo hold that morning, but he was far scarcer than the rat droppings, and despite his interest in getting off-planet, he hadn't shown any curiosity as far as the repairs went.

"Such as?" Alisa asked.

"A lot of equipment has already been repaired. It's jury-rigged, so you can tell there was a problem, but the patches are efficient enough that they don't need me to do anything, at least not until genuine replacement parts can be found."

"My mother was good at making do. She was half engineer and half pilot, all self-taught. She had a real knack for keeping this boat in the air. Until the end." Alisa grimaced.

Mica sat up and opened a panel. She pointed to a circuit board and a snarl of wires that had been tamed with wire ties. "Do you know if that's her work?"

Alisa shrugged. She'd never had much passion or aptitude for fixing things, despite her mother's attempts to teach her how to maintain the ship, so she didn't even know what she was looking at. "She might have. The last four years that she flew freight, I was away in college. She was out here on her own, so I don't know what she had to deal with."

"But you said life support was definitely wrecked, right?"

"Yes," Alisa said, her voice tight. Life support had been what failed, what had resulted in her mother's death. Another long-hauler had found the ship adrift and reported it to the authorities. Alisa's mother had been found dead inside, the carbon dioxide levels off the chart. Angry and devastated, Alisa had almost left it out there, but it had been drifting close to Dustor, so she'd hitched a ride to claim it and had worn a spacesuit to fly it to the planet where she'd sold the old freighter to the highest bidder.

"I've run several tests. Nothing's wrong with life support now."

"You're sure?"

"There are patches a-plenty. I can see that someone put a lot of work into fixing the system."

This time, Alisa was the one to glance toward the empty hatchway. "Are you implying that our passenger did it?"

"It wasn't the rats."

Alisa rocked back onto her heels. "From what I've heard, most soldiers who go into the Cyborg Corps are taken in young, before they've earned degrees or had much time to learn a trade. And their superiors don't really encourage them to educate themselves, not in intellectual subjects, anyway. I always had the feeling that the imperials were afraid of their own creations. Didn't want them getting thoughts in their heads about turning on their superiors or taking over installations."

"Maybe I'm not the first engineer he's had up here, fixing things for him."

"You're fixing things for *me*, not for him. Don't you forget who's not paying you a single tindark for your work."

Mica snorted. "Whatever gets me to a civilized planet. The employment prospects here are horrible."

"The prospects for everything here are horrible."

"That's the truth. I just hope we don't get off Dustor and find out that it's the same everywhere."

Alisa frowned. "Even if things aren't as smoothly run as they might have been when the empire was in charge, humanity has its freedom now. That's worth some inconveniences."

Mica waved her hand in the air. Alisa wasn't positive that was a sign of agreement.

"Just keep an eye on our brawny buddy," Mica said. "If he wasn't the one fixing things, I'd like to know what happened to the *last* engineer he had in here."

Alisa's gaze drifted back to the tidy wires. "Are you *sure* you want to know that?"

"Maybe not, but it would be good to know how many extra deadbolts I need to install on the hatch to my cabin."

Alisa smiled, though she had no idea if deadbolts would stop a cyborg. She had been flying over a battlefield once and had seen one lift a tank off a comrade.

"Since the ship is apparently already half-fixed," Alisa said, "does that mean that we can get out of this junk cave soon?"

"Should be ready by tomorrow."

"Excellent. I'll see if I can get enough reception to access the city-net and put out flyers for passengers."

"Don't forget about security guards. In case the deadbolts don't work."

"Pessimist," Alisa said.

Mica snorted again. "Optimist."

CHAPTER FOUR

The light of two of the system's three suns beat down upon Alisa as she weaved through the city, back toward the crowded ship docks, her rented hoverboard hissing and sputtering. She led it along behind her like a dog on a leash. A drunken dog with a limp that liked to bump into passersby. People of white, brown, and mixed skin colors cursed her in an amalgam of Russian and Chinese that was the planet's native language. Alisa apologized in Standard, lamenting that nobody seemed to notice or care about the Alliance jacket she wore. She'd helped free these people, damn it. A little respect would have been nice, drunken limping hoverboard or not.

At least the storeowner had been sympathetic to war veterans, and after looking at her military ID, he had been willing to give her the supplies on credit. She'd promised to pay him back as soon as their passengers signed on, which, she hoped, would be before the end of the day. If nobody showed up, she would have to find a way to hustle for some coins. She wondered how the cyborg would feel if she asked him to pay his way.

Alisa was relieved when she spotted the *Nomad*, the suns throwing rays onto its bronze and silver hull. The craft looked old in the harsh desert light, but reputable. It had never belonged in that junkyard with those derelicts, and even though she couldn't help resent it, and even fear it, for how it had betrayed her mother, she admitted that the ship still deserved to be out here in the light of day.

The hatch stood open and the ramp down, inviting people in. People who could pay. Alisa hurried toward it, hoping numerous well-heeled passengers had signed aboard while she had been shopping for supplies. She supposed it would be foolish—or overly optimistic, as Mica would say—to hope that their cyborg guest had disembarked, changing his mind about riding into space with them.

As she neared the ship, a commotion broke out in front of one of the merchant tents set up along the open-air docks. A gun fired, and people scattered.

"Thief!" a woman cried and lunged out of the tent holding a blazer rifle in both hands, a faded yellow dress flapping around her legs as she ran.

People sprinted away from her. Alisa pulled out her own gun and jumped behind the hoverboard for cover while looking for the thief. A young man was racing down the promenade, zigzagging and gripping his injured arm. Alisa hesitated to shoot since she couldn't tell if he had truly stolen anything and since she didn't have a stun gun. The proprietor did *not* hesitate. She fired, heedless of the nearby people. Her aim was better than Alisa would have expected, and a bolt of energy slammed into the man's back. He tumbled to the cracked cement walkway. The woman stalked toward him, her head held high, ignoring the people giving her alarmed looks. When she reached the man, she patted him down, pulled a gold chain out of his pocket, and stalked back to her tent.

Alisa kept expecting the sounds of sirens or at least for a couple of automated police patrollers to show up, both to see if the thief had survived and to take the woman into custody. Killing someone for stealing had never been legal.

Slowly, as the crowds returned to the promenade and as nobody came to do something about the thief, who was probably dead by now, it dawned on Alisa that *imperial* law wasn't being enforced anymore. After all, the empire had fallen. She knew from watching the news holos while she had been recovering that there was a three-planet government that the Alliance had set up on the most industrious and resource-rich planets, but they were a long ways from here. Alisa had no idea what passed for the law out here now or even if the Alliance had influence here. Someone must have stepped in to fill the void of the missing imperial government, but she didn't know who.

"That'll teach you to be unconscious for two months," she muttered.

Alisa was lucky to have survived that final battle and to be walking again, but she couldn't help but feel a little bitter over the mediocre medical care the hospital here had been able to provide. Had she gone down on a more sophisticated world, with all of the modern medical tech, she might have been out in a week or two.

She tugged the hoverboard into motion again. She was alive now and had her health back. That was what mattered. That and the fact that she was going home to be with her daughter again. Focusing on that made it easier to avoid thinking about the fact that Jonah was gone and that there was no longer a home waiting for her back on Perun. She hadn't figured out yet what she would do after she had Jelena back.

When Alisa led the hoverboard up the *Nomad's* ramp, she found Mica on her hands and knees in a corner of the spacious cargo hold, a welding mask pulled over her face. She gripped a soldering gun in gloved hands, navigating a seam along an interior bulkhead.

"Does that mean we're not as ready for space as I was hoping?" Alisa asked, looking around as she brought the supplies inside.

She did not see the crowd of passengers she had hoped would be waiting, but perhaps they had already been shown to their cabins? She *did* see a row of burly men lined up against the bulkhead next to the stairs that led to the upper decks. The big open cargo hold took up the bottom two-thirds of the ship, with only the engine room sharing space with it down on this level. Living quarters and navigation lay up top. There was nothing as fancy as an elevator on this old ship.

Some of the men leaned against the bulkhead while others sat on duffel bags or hover cases. Several of them were eyeing Mica's butt as she worked, though the appraising gazes turned toward Alisa as she walked in.

"Just doing some finishing touches," Mica said, kneeling back and pushing up the mask. "Your applicants for the security gig have showed up." A sour twist to her lips suggested she might have been aware of the butt inspections.

"Thanks." Alisa lowered her voice, walking over to talk privately to Mica before speaking with them. "Have any prospective passengers interested in rides off-world come along?"

"Plenty have come along." Mica pulled her mask back down. "None that have had coin."

"Ah." A queasy feeling crept into Alisa's stomach. How could she hire security guards when she didn't have any money and wasn't guaranteed to have any coming in? As it was, she wouldn't be able to pay back the storeowner if she didn't get at least one passenger. She had put an offer out, saying she was available for carrying freight, but she couldn't imagine what freight someone might have to export from Dustor. The desert planet wasn't known for its industry. Or anything else. Other than its utter lack of mentions in tourism brochures.

While mulling over her bleak options, Alisa parked the hoverboard for later unloading and walked toward the men. None of them looked like the sort who would appreciate it if she told them she had published the notice in error and that she didn't have a position open after all.

Movement near the hatch drew her eye, and she paused.

A man in a gray robe was walking up the ramp. He peered inside, tapped a black-and-gray beaded earstar, checked something on a holo that popped up before his eyes, and finally looked back into the hold.

"Are you seeking passage to Perun?" Alisa asked, holding up a finger toward the job applicants. On the chance this man had money and wanted a ride, she wasn't going to risk letting him wander off to another ship. Most of the craft docked here hadn't looked spaceworthy—there was a dirigible a few docks down—but she had seen one other freighter, possibly also accepting passengers.

"I am," the man said, taking a few more steps to the top of the ramp.

"What's she want to go to Perun for?" one of the applicants muttered. "Empire's still got its clutches sunk in there."

"I don't care, so long as she's hiring," another said.

"She's not the captain, is she? I'm not working for a skirt."

"A skirt? That looks like a uniform to me."

Alisa ignored them and headed toward their potential passenger, though she took note of the men who didn't sound enthused about working for her.

"I'm Captain Marchenko," she said, touching her palm to her chest, then lifting it toward the newcomer.

"Dr. Alejandro Dominguez," he said, returning the gesture. He was a handsome man with bronze skin, his hair more gray than black, and she judged him in his early fifties. He carried a satchel and duffel over his shoulder, not bothering with a personal hoverboard.

"A doctor?" Alisa looked down at his long gray robe, a simple rope belt tying it shut. She wouldn't object to a doctor on board, not in the least, but she had taken him for a monk with that attire. He even wore a silver pendant with the three suns clustered on it.

"I was a surgeon for many years, though I mostly do research now and seek to better understand the path the gods have set us upon." He lowered his bag so he could press his hands together in front of his chest and bow.

One of the applicants, the one who had been complaining about skirts, muttered something about religion and lectures.

Alisa was curious how a monk doing research had ended up on this dustball, as there weren't any monasteries or libraries, as far as she knew. Maybe he'd been marooned at the end of the war, the same as she. She wouldn't ask. She wasn't going to risk offending a paying passenger.

"It's two hundred tindarks for the ride," she said. "Sound reasonable?"

That might be on the high side, but she had little concept of what was fair these days. Her mother had only rarely taken on passengers, and that had been years ago. Since then, Alisa had ridden for free on military transports when she hadn't flown in her own craft. But she figured she should start high, since people liked to haggle.

"A little steep," Alejandro said, "but you *are* the first ship that's been heading to Perun in the two months that I've been seeking passage." His expression turned wry.

Between that comment and the one the job applicant had made, Alisa was starting to wonder if everyone else knew more about what was going on back on her home planet than she did.

"It's brave of you to take the trip," Alejandro remarked, glancing at her jacket. "You won't be welcome there now."

"So I expect." Alisa shrugged. She wasn't about to explain her situation to a stranger. "You look respectable, but I'm going to have to ask for payment in physical currency and up front. I hope you can understand. Food and a private cabin are included," she rushed to add, hoping to soften her demands. Besides, it would be easy to offer a private cabin, since she had so few passengers.

"Ah, of course. Give me a moment." He lifted the flap of his satchel and poked around inside. Given the number of scrolls, books, and pouches stuffed inside, it might take him a while to locate his purse.

Feeling relieved that he hadn't objected, Alisa returned to the applicants. She could afford to hire one now and to pay back the storeowner. Things were looking up.

Despite their earlier mutterings, they all straightened as she approached, adopting a modicum of professionalism. They were all male, all brawny, and all even scruffier and more disreputable-looking than the cyborg. Maybe her plan to hire one of them to keep him in check was a silly one.

"Who's got his own combat armor?" Alisa asked.

She had asked for it in the ad, even though she hadn't known if she would be lucky enough to get it, since a full suit cost thousands of tindarks. Even army veterans rarely had a suit of their own since theirs had been issued by—and returned to—the military. Usually, only well-off mercenaries and security guards working for big companies had the gear. Still, she spotted a couple of men with cases, and that stirred her hopes. A man in a quality suit of combat armor might just beat a cyborg in a fight. She hoped a fight with the cyborg wouldn't be necessary, but if it was, she wanted someone who could handle him, or at least delay him while *Alisa* shot him.

Two hands went up. The shoulders of the other seven men slumped.

"Sorry, fellows," Alisa told them. "It's going to be a requirement for the position."

If nobody had shown up with combat armor, it might not have been, but she had to take one of these two men, given the choice. Not only because of her cyborg issue, but because the ship's spacesuits had long since been stolen, so if they needed any repairs done mid-route, it would be useful to have someone who could tramp around out on the hull. Any combat armor worth its price ought to have magnetic boots and be rated for space. One never knew what kind of trouble would latch onto a ship out there.

The two men lowered their hands as the seven rejected applicants walked past the doctor and headed down the ramp. Mica had come over to talk to Alejandro. Hopefully, she would collect his payment and see him to a cabin.

Alisa turned her attention back to her remaining two applicants. One was a pale-skinned fellow with a smug smirk. He had a handsome face and looked like he knew he had a handsome face. Alisa was fairly certain he had been the one making comments about working for women.

The other applicant was a stocky, brown-skinned man with a wild tuft of blond hair that she assumed was dyed or otherwise modded. "Tommy Beck, ma'am," he said, slapping a hand to his chest, then holding it out in greeting. "Served four years in the fleet, got out, did some private gigs, then fought for the Alliance for all four years of the war." He glanced down at the collar of her jacket, taking in her rank. "It'll be good to work for a real officer, not someone who bought a ship and figures that qualifies him for something."

The other man snorted. "You don't have the job yet, Beck. But I see they taught you how to kiss ass real well during that war."

"You don't have a problem working for a woman?" Alisa asked the pretty boy before Beck could retort—or do something with the fingers he had just curled into a fist. She was already fairly certain she would reject this clod on principle, but she ought to ask to see their résumés, if they had brought them, and perhaps for a demonstration of their skills.

"Draper," the man said, his gaze dipping to her chest. Instead of looking at the rank on her collar, he was more interested in studying her breasts. "Done all *kinds* of work for women," he said. "I'm sure I can keep you pleased."

The attention made her wish she still had her wedding ring, but she had always taken it off when she handled the flight stick of her Striker. It must have fallen out of her pocket during the crash, because it hadn't been there when she had awoken in the hospital and poked into her uniform. Either that or someone there had looted her unconscious form—considering that all of her valuables had been missing, that did seem to be a possibility. Alisa remembered how distraught she had been, worrying that Jonah would be disappointed at the loss of the ring. That had been before the letter had come.

"I don't think a man whore is what she's looking for," Beck said. "At least that wasn't listed in the job description."

"Suck my asteroids, Beck."

Draper stepped forward, raising his arm toward Alisa. To put around her shoulders, she realized with displeasure. She stepped back, but he still got close enough to drop his hand onto her shoulder. She could have scurried away and avoided him completely, but didn't think it would be seemly for the captain to be seen fleeing the prospective employees.

"Happy to advise you on security matters, Captain," Draper said, squeezing her shoulder and using his grip like an anchor to ooze closer. "Lots of pirates and gangsters out there these days. It's not safe anymore to fly between here and Perun. Mafia's got ahold of one of the Perun moons, you know." He squeezed her shoulder again.

Alisa dropped her hands to her hips, her fingers an inch from her Etcher. She leveled a flat look at him, trying for the stern authority of an experienced commander even if she'd never led anything more than a squadron of pilots, men and women who had been too busy worrying about peppering the defenses of imperial cruisers and dreadnoughts to challenge her authority. Draper wore a weapons belt, too, and even though he acted like a sleaze, was probably a quick draw. He had muscles, not just a pretty face.

"Why don't you take your hand off her, Draper?" Beck said, stepping forward.

"Why don't you contemplate your tiny prick, Beck?" Draper oozed even closer to Alisa, sliding his hand down her back. "How about a tour of the ship, Captain?"

That hand was on its way south to her ass. Alisa's reflexes overrode her desire to appear cool and nonchalant. She tried to move to the side, her fingers touching the butt of her gun. He moved more quickly than she expected, clasping her wrist before she got the weapon all the way out of her holster.

"No need for impoliteness, Captain. I'm just being friendly. I expect you'll need a friend out there." His other hand continued downward to squeeze her ass.

She stomped down on his foot, glad he wasn't wearing his combat boots now because he winced satisfyingly and released his grip on her butt. He still had her wrist, though, and that wasn't acceptable.

Something crashed into Draper before she could decide on her next move. Beck.

He rammed Draper with his shoulder, and both men flew away from her, tumbling to the ground. Draper cursed, but that was all he had time for. A punch slammed into his solar plexus. He snarled and returned the attack.

Alisa skittered out of the way as they thrashed about, heads clunking against the metal decking, flesh smacking against flesh. She kept her hand on her Etcher, though she didn't break up the fight. First off, she didn't know how she could—they wouldn't even hear her if she shouted at them to stop, and she had no intention of shooting them. Second, for good or ill, she was getting a preview of their unarmed combat skills.

She looked over at Mica and the doctor, hoping their new passenger wouldn't be alarmed by the display. His eyebrows were arched, but he didn't seem worried. Mica didn't look surprised by the wrestling match. She had probably heard a few more unsophisticated comments from the applicants while she had been waiting for Alisa to return.

"Part of the interview process," Alisa called over to the doctor. "We're taking on crew."

"Of course," he murmured.

She remembered his religious pendant and hoped the sight of men pummeling each other wouldn't disgruntle him, at least not until after he had paid. She had never considered herself overly religious—even if she'd caught herself praying right before that crash—and didn't know all of the rules of the monastic lifestyle, but she was fairly certain violence wasn't encouraged. Three of the ten edicts handed down from the founders had to do with living peaceably with one's neighbors.

The men rolled in her direction, cursing and snarling, and Alisa had to move out of the way again. Droplets of blood flew, spattering her deck and making her rethink her decision to let them settle this themselves. Maybe throwing some water on them or hitting one of the ship's alarms would break them up.

Draper came out on top, straddling Beck's torso and gripping his neck with both hands. Blood smeared Beck's face, but he tried to fight back, twisting and bucking, doing his best to thrust Draper away from him. He gripped the other man's arms, shoving at the hands wrapped around his neck. But Draper had him pinned effectively, and Beck's face was turning red.

Alisa grimaced. She had hoped the man with manners would prove the better fighter and come out on top. She supposed this was typical of the universe, that the bigger asshole ended up being the stronger man. Draper's eyes were filled with an alarming glee as he tightened his hands around Beck's neck. Alisa had the sense that he'd killed plenty of men in his life, and that he liked doing it.

When it became clear that he wasn't going to stop squeezing Beck's neck until he passed out—or worse—Alisa stepped forward, coming in from behind him so she would catch Draper by surprise. She pressed the muzzle of her Etcher against the side of his head, suspecting he would ignore her without the authority of a weapon behind her words.

"Interview's over," she said, keeping her voice as calm and full of steel as she could. "Let him go."

Draper eyed her, his hands still around Beck's neck. Beck's face had turned from red to purple.

Draper sneered. "You ever shoot anyone, girl?"

"Eighty-seven enemy pilots during the war," Alisa said, meeting his eyes, "and the asshole in the junkyard the other day who also thought women wouldn't kill."

It had been easier out in space, with distance and a cockpit keeping her from looking into the eyes of the person she was targeting, but she could kill in self-defense, and she could do it to keep this creep from murdering someone at her feet.

"Get off my ship," she said. "I won't ask again."

Seconds passed as Draper scrutinized her face—and her gun, probably thinking he might be able to knock it away before she could shoot. In the end, he released Beck. Alisa stepped back so he could get up, but she kept her Etcher trained on his head.

Draper rose to his feet, a knot swelling at his temple. Beck was the worse off, with his split lip bleeding as he wheezed for air. At least he could get that air now. He sucked in deep breaths as he rolled away from the other man.

Alisa, keeping her eyes on Draper, nodded toward the hatch. "Thanks for applying for the job, but you're not hired. Beck, you're hired."

Draper curled his lip. "What, because he didn't look at your tits?"

"Among other things," Alisa murmured.

"I'm the better fighter. You let womanly sentiment decide who you hire, and you'll get screwed by the first pirates you run into."

"I'll risk it."

"Stupid bitch," Draper grumbled and headed to his case of armor.

Alisa gritted her teeth, half-tempted to shoot him in the leg, if only because letting him disrespect her would make her look weak in front of her people. But this wasn't the war, and he wasn't an imperial soldier molesting innocent settlers and supporting an oppressive regime.

Draper slapped a button on the side of his case, and it floated into the air. "Follow," he said, and walked it out the hatch, not looking back.

Alisa let out a sigh of relief when he disappeared from sight. Beck found his feet, his breathing returning to normal and his skin back to brown instead of red or purple.

"Ah, thanks, ma'am," he said, wiping his sleeve across his bloody mouth. He wore a sheepish expression, and she could tell she wasn't the only one concerned about coming across as weak in front of the others.

"You're welcome. Grab your gear, and I'll show you where to stow it." Alisa turned toward the doctor, intending to take him to his cabin at the same time—he had fished out a small pouch of physical currency and was presumably ready to pay.

Movement at the top of the stairs leading out of the cargo hold caught her eye. The cyborg. How long had he been watching from the walkway up there? She didn't think he had been up there when she had first walked in—maybe the sounds of the fight had drawn him.

He walked down the stairs, his expression as chilly as ever, especially when he glanced toward Alisa and Beck.

Beck stirred, his gaze locking on the cyborg's uniform—on that patch that proclaimed what he was. The cyborg strode toward Alisa. Beck drew a blazer.

Alisa flung up her hand. "He's not—"

But Beck was already pointing the blazer, and the cyborg blurred into action before she could finish her sentence. She knew he was fast from her own experience with him, but watching from the side was just as alarming. In the split second it took Beck to raise his blazer, the cyborg burst across the distance between them, disarmed him, and rammed his back against the bulkhead.

"Shit," Alisa muttered and jumped over to stop the incident before it could escalate, before poor Beck ended up with a hand wrapped around his neck again. "Cyborg," she said, wishing she had gotten his name, "this is Tommy Beck. I just hired him to help with security, so I'd appreciate it if you didn't mangle him."

Those cool blue eyes turned toward her. Beck tried to knee his assailant in the groin, but the cyborg easily deflected the attack by shifting his leg. He didn't even look at Beck, his eyes remaining fixed on Alisa.

"This ship doesn't need security," he said. "It has me."

It. The ship. He hadn't said that *she* had him. That was certainly no promise of loyalty. Alisa would not point out that the main reason she wanted to hire security was to handle *him* if he decided to betray them. Even if he hadn't done anything to bother her or Mica so far, she couldn't forget what he was, someone who had sworn himself to the empire and the imperial fleet, accepting all those implants in exchange for a lifetime of service. What would happen if they ran into ships loyal to the empire? Or even pirates who had been imperial soldiers and were now reduced to surviving by preying on others? She couldn't know that he wouldn't turn her and her people over to former imperials if given the chance. It wasn't as if he had wanted to share this ship with anyone. She just wished she had a Starseer to use against him instead of Beck, who, as polite as he was, had now been bested twice in as many minutes.

She sighed, fearing Draper might have been right, however much of an ass he was. Maybe she was letting sentiment overrule logic.

All she said out loud was, "You're getting off at the first stop, right?"

The cyborg kept staring at her, and again, she had that uneasy feeling that he could read her mind. Yes, a Starseer would have been the ideal opponent to keep him in line, but those people were rarer than Teravian diamonds, and they didn't hire on as security on rusty old freighters.

The cyborg released Beck, taking the man's blazer with him when he stepped back. He clasped it with both hands as he stared Beck in the eyes, then flexed his forearms and bent it in half with a pitiful squeal of metal. The cyborg dropped the broken lump onto the deck and strode back to the stairs leading out of the cargo hold.

"Fucking imperial mech," Beck growled, glaring after him.

Alisa noticed that he didn't say it very loudly.

She rubbed a hand down her face and glanced toward Mica and the doctor again, wondering what their passenger's expression would be this time.

Alejandro was watching the cyborg's back as he climbed the stairs, his dark eyes closed to thoughtful slits. Alisa couldn't read the expression, but almost thought there was recognition in it. That made her uneasy because it implied that their passenger might have been associated with the empire. What if he'd been a doctor—a surgeon, he'd said—for the military, and he had seen many cyborgs?

Alisa shook her head. What did it matter now? More than seventy percent of the system had been loyal to the empire, or had at least kept their mouths shut about the draconian laws the empire had imposed. Only fifteen or twenty percent of the system's population had joined the Alliance openly and fought to put an end to imperial rule. Alisa was proud of what they had accomplished, as were many, but she would have to keep in mind that many people she encountered in the future would not be. She would have to be careful going forward, and it might be smart to stop wearing her uniform jacket.

"Captain, I, ah—I appreciate the job," Beck said, "especially considering…" He stepped away from the bulkhead, frowned down at his broken blazer, and rubbed the back of his neck. "Well, you haven't seen my best yet, that's for sure, but I'm a decent fighter, especially in combat armor. Got a mind for all the connections and wiring in the helmet. My superiors always said so. And I'm decent with a wrench too. You won't regret hiring me. Oh, and just wait until you taste my barbecue."

Alisa blinked, looking away from the doctor. "Pardon?"

"I'm an excellent grill master." Beck managed a smile, though his puffy lip made it lopsided. "Make my own sauces and marinades. Brought my portable grill along too." He pointed his thumb at a duffel resting beside his armor case. "If you can provide fresh meat, I can work magic on it."

"I'll keep that in mind, Beck." She patted him on the arm. "Grab your gear, and I'll show you and the doctor to your cabins."

"Yes, ma'am."

As she walked away from Beck, she told herself that this would work out. He was polite and respectful and wouldn't likely be trouble as long as she could keep him from plotting the cyborg's death. Those traits were worth more than all the fighting prowess in the universe.

When she approached Alejandro, he tossed her the coin purse. Alisa caught it, feeling like they were back in medieval times on Old Earth. She looked forward to returning to a planet with a decent banking system and checking her account to see if she had any money in there. The Alliance hadn't had much to pay its troops with, but she and Jonah had both had regular jobs before the war.

"Glad to have you aboard, Doctor," she said.

"You can call me Alejandro," he said. "As I said, I'm mostly retired. Research, you understand."

"Of course." She hoped she could talk him into serving as a medic for them if they ran into trouble. If nothing else, Beck's lip could use some attention. "I'll get your bag."

She reached for the duffel at his feet, but he rushed to step in front of her, blocking her from it.

"Not necessary," he said quickly. "I'll get it."

"Uh, all right." Alisa quirked an eyebrow at Mica, who shrugged.

As the doctor shouldered the duffel, someone else walked up the ramp, a woman in boots and a simple green dress. She rolled a wood and brass trunk behind her, the sides plastered with stickers featuring everything from razorback ducks to garden plants to DNA double helixes and diagrams of elements from the periodic table. A few customs stamps from different planets were mingled in.

"Is this the *Star Nomad*?" she asked, pushing one of two long, black braids behind her shoulder.

"Yes, I'm Captain Marchenko. Need a ride to Perun?"

The woman glanced over her shoulder. "I do, indeed."

The crowd had thinned out on the promenade as the last sun dipped toward the horizon, the desert temperature already starting to drop. Alisa didn't see anyone following the woman.

"I'm Yumi Moon, a traveling science teacher seeking employment. How much is the fare?"

"Two hundred tindarks. Physical coin."

Yumi hesitated. "Tindarks? Not morats?"

"Imperial money's no good here." Alisa couldn't imagine that there were many places left where it was.

"I have one hundred tindarks," Yumi said. "Will you take the rest in trade? I have merchandise worth well more than you're asking."

She patted the side of the trunk and smiled hopefully. She looked to be a few years younger than Alisa, in her late twenties perhaps, though her smooth, bronze skin made it hard to pin down.

Alisa almost asked what kind of merchandise, but did she truly care? She would have taken Yumi on for a hundred. Still, a good businesswoman ought to haggle, right? "One hundred in coin and one twenty in trade, since I'm sure it'll take me a while to find a buyer for whatever it is you've got."

"Probably not that long. Your crew may even be interested." Yumi smiled again. "But I agree to your terms." She stuck out her hand, but paused before extending it fully. "Providing you're leaving soon?"

"Taking off by midnight." Alisa could have left that moment—nobody here wanted to hurry to Perun more than she did—but she would wait a little longer in the hope that a few more passengers wanted rides. However unrealistic the wish, she hoped someone had taken her up on her offer to haul a load of cargo, too, as freight was easier to manage than people and rarely required food and fresh towels.

"That should be fine." Yumi rested her trunk on the deck and fished out a few coins. "Here. I'll be right back. I'm going to get my chickens."

"Ah, chickens?" Alisa asked.

"They're absolutely fabulous in space. Did you know chickens came across the expanse from Old Earth? They're one of the chosen creatures. Their droppings make wonderful fertilizer, and we'll have eggs every morning. You'll be delighted."

"*Chickens?*" Alisa asked again, horrified at the notion of them running around the cargo hold. Or worse, getting loose and pecking at wires in engineering. Had chickens ever caused a catastrophic engine failure?

"You'll be delighted," Yumi repeated and trotted down the ramp.

"They better not fertilize my ship," Alisa called after her.

All she got for a response was a cheerful wave over the shoulder.

"Chickens?" Mica asked, coming up beside her and gazing out at the reddening sky over the city.

"Looks like we'll have a cargo, after all." Alisa grimaced, hoping the woman only had a *few* chickens. She could fence off portions of the cargo hold in a pinch, but was already wishing she'd haggled and demanded even more of a payment. After all, chickens were passengers too. "Any trouble getting people settled in?" she asked.

"Not really, but Beck refused to bunk next to the cyborg—you get his name yet?"

"No."

Mica raised her eyebrows. "Are you going to?"

"If he wanted us to know, he would have offered it."

"Mm. You didn't mention to the passengers that there's going to be a ten-day diversion, did you?"

"I thought I'd wait until after we're in space and their money is in the vault." Alisa gave an apologetic shrug. "I'm a touch desperate right now."

"I wasn't judging you."

"Are you sure? Your nose wrinkled dubiously."

"I have a nervous tic."

"You're nervous about something right now?"

"No."

"Oh." Alisa thought about mentioning what quirky people engineers were, but decided to let it go. "At least things are looking up. We might get more passengers tonight. One more, and we could even turn a profit on this trip."

"You have a lot of patches that should be swapped out for replacement parts," Mica said. "Expensive replacement parts. If you want to keep this barge in the sky, you need to sink some money into it."

"Mica, are you trying to squash my optimism with your pessimism again?"

"Just stating the facts."

"That was a yes, right?"

Mica's nose wrinkled again.

A commotion arose among the people passing along the promenade near the base of the *Nomad's* ramp. Alisa's first thought was that Yumi was returning with her chickens, but she didn't see the woman. She did, however, see two men in gleaming silver suits of combat armor, the square panels on their arms signaling weapons ports that could be lifted for firing. As if that wasn't enough, they both carried massive assault rifles. One also wore a bandolier of grenades. Thanks to their helmets being tucked under their arms, Alisa had no trouble seeing the thick girths of their necks and their I-can-break-granite-with-my-teeth jaws. She would have believed they were cyborgs, but they might just have been gym enthusiasts. Either way, she hoped they continued past her ship.

They stopped at the base of the ramp and looked up at her.

"Any chance they're here to apply for the security gig?" Alisa murmured.

"They're late if they are," Mica said.

Judging by their matching suits, suits that had likely been issued by some wealthy employer, Alisa doubted they were looking for a job. She thought about hitting the button that would withdraw the ramp and close the hatch, but the men were already halfway up. They would probably tumble inside, exactly where she did not want them.

"You fellows looking for someone?" Alisa asked.

She remembered the nervous glance that Yumi had sent over her shoulder and her desire to leave town quickly. She wasn't a thief in trouble, was she?

"Yup," one of the brawny men said.

They stopped a few feet lower than Alisa on the ramp, but even so, they were tall enough to look down at her. The speaker produced a palm-sized netdisc. A holographic display popped into the air above it, and a familiar face with brown skin and blond hair rotated to face Alisa. Tommy Beck.

"We're looking for this man. You seen him?"

"No," Alisa said without hesitating. She did not look to the side to see if Mica wrinkled her nose this time. Maybe it wasn't wise to hide someone that she knew nothing about, but Beck had bowled into Draper on her behalf, and he seemed like a decent fellow. These men seemed like they pummeled sabertooth *rawangas* to relax, when they weren't busy ripping people's heads off and shooting them.

"Boss figures he's heading off-world," the speaker said, his gaze scouring the cargo hold behind Alisa. His buddy drummed a beat against the double barrels of his assault rifle. "There are only three ships that have filed flight plans with the dock master that say they're going to break atmo in the next twenty-four hours."

The flight plans for the ships docked here shouldn't have been public information. These men did not look like police, so it made Alisa uneasy to know they had gotten that data somehow.

"Haven't seen him," she said with a shrug, refusing to show her unease. "Who do you work for? I can let them know if he comes by before we leave."

"The White Dragon," the man said, his tone challenging.

Alisa wished she could say that she hadn't heard of them, but the mafia organization was large enough—and cruel enough—that it often made the news. She kept her face from showing any expression, but doubts danced in her head. She wouldn't have pegged Beck as someone who would poke his nose into hornets' nests, but if he had, then she would be a fool to keep him on her ship. Just because he'd stood up for her wasn't a reason to position herself in the crosshairs of the mafia.

"Got a contact number?" she asked nonchalantly.

The man poked something in his holodisplay, and the image of Beck disappeared. A laser beam shot out of the disc and burned into the wall next to the hatch controls. Alisa jumped and opened her mouth to protest, but the device finished quickly, leaving a name and comm code etched into her hull.

"Contact number," the man said dryly. "We'll be checking the cameras. If we see that he did, indeed, board your ship, we'll be back."

The silent man smirked and tapped one of his grenades.

"Great," Alisa said, "maybe next time, you can etch a Banakka board on my wall, and we can play a few rounds."

Neither of them smiled. Nobody on this planet appreciated her humor.

"If you're lying, you'll regret it," the speaker said. "Lying isn't healthy, you know."

"Yeah, I hear it hardens your arteries and gives you cavities."

He scowled at her. "You looking for trouble, girl?"

"No. Look, I told you, I'll let you know if I see the man. I'm helpful."

After a long glower, the thugs stalked back down the ramp and strode to the next ship docked along the promenade. People skittered out of their way as they passed. If they didn't, the men shoved them out of the way with enough force to knock them over.

"Why does our trip to Perun keep getting more complicated?" Mica asked.

"I don't know, but I really don't want to play Banakka with those two." Alisa thumped a fist on her thigh. She'd wanted more passengers, but lingering here wouldn't be a good idea, not now. Besides, the passengers and crew she had already taken on were looking to be trouble enough already. "I'm going to run my preflight checklist. As soon as Yumi gets back with her feathered cargo, let me know. We're shoving off." She would have to electronically transfer the funds she owed the storeowner once she had an account set up again.

"No arguments here."

As Alisa headed for the steps, she spotted the cyborg up on the walkway again, looking down on the cargo hold. Yet another exchange that he had probably witnessed. She supposed it would be pointless to fantasize about him smashing the hells out of those two thugs in their sardine cans. No, he had disliked Beck instantly, so he wouldn't defend him. The cyborg was probably thinking about tossing him out the airlock at the first opportunity.

Alisa grumbled to herself, taking the steps three at a time. The sooner they got off this dustball, the better.

CHAPTER FIVE

The *Star Nomad's* compact NavCom cabin would have been deemed small in comparison to the bridge of a dreadnought or other warship, but it felt large after the cockpits of the one-man Strikers that Alisa had flown in the Alliance army. There were seats for the pilot and the co-pilot, and a fold-down seat behind them at the sensor station. The monitoring station for the cargo hold, life support, and fuel management was also back there. Displays and controls were hardwired into the consoles—no fancy holo-nav systems on this old ship.

Memories of her childhood and learning to fly washed over Alisa as she sat in the pilot's seat, guiding the *Nomad* toward the clouds. It was comforting that the navigation and thruster controls were so familiar.

As they gained altitude, her thoughts shifted from her memories and into the present. She worried that she had dug her own grave by not tossing Tommy Beck into his armor case and dumping him out on the promenade before taking off. On the way up to NavCom, she *had* stopped outside of his cabin for a long moment and considered telling him to get out. But who else would stand up to the cyborg if she needed it? A fifty-year-old doctor turned monk? A chicken wrangler? The engineer who'd told her she was spaced if she took the cyborg on to start with?

Besides, Alisa couldn't get past the fact that Beck had defended her against Draper and his intrusive paws. Handing him over to the mafia would be a poor way to thank him for that. She would take him to Perun and drop him off there. There were billions of people on that planet. He could get lost, disappear. And if the White Dragon mafia caught up with her later and had revenge in mind, she would tell them that he had stowed away. Any camera footage those thugs got ahold of would only show the promenade and possibly her ramp. Even if they'd had spy boxes or other aerial cameras, she doubted they would have been able to record much of what went on inside her ship.

As the *Nomad* gained altitude, Alisa waited for a communication from the dock master that would clear her to leave the planet. Maybe she wouldn't get one. Dustor wasn't that populous, with few ships coming and going, so the likelihood of a crash was small. Still, she spun in her seat enough to check the sensor display, to make sure there wasn't anyone else intruding upon her flight path. Igniting the thrusters to break out of the atmosphere used a lot of fuel, and she didn't want to have to abort in the middle of the burn.

Her heart lurched when her eyes locked onto the sensor display. There weren't any ships ahead of her, but there was one behind her. *Directly* behind her.

She bit her lip, thinking of the White Dragon thugs. They couldn't have already checked those cameras, could they have? It had been less than a half hour since they had walked away from her ramp.

Alisa flicked on the ship's intercom. "Beck, come join me in NavCom, please. Mica, you'll want to camp out in engineering if you aren't already there."

"Where else would I be?" came her immediate response. "Petting the chickens?"

"They are kind of cute," Alisa said, glad Mica was already at her station.

The ship following them might be nothing, just someone else using her same flight path, intending to head out. But she remembered what the mafia thugs had said, that only three ships were taking off in the next twenty-four hours, and that she was one of them. What were the odds that one of the other two had left minutes after she had? Would the dock master have approved that? Usually they kept a window, to avoid accidents.

"If I find feathers or fertilizer in my engine room," Mica said, "they're going in a stew pot."

Alisa did not respond. The intercom system broadcast ship-wide, and their chicken-loving passenger might not care for the conversation. She glanced at the sensor display again. The other ship had picked up speed and was closing the gap. If it had weapons, it would be within range to use them soon.

She drummed her fingers on the console. If she kept going up, there was nothing but a whole lot of empty space out there. Nowhere to hide.

She shut off all of the autopilot assists and took the flight stick.

"We're going to take the scenic route," she mumbled to herself, or maybe to the plush stuffed spider that dangled from a wire above the co-pilot's seat. It had been her mother's good luck charm. Alisa had almost torn it down when she had been recovering the body and deciding what to do with the *Nomad*. Ultimately, she had left it there, taking it to the junkyard along with the ship. It was a testament to the thing's hideousness that Finnegan had not removed it when he had been selling the spacesuits and other valuables.

"You called for me, Captain?" Beck asked from the hatch.

"Come in. Have a seat." Alisa did not look at him. She had steered the ship almost straight down, heading for a network of canyons that scoured the beige, sandy landscape south of the city, and she would need her concentration. "Know anything about the White Dragon mafia?"

"Shit."

"I'll take that for a yes."

Alisa checked the sensor display again. The white dot that represented the other ship had changed course. It was following them. No mistake.

She raised the shields and banked, diving for one of the larger canyons. The freighter handled sluggishly compared to her military Striker-18. She reminded herself she was flying a big box, not a small, sleek combat vessel. She also did not have weapons, so there would be no dogfights between the walls of the canyon. The best she could hope for was to find a hiding spot—if they found a ledge they could slip under and turned off all of their power, they might disappear from the enemy's sensors. Maybe. It depended on how good those sensors were. Some of the high-tech imperial stuff could find a tindark coin dropped on the opposite side of a moon.

"Care to explain?" Alisa asked as they dipped below the rim of the canyon, the pale sandstone walls to either side jagged and dangerous. Whatever river had carved out the terrain feature was dried up now. Unlike on the featureless sandy surface of the planet, an area scoured by wind too often to support plant life, all manner of cactuses rose from the bottom of the canyon. Too bad a fifty-meter long freighter couldn't hide behind a cactus.

"You want to hear about it *now*?" Beck asked as he strapped himself into the co-pilot's seat. He gripped the armrests as he frowned at the striated walls streaking past on the view screen. Here and there, arches and pillars created obstacles for Alisa to weave through.

"Better now than after we crash and die," she said.

Beck shot her an alarmed look.

She thought about pointing out that she wasn't doing much yet, just following the contours of the canyon and checking the sensors. Not surprisingly, their pursuer was tracking them from above, flying over the arches instead of dipping under them. Alisa tapped a button and tied into the planet's satellites to get an idea of the terrain ahead, hoping to find a cave or ledge large enough to hide her ship. She also hoped that the White Dragon pilot wasn't a native of the planet who knew every nook and cranny by heart.

An alarm flashed on the co-pilot's station. Weapons locking onto them.

Alisa dipped the craft lower as a sizzling bolt of energy streaked over them. It slammed into a canyon wall, and rock exploded, pelting their shields. Pulverized dust clouded the air until they passed the area.

"I'm sorry," Beck said. "I didn't think they'd catch up with me so quickly. I didn't mean to endanger you."

"Story," Alisa said, zigzagging them over the dried riverbed below, trying to make a difficult target.

"The war ended and didn't leave me bursting with cash," Beck said. "You know how it was. Fighting for freedom, not coin."

Alisa knew all too well. She nodded for him to continue. Up ahead, a small canyon converged with their bigger one.

"Well, I've been a fighter for a long time," Beck went on, "but it's not my passion, not like food."

"Food?"

"Cooking—grilling especially. I told you I make some fine flavors. It had long been a dream of mine to go commercial with some of my sauces, get them in the groceries on all the main planets, sell enough to retire from fighting."

Another bolt of energy sizzled after them. Alisa turned abruptly, banking hard to take them around the sharp angle and up into the smaller canyon. She clipped the top of a tall pole cactus, leaving it on its side. Three suns, she'd forgotten what a behemoth the *Nomad* was. Out in space, where everything was on a galactic scale, it did not matter as much, but she would feel like an idiot if she wrecked her own ship without having suffered a single blow from the enemy.

Beck's fingers tightened on the armrests, and he paused in his story.

Alisa spotted what might be a ledge on the satellite map. She increased her speed.

"When I got out, nobody was hiring fighters," Beck said. "I figured that was a sign from the stars, time to take a shot at making my dream happen. I wanted to open a restaurant, to prove that my sauces were brilliant. I'd get people talking about them, figure out which they liked most, which ones would be the most likely candidates to sell on the interplanetary market."

Alisa tipped the freighter on the side, flying along the wall to avoid fire from above. Another crackling bolt slammed into the middle of the dried river.

The canyon was growing narrower. Piloting would get tougher, but their enemy should have a tougher time shooting down between the walls too. She hoped.

"I didn't have the funds to open the restaurant on my own," Beck continued. "I thought about selling my combat armor, but it's more than ten years old and has some dents and scrapes that won't buff out. The secondhand place didn't want to give me anything close to a fair price. A man was there when I was trying to make the sale and asked what I needed the money for, then said he knew someone who might give me a loan if I didn't mind a hefty interest rate." Beck flexed his fingers on the armrests as the *Nomad* dipped below an arch, the shields bumping the bottom edge on the way through. "I was enamored with my idea and figured I could handle the interest. In truth, I could. I took on a partner with experience in restaurants, and we weren't open a month before we had more business than we could handle. Considering how screwed the economy is on Dustor, I figured that was damned impressive, and it would only be a matter of time before I could start my sauce line."

If Alisa had not been busy avoiding fire, she would have given him some incredulous looks. It wasn't that she blamed a man for having dreams, but what kind of combat specialist fancied himself a chef?

"One night, we had a special guest come by, the man who had indirectly financed my business. Weeks had passed, and I never had any idea the mafia was behind it. I thought I'd been taken on by some benevolent angel investor, albeit a greedy one." Beck snorted noisily. "Turns out, this was one of the six brothers that founded the White Dragon Clan. He loved good food, and I figured things might turn out all right. I'd feed him an excellent dinner, and he would know that he had made a wise decision by investing in my enterprise. That was before some enemy of his decided to poison him that night, using my food to hide the drugs. He—"

"Hold on." Alisa raised her hand to pause his story and hit the intercom. "Mica? I know we packed light, but is there anything down there you can use to make some explosives? I have an idea that may or may not work."

She eyed the satellite imagery again, considering a ledge ahead of them. There was no way to tell how thick it was or how much space was underneath it. She might very well reach it and find out it was only a plateau, but the way it thrust out into the canyon and halfway over the riverbed gave her hope.

The "Uh" that Mica responded with did not sound promising.

"I have DZ-4 bombs," an unexpected voice said over the intercom. The cyborg.

"Get them. I need you to meet Beck at the hatch." Alisa doubted the cyborg would appreciate taking orders from her, but their pursuer chose that moment to fire again. The energy bolt blasted past without going anywhere near them, but it slammed into the top of a cliff up ahead, and rubble rained down as the *Nomad* passed. The thumps of the pieces bouncing off the shields resounded throughout the ship.

"I'll be there in less than a minute," the cyborg said. He sounded unperturbed, as if he had been fired on a thousand times in his life. He probably had.

"You have any explosives, Beck?" Alisa asked.

"No, but I can blow the hells out of a man with the blazers built into my armor. Might be able to put a dent in some ship's shields if I have long enough." He unfastened his harness and stood.

"Go with the cyborg. Help him plant explosives. If my plan works, we won't need you to go toe to toe with a ship."

"The mech?" Beck scowled.

"We're all on the same side. *Your* side." Alisa turned a frosty look on him, hoping to remind him that he had brought this upon them. She didn't want anything except cooperation from him.

"Right. We'll get it done." He ran out the hatchway.

Alisa tapped the intercom. The ledge was coming up. She would have to work quickly and hope the shields could take a couple of hits from the mafia ship. The canyon narrowed further up ahead. Good. That should make her actions more believable.

"Brace yourselves, everyone," Alisa said. "We're about to get hit."

"Pardon?" Mica asked.

"Trust me." Alisa nudged the flight stick and took them upward, hoping it would look like they were giving up on the canyon and fleeing back to the city.

The White Dragon ship reacted even more quickly than she expected, the pilot firing at her with glee. Her fingers twitched, wanting so badly to take evasive maneuvers, but she forced herself to stay on a straight and predictable course.

An energy bolt slammed into their starboard side. An alarm flashed on the console, warning her that the shields had dipped below fifty percent power.

Alisa was too busy with other controls to do more than glance at it. She hit a button to vent exhaust at the same time as she spun artfully, corkscrewing back down into the canyon. She leveled them out just enough to pilot them toward the ledge at the same time as they lost elevation.

Footsteps clanged on the deck behind her, and she glimpsed Alejandro racing to NavCom, gripping the hatchway with both hands as he stared at her. The artificial gravity compensated for the spinning, but the ship still jostled back and forth.

Busy concentrating, Alisa did not acknowledge him. She leveled further just before they slid under the ledge, the thrusters skipping off the ground. Alejandro cursed, nearly tumbling to the deck.

The ledge was barely high enough for the *Nomad* to slide under. Alisa reversed the thrusters, halting them far more abruptly than the ship was designed to do. This time, Alejandro almost ended up in her lap. Alisa vented more exhaust, hoping it looked like smoke from above.

"Cyborg, Beck, you're on," she said, hitting the control to open the hatch even as she settled them onto the ground under the far end of the ledge. Their nose peeked out, but not so much that the White Dragon ship should be able to tell that the *Nomad* had landed with control instead of in the crash she'd done her best to simulate. "Plant some explosives on the ceiling of the ledge, right behind us, right where you would land if you were an enemy ship coming down to check us out. Set a delay if your bombs don't have a remote detonation capability."

The men did not respond, but she flicked on the exterior cameras and saw them running down the ramp in the direction she had indicated.

"You *pretended* to crash," Alejandro said slowly, also watching the camera.

"Yeah. Did you come up here to pray for us in case we were really going to crash?"

"Actually, I was going to call you a maniac and try to wrest control of the ship from you."

"Are you a pilot?"

"No, but I felt desperate." He shrugged, his hand wrapped around his pendant. "I haven't been in many battles."

Alisa thought about pointing out that this was tame as far as battles went, but it wasn't over yet. They could still end up in pieces littered up and down this canyon for miles.

"They're hovering over us now," she said, watching the sensor display. She flicked several switches. "I'm killing all non-essential power so we look dead, but not everything. If they decide to blow this ledge to Old Earth and back, we'll need to take off. I'm hoping they have orders to bring Beck back alive for his punishment."

Alejandro scratched his head. "I...feel like a planet that got left off the map."

"He failed to explain that the mafia is after him before he accepted his new job."

Alisa watched the camera as they spoke, wincing when she realized how high above them the underside of the ledge was. The *Nomad* fit with ten feet to spare, and the ship itself was over thirty feet high.

As she was trying to remember if there was collapsible grav scaffolding somewhere in the ship, the cyborg ran to the rock wall. It was vertical with few obvious handholds, but he climbed up it as if there was a rope ladder hanging there for him. Beck could only stand and watch, pointing his rifle vaguely down the canyon at the cactuses poking up on either side of the riverbed.

Alisa glanced at Alejandro. He was watching the camera too and did not appear surprised. She remembered that hint of recognition she'd glimpsed on his face when he had first seen the cyborg. She wasn't sure if it had been because he recognized him specifically or just that he was familiar with cyborgs.

"You haven't met him before, have you?" Alisa drummed her fingers as she watched him switch from vertical to horizontal, still finding hand and footholds as he maneuvered far enough out along the ceiling of the ledge that he could plant the bombs where she had requested.

Alejandro hesitated, then shook his head.

She almost pressed him further, but the blip that represented the other ship moved. "They're coming in to check us out more closely," she announced. "Or, with luck, to land and try to board us."

"That's what you consider lucky, is it?"

"Hurry up, boys," she muttered, her hand hovering over the external comm. She was about to warn them that they didn't have much time, but the cyborg let go of the ledge then. He dropped forty feet, twisting in the air to land on his feet. He crouched deeply to absorb the impact of the landing, but anyone else would have broken both legs trying that move. "Must be nice to be able to do things like that," she mumbled.

"They give up much in exchange for their abilities," Alejandro said dryly.

The words made her think he might know a lot more about it than she did, but even if there had been more time, she wasn't sure she would have asked for details. Cyborgs were the enemy. They had been long before the war had started, acting as tools of death for the empire, assassinating those who didn't precisely obey imperial law. She had no wish to humanize them and think of them as anything except monsters to be avoided.

A shadow fell across the canyon. The other ship coming in. To land, Alisa hoped. They could have fired from up above without dropping into the canyon.

Beck and the cyborg raced up the ramp and showed up on the interior cameras in the cargo hold. Alisa flicked the switch to close the hatch, then moved her hand toward the buttons that would turn main power back on and raise the shields. She was tempted to hit them now, as the enemy ship lowered itself toward the ground, but that would register on their sensors. The *Nomad* couldn't play dead in the water and have the shields up at the same time.

Sweat dampened her palms. They could have withstood a few more blows with the shields up, but without them, that energy weapon would blast a hole in the hull and possibly kill them all.

"He better be one damned amazing grill master," Alisa said. She expected a feast if they got Beck out of this.

"Pardon?" Alejandro asked.

She shook her head. Beck could explain his story to the others later, assuming they survived this.

The enemy ship came into view, a sleek black vessel with dozens of weapons protruding from the hull and a gun turret on the top. It hovered briefly, eyeing them.

Alisa grimaced, wishing she had shoved the *Nomad's* nose into the wall and brought down some rocks around them. They probably looked like they had landed instead of crashing. At the least, she should have had the cyborg kick some dirt onto the hull while he had been out there.

"The explosives can be remotely detonated," the cyborg said over the intercom. "Tell me when."

"I will," Alisa said. Reminding herself that he hadn't agreed to accept her as his captain and follow her orders, she made herself add a "Thank you."

She wasn't surprised when she didn't get a "You're welcome" in return.

The other ship landed. Ten feet away from the ledge.

"Damn." Alisa thumped her fist on the console. She had hoped they would creep under the ledge, and that she could bring it down on the ship as the *Nomad* flew away.

"Now what?" Alejandro asked.

She held up a hand, hoping...

There. A hatch opened in the belly of the black ship, and a ramp lowered to the ground. Six men in combat armor followed by six more men in regular clothing came out. Judging by all the weapons they carried, both sets of men had raided their armory on the way out.

"They really want you, Beck," Alisa said.

"But they're not getting me. Right, Captain?" Beck responded from the cargo hold.

"Let's hope not. Got your rifle ready?"

"Always."

The squad of men marched toward the *Nomad's* hatch.

"This is as good as it's going to get," Alisa said. "I hope it's enough."

"Captain?" Beck asked.

Alisa waited until all of the men had walked under the ledge and were passing beneath the bombs. "Now, Cyborg."

The explosives blew before she finished the words, the boom thunderous in the confined canyon. It was a good thing she had already been pounding the button to raise the shields. Power surged through the ship, the thrusters activating as she took them out as fast as she could. Huge boulders tumbled down from above, slamming to the ground around and on top of the White Dragon men. They slammed into the top of the *Nomad*, as well, a cacophony of bangs sounding as the shields deflected them.

"Fly back over the other ship," the cyborg ordered over the intercom, "and open the hatch."

"What?" Alisa balked more at the idea of opening the hatch while they were in the air than in doing whatever it was he had in mind.

"Do it," he ordered, his voice resonating with the authority of command.

Alisa found herself obeying before she had time to debate whether she *should* obey or not. He must have a plan to take out the ship. It would keep them from being followed, but...

She swallowed as she flew straight up, did a loop, and twisted to head back in the direction they had come from—it was the only way to turn around in the narrow canyon. She piloted toward the ship parked next to the destroyed ledge, the rocks crumbled atop the men down there. Those in combat armor might have survived. The rest would have been pulverized.

An alarm sounded. The hatch opening. The cyborg had hit the button himself from down there. She could override it, but should she?

The enemy ship hadn't moved yet. Its pilot was probably staring in horror at the collapsed ledge, but any second, he would realize how vulnerable they were. He would pull their ramp in, shut their hatch, and power up the shields. That could be done in seconds.

Realizing they would only get one chance, Alisa swooped down over the mafia ship. Her momentum took her past it quickly, and at first, she didn't think that anything had happened. Maybe the cyborg had missed his opportunity.

Then another alarm blared on her sensor panel, warning of an explosion right behind them. Her rear camera caught the inferno that lit up when the bomb blew right on top of the ship, its shields not up to deflect the power. Black smoke billowed, and chunks of the hull flew up and down the canyon, ricocheting off the rock walls.

The ship was likely salvageable, but Alisa doubted it would be flying after them today.

The alarm warning about the lowered ramp stopped going off. The cyborg had pulled it back in and secured the hatch. Alisa set a course into the nav system, more than ready to hand the piloting over to the computer. They shouldn't need any fancy flying to escape the atmosphere.

She slumped back in her seat, realization setting in. Enough of those people would survive to report back to their mafia bosses, to identify the ship that had attacked them—that had *killed* some of their people.

They were criminals, and she didn't believe that what she had done was morally wrong, but she *did* believe there would be repercussions for this choice.

"We won the war," she mumbled. "There were supposed to be parades. Instead, I got stuck on this dustball, and now the mafia is going to be after me." She groaned and scrubbed her hands over her face. Taking on Beck had been a mistake. Not shoving him back out after she'd known about his troubles had been a bigger mistake.

"Parades are for heroes," Alejandro said. "There are no heroes in war. Just tools being used by one organization or another."

Alisa had forgotten he was there and regretted speaking aloud, but his words rankled. She turned toward him. "I dare you to say that in front of your cyborg buddy."

"I doubt he would disagree."

"Well, I do. I'm not a tool. I wasn't brainwashed into joining the Alliance and fighting against the tyranny of the empire. I saw that tyranny firsthand. Security everywhere you looked. Supposedly to keep down the bad people, but just as surely oppressing and terrifying good imperial subjects. Subjects afraid to say the wrong thing, afraid they'd be made to disappear. I watched friends disappear when I was in college. Others spoke up and came back with half of their memories gone and a new personality. If you think we were tools to fight that, you're the delusional one, Doctor, not me. The only semblance of freedom was for those who could take to the skies." Alisa touched the console of the ship, of her *mother's* ship. Mom had known that truth long before she had.

"I simply meant that heroes find a way to change the world for the better *without* killing." Alejandro walked out, leaving her alone in the cabin.

Alisa preferred that because tears of frustration, or maybe tears of sorrow, were pricking her eyes. She had lost her husband, she was billions of miles from her daughter, and in the span of a week, her life had gone from confusing and frustrating to terrifying and ominous. She'd assumed that once she reached Perun, she could walk into her sister-in-law's apartment and retrieve her daughter, but would that just be putting Jelena in danger? After this, the mafia would put a bounty out for the destruction of the *Nomad*—maybe for her death. She could be looking over her shoulder for the rest of her life.

She dropped her face into her hands. All she wanted was to go home. Why couldn't home be there, where she had left it?

CHAPTER SIX

As the night cycle deepened, Alisa gazed at the old-fashioned photograph in her hand, the photo she had carried in her flight suit all through the war, the paper now creased and wrinkled. The picture was of her, Jonah, and Jelena, taken four and a half years ago, before the war and back when the universe had made sense. It hadn't been an ideal universe, but it had been knowable. Understandable. The future was something different now, something uncertain and scary.

She closed her eyes, retreating into the past.

Alisa opened the door to the sound of giggling. She walked into the apartment, a bottle and a box cradled in her arms, her laundry in a bag over her shoulder, the clothes needing attention after her week flying her DropEx delivery route. When she glimpsed Jelena floating in the air on the other side of the couch, her arms outstretched like an airplane, she set her belongings down and walked over to investigate.

Jonah lay on his back on the floor, his bare feet creating a shelf to prop their daughter up as he held her hands and gyrated his hips to give her a ride. Another round of giggles burst out as she swooped low over the coffee table.

"Alisa," Jonah said brightly, his eyes gleaming with good humor.

"Mommy's back!" Jelena blurted, wriggling on Jonah's feet.

"I'm back," Alisa said, tamping down a grin and trying to look stern. "School starts next week. I thought you two were going to practice reading while I was gone."

"We're taking a break. We've been working for hours." Still flat on his back, as Jelena waved at him to make her swoop sideways again, Jonah fished under the couch, pushed a couple of toys aside, and produced a netdisc. "See? We still have a book open."

"Mmhm, and is it hard to read a book that's under the couch?"

"Not at all. Jelena has excellent *eyes. The delights of youth."*

Alisa's grin slipped out, and she shook her head. "I got champagne and bonbons on the way home, so we can celebrate your promotion, Professor *Chaikin." She considered his position on the floor and how he appeared to be having as much fun as Jelena. "Perhaps juice bulbs and candy planets would have been more appropriate."*

"Not at all. The champagne is very thoughtful, thank you." Jonah lowered Jelena to the floor, his eyebrows rising as he looked toward the chocolate box. "Are you sure the bonbons were purchased with me in mind?"

"Of course. You get the ones with the weird fillings that I don't like."

Jelena ran around the couch and hugged Alisa's legs. "Mommy, I was flying. Just like you. Did you see?"

She reached down and picked Jelena up for a hug. "I did see. And if you had a few thousand tons of deliveries in your cargo hold, it would have been exactly *like me." Her tone must have sounded unintentionally wry, or perhaps bitter, because the humor faded from Jonah's face.*

"You're not feeling restless again, are you?" he asked, coming over to add his arms for a family hug. "Flying an airplane instead of a spaceship?"

Alisa hesitated, but shook her head firmly and smiled. "Not at all. It's bad enough being away for a week at a time. If I left for months, Jelena would never *learn how to read."*

Jonah snorted and kissed her, not denying it.

Footsteps sounded on the deck outside of NavCom, and Alisa slid the photo back into its usual spot in her jacket pocket. Six months after that arrival home, the war had officially started, and the Alliance had sent out its recruiting flyers. Pilots had been in high demand. Even though she had loved spending time with her family, she had not hesitated long before signing up. She'd told herself—and Jonah—that she wanted to ensure a future of freedom and opportunities for Jelena, and she had genuinely believed that, but looking back, she realized she had also been eager for a chance to fly among the stars again. Jonah had understood, probably more than she had at the time.

The hatch opened, and Alisa rested her hands on the controls, pretending to be doing something. It had been several days since they'd escaped their encounter with the White Dragon ship and left Dustor behind, and the first of the asteroids was now visible on the view screen. She truly *would* have to do something soon, but the cyborg had yet to give her directions beyond the Trajean Asteroid Belt.

"You all right, Captain?" Mica asked, flopping down in the co-pilot's seat.

"Fine. Why? There some trouble I should know about?"

"Not really, but I think people are wondering if the captain shouldn't be doing more captaining instead of hiding up here in navigation. Beck was asking if he should be doing something, too, and I've heard our two passengers rumbling a few times, wondering how long this delay will be and when we'll be heading to Perun."

"You tell them to ask the cyborg?"

"No." Mica snorted. "You still don't know his name?"

"I don't want to know his name."

If Alisa knew his name, she might have to stop thinking of him as *the cyborg*, and she didn't know if she wanted to do that. He had been useful during the fight with the White Dragon ship, and he hadn't caused any trouble yet. She almost wanted him to cause trouble, wanted him to live up to what she expected from a soldier in the Cyborg Corps. But he just kept to himself, staying in his cabin, not dissimilarly to the way she was staying in NavCom and ignoring the rest of the ship. She didn't want to *captain*. She was far more comfortable piloting. Besides, did a crew of three need a captain? Mica seemed to get the job done without anyone telling her what to do, and Beck...well, she supposed she could find some work for him, but in truth, she had only hired him to be an extra gun if they ran into trouble.

"The cute girl with the chickens is wondering when you're going to collect the second half of her payment. She seems proud of whatever it is. I'm starting to get an inkling."

"Oh?" Alisa was about to ask for clarification on the payment but found her humor piqued and instead asked, "You think she's cute?"

"She's a kook. She had the hatch to her cabin open this morning as I was walking by, and I heard this heavy breathing. My first thought was that she'd dragged Beck inside for a rousing round of sex, but she was just lying on her bed, making herself hyperventilate. She had some quirky drum and flute music going. When I asked what she was doing, she said, 'experiencing euphoria' and invited me to join her." Mica made a disgusted face.

"I don't know how you turned down an offer like that. Especially from someone cute."

Mica sighed at her.

"Her name is Yumi," Alisa said. "That one I know, at least."

"Congratulations. There's a smoky sweet smell wafting from her cabin now. Reminds me of the dorms at BKU on Arkadius. I'm guessing your payment will come in the form of special herbs. Or perhaps in psychedelic mushrooms."

"Probably ones that she grew herself," Alisa said, not fazed. Who was she to judge when she'd traded her prescription painkillers for a gun and chocolate? "With the help of chicken fertilizer."

Mica shifted toward the view of the asteroid belt. "Do you know where we're going in there?"

"No."

"Shouldn't you ask?"

"I was hoping the cyborg would come up here and tell me, so I wouldn't have to go knocking on his hatch. I used to play house with my stuffed animals in that cabin he's claimed. I don't want to see what he's done to it."

Mica grunted. "You played house?"

"Well, I played ship and made the stuffed animals my crew. We battled smugglers and pirates together."

"And now you're doing it in real life."

Alisa grimaced. "When I was six, and my stuffed crew and I defeated the bad people, vengeful friends of the bad people didn't come after us later."

"Six-year-olds tend to be shortsighted."

"Yeah. Why don't you go talk to the cyborg for me?"

"No, thanks. You're the captain."

"I don't suppose you'd go if I ordered you to go?" Alisa asked.

"Probably not. We're not in the military anymore, and I doubt you're going to fire me. Mostly because you're not paying me."

"This is true." Alisa flexed the tense muscles in her shoulders. She had been sitting up here for too long. "You going to stick with me after we make it to Perun? Or are you getting off there? I know we only talked about getting there, not what would happen after."

"I figured you'd reunite with your husband and kid and live happily ever after." Mica frowned at her. "I'm not misremembering that, am I? I thought you mentioned a family back when we were on the *Silver Striker*."

Alisa stared numbly at the asteroids looming ahead. She had forgotten that Mica didn't know. They had fallen into working together easily, as they once had when they had been new lieutenants on a big ship, intending to do big things to stop the empire.

"I'm going back for my daughter," Alisa said. "My husband was a civilian casualty in the Perun Central bombing."

"Ah. I'm sorry."

Alisa flicked a hand in acceptance, not wanting to speak further about it. She had spent the first month of her rehabilitation in denial over his death, until the vid images had come in on the news, showing the devastation to the city, which had prompted her to find pictures of the destruction of her own neighborhood. She'd also found Jonah's name in an obituary. That had made everything depressingly real. She had spent the second month of rehabilitation mourning his death, regretting that she hadn't had a chance to say goodbye, and regretting that she hadn't told him often enough what an amazing person he was. It would take her a long time to stop missing him, but now she needed to focus on the future instead of living in the past.

"After I get Jelena, I'll figure the rest out," Alisa said. "I'm not sure what else I'm qualified to do except for piloting, and whether it was entirely legal or not, I do have this ship now."

"I was planning to look for work," Mica said. "I'm qualified for a lot."

"Are you sure? Some people demand optimism from employees."

"I've yet to see that in a job description."

"You have to read between the lines. It's there."

"We'll see," Mica said. "I'd like to do something a little more interesting than keeping an ancient freighter smothered in shag carpet in the air."

"That carpet is only in the rec room."

"No, it's in my cabin too."

"That's velvet carpet. That room was rented by a—well, I wasn't supposed to know what she was, but a lady rented it for a while and saw clients when we visited planets and space stations."

"It's purple. It's gross."

"Stick around, and I'll let you remodel."

Mica curled a lip. "It's not that I don't appreciate the job offer, Captain, but…you know I'm from a mining colony, right? Grew up on a moon strip-mined half into oblivion."

"I figured it had to be something like that when you've got a name like Mica Coppervein."

"Yes, we all got named after our colony, not our parents. We weren't supposed to think too much about being individuals, just about making sure the colony succeeded, that the valuable ore got taken out and sent back to the empire." Mica sneered slightly. "The empire always took so much, left us so little. There was never enough to go around. We worked hard all day and into the night, and we were always at least a little hungry."

"But you got out and found yourself an education," Alisa said, though the latter was an assumption. Mica had been a lieutenant in the war, so she ought to have a degree.

"I won the lottery. The children all got some education, enough reading and math to understand the equipment and fix it if things went wrong. There were tests to select the brighter kids. I was one of those, but that didn't necessarily mean anything. The timing was just right for me. Every few years, the empire came around with some scholarships. They wanted the best and the brightest for the fleet, and they weren't above finding those kids on remote holes. With the help of the foreman, they picked one kid to go away and get an advanced education. That was me."

"Were you supposed to go back and help your people one day?"

Mica shook her head. "It was about helping the empire, not my people. Besides, nothing's changed there in fifty years. Maybe five hundred. They're not looking for revolutionaries to return and stir up the colony. No, after you finish school, you're supposed to be so grateful for the opportunity that the empire gave you that you're eager to go to work for *them*." Mica looked at her hands. "I was grateful that fate had given me a chance, but I couldn't ever love the empire. I just figured I'd take what I'd been given and do some good with it somewhere. First, that was joining the Alliance and fighting for a better way of life. Now…I'm not sure yet, but I have to do something meaningful. I can't waste what I was given when thousands of my people are never given anything."

Alisa reached over and squeezed her shoulder. "I understand. We'll get to Perun, and you'll find your destiny."

"A whole heap of trouble, more like."

Alisa smiled and pushed herself to her feet. "I guess someone has to talk to our cyborg."

"Good luck. I'm still not convinced he's not going to kill us all in our sleep."

Alisa paused with her hand on the hatchway. "Has he done something to make you think that's likely?" She had not seen it, but she'd also been spending her time isolated in NavCom.

"Besides regarding us all with disdain?" Mica asked.

"Yes."

"No. I'm just being pessimistic."

"Rare."

"Yes."

Alisa headed into the corridor, turning down the first of two dead-end hallways that led to crew quarters. The hatch to her mother's cabin was still locked. Alisa had left it that way, not having the courage to go in there and look around six years ago. She still wasn't sure she had the courage.

Before she made it to the cyborg's cabin, Beck stepped out of his hatchway, almost running into her.

"Sorry, Captain. I was just cleaning my armor." He raised his eyebrows, appearing quite eager to please. "You have anything more that needs doing?"

"I don't know. What can you clean besides armor?"

"I was in the military for a long time. I've cleaned just about everything. Not real fond of lavs."

"Surprising."

He gave her a salute, not seeming to realize that neither of them were in the Alliance army anymore, and started past her. She continued toward the cyborg's hatch, but Beck stopped her with a soft word.

"Captain?"

"Yes."

"I—ah. I just wanted to let you know that I appreciate that you didn't kick me off the ship." Beck made a face, his forehead creasing. "I think maybe you should have."

"I can't do that until I've tasted your grilling."

"All I need is some fresh meat, and I can make a feast."

"Maybe there will be something interesting on one of the asteroids."

Beck scratched his head. "You've got an odd sense of humor, Captain."

"I know. I'm not finding folks as appreciative of that as you'd think."

"Well, I'm appreciative that you didn't hand me over to the mafia. I'm not the brightest sun in the galaxy, and sometimes I get a bit impulsive. I didn't mean to bring my troubles to you, but you just let me know if there's a way I can repay that favor. Anytime. I'm your man."

Alisa hadn't intended to keep him onboard past Perun, and she doubted she would need many favors repaid in the next week, but she smiled and said, "I'll let you know. Might need someone to stand in front of me if there are any White Dragon thugs waiting for us when we land."

He grimaced. "Did you have to file your flight path with the authorities before we left? I've heard the mafia owns the authorities on Dustor. I've heard that *now*. I was blissfully ignorant of such things a few months ago."

Yes, and if the mafia brutes had been able to gain access to the security cameras on the docks, who knew what information they could gather?

"I did file a flight path—that's the law, after all—but I didn't mention our detour to, uhm." Alisa waved toward the cyborg's cabin. "I'm about to find out where."

Beck curled a lip at the hatch and took a step back, like he wanted to flee in the other direction, but he braced himself. "You want me to go in with you to talk to him?"

Yes, she thought. "No, I doubt he'll kill his pilot. *Before* he reaches his destination."

"Holler if you need me." Beck saluted again and headed into the lav at the end of the hall.

If he was going to clean it, she would consider giving him a raise. She had unfortunately noticed that someone's space rations hadn't been agreeing with him or her overly well.

Alisa continued in the opposite direction, to the last hatch at the end of the hall. She lifted her hand to knock, but paused when a thump reached her ears. Another thump followed and then an abbreviated yell. It almost sounded like people were doing battle inside.

Since Beck wasn't in there, she couldn't imagine who else the cyborg would be beating on, but she rushed to knock loudly, hoping to deter him. The noise halted immediately. Several long seconds passed, and Alisa shifted her weight, images of what she might see tormenting her mind. She reached for the latch. Even if it was locked, she had access to all of the spaces on ship.

But the big metal hatch opened before she had more than brushed it. She jerked her hand away as the cyborg's large form loomed in front of her, and she inadvertently took a step back. He was barefoot and bare-chested, revealing a torso so chiseled with muscles that any bodybuilder would have envied him.

He looked completely human, no sign of machine parts integrated underneath his flesh. If he didn't give himself away by jumping off buildings or wearing that Cyborg Corps uniform, a person might spend a lot of time with him without ever knowing. A part of her wondered if she would be able to feel the difference between human and cyborg if she ran her hand down the ropy muscles of his arm. Not that she had any wish to do so. Even before she had fallen in love with Jonah, a kind and peace-loving man if ever there was one, she had preferred artists and creative souls to the brawny hulks that hurled weights around the gym.

Realizing she was staring at his pecs as these thoughts flitted through her mind, Alisa jerked her gaze up to look at his face. Only when she saw his ruffled hair sticking up on one side and a pillow crease on his cheek did she realize he had been sleeping. It *was* late in the night cycle.

Though puzzled as to what that thumping had been about if he had been sleeping, she straightened her spine to address him. "We've reached the T-belt. I'll be needing some more specific directions unless you want to simply tour the rock field. Even if you do, our other passengers might object to that."

Down the hall, Beck came out of the lav. The cyborg's gaze flicked in that direction, then he stepped back into his cabin, holding his hand toward the interior.

It took Alisa a moment to realize that he was inviting her in. Her gut knotted at that. She didn't *want* to be alone with him. Memories of the Battle for Atlar-Sharr sprang to mind, of the way the *Merciless*, the ship she had been flying, had been irreparably damaged and then captured, despite all the fancy piloting she'd been able to muster. She and a handful of the command crew from the bridge had made it to an escape pod, but not before they had seen a troop of Cyborg Corps soldiers tramping through the corridors, ruthlessly slaughtering the men who fought back, who tried to buy the captain and the lieutenants time to escape. She remembered feeling like a coward for leaving when others had remained to fight the monsters, but she had been following orders. Besides, she had been too terrified to run off and pick a fight with the stone-faced killers. She would have run, orders or not.

The cyborg was looking down at her, still holding his hand out, the expression on his face somewhere between ironic and impatient.

"You want to talk in private?" Alisa asked. "I don't think there's anyone in the rec room."

Somehow, talking in a common area seemed safer than talking in his cabin. With the hatch closed.

"This won't take long." He stepped away from the hatch and grabbed a shirt off the back of a chair tucked into a small, built-in desk. It and the bunk were the only furnishings in the room, though a trunk and a large red case had been secured in a corner.

Alisa's heart kicked into double-time when she realized what that case was. Combat armor. The crimson combat armor that the Cyborg Corps soldiers wore in battle. The exact armor that those cyborgs who had mown down the crew of the *Merciless* had worn, the dark color masking the blood that spattered it, the blood of the slain, the crew, people she had worked with, had come to know.

Oblivious to the fact that Alisa was on the verge of hyperventilating, the cyborg opened the trunk and pulled something out of a pocket in the lid. A netdisc. He thumbed it on, scrolled through images on the holodisplay that came up, and set it on the desk. An oblong rock covered in craters—an asteroid—floated in the air.

Alisa took a deep breath to steady her nerves and made herself ease into the cabin.

The cyborg folded his arms over his chest and leaned against the back wall, intentionally giving her space, she sensed. Maybe he knew that he was the stuff of nightmares, of terrifying memories that would never fade completely. Did he care at all? Or did he love the reputation he had?

She glanced at the bed as she drew closer to the desk, at the rumpled sheets, wondering again what he had been doing when she had knocked. Vigorously masturbating? She smirked and almost shared the thought with him, but managed to clamp down on her irreverent tongue before the joke came out. She already knew what he thought of her humor.

"Those are the rough coordinates," the cyborg said. "And that's the asteroid."

Now that Alisa could see it better, she noticed how fuzzy and degraded the image was, as if someone had taken a picture of a holodisplay of an asteroid. She experienced the first inkling that maybe he wasn't supposed to have this information or be visiting this place. Back in that junk cave, all she had envisioned doing was dropping him off somewhere, but now she wondered if he was going to be even worse than Tommy Beck in involving her and her ship in something dangerous.

No. She wouldn't allow that. She *would* drop him off. The asteroid spinning slowly on its axis didn't look like the kind of place where someone could arrange a transport, but that was his problem.

The cyborg leaned toward the desk and swiped his fingers through the holodisplay, bringing up more images. "I've pieced together a map of the inside from various notes and snatches of conversations I heard over the years."

"Map of the inside?" Alisa stared at him, forgetting her unease in his presence as incredulity replaced it. "You want me to fly *into* one of those holes?"

"What did you expect?"

"A space station floating around out here somewhere. Or a mining facility on the surface of an asteroid. Someplace to drop you off and get—" She stopped herself from saying *get rid of you*, though those were surely the words that had been in her mind.

His eyes closed to slits. Yes, he knew what she had almost said.

"My visit won't take long," he said. "The person I seek will either be there and have the answers I want, or he won't."

"Be there? Inside of the asteroid?"

He nodded once.

"And if he's there, will you be staying with him?" She resisted the urge to make an innuendo. She didn't know why sexual comments kept popping into her head. Her humor had odd timing.

"Can't wait to get rid of me?" He leaned back against the wall, again assuming his relaxed pose with his shoulder against the wall, but his jaw was clenched, his face lean enough that she could see the muscles tightening.

"Look, I just want to get to Perun."

His gaze flicked down to her jacket. "You're not going to be welcome there."

"Better than not being welcome anywhere," Alisa retorted before she remembered that if there was anyone in the galaxy she didn't want to irk, it was a cyborg.

He did not move, but that stillness no longer looked relaxed.

"You think you're so fucking brilliant, don't you?" he asked softly, his voice hard. "Took down the mighty empire, destroyed three hundred years' worth of order, tradition, safety. And how did you do it? Not with force, not in honorable battle, but through guerrilla tactics, spying, and treachery." He took a step toward her, his arms lowering, his fingers curling into fists at his sides. "As if that's something to be proud of, as if it hasn't always been easier to destroy than to create, to build."

Alisa took a step back, but her shoulders bumped against the hatch. She wondered if Beck was still in the corridor.

"Did you ever stop to wonder if you were doing the right thing?" the cyborg demanded, his voice still soft. "If your people had the manpower and wherewithal to replace a stable government? I sincerely doubt it, judging by what's cropping up in the empire's absence. Those sadistic morons down in that junkyard that enjoy cutting on visitors and roasting the pieces they cut off over a fire, those are only the tail of the comet. There's much, much worse out there. Your *security guard*—" he sneered, putting mocking emphasis on the words, "—found out that the White Dragon Clan rules on Dustor, and they're not even the worst of the degenerates out there taking advantage of the void, using intimidation and cruelty to cow people, to carve up the system into kingdoms, each more vile than the last."

He truly looked pissed now, and Alisa wanted to sprint into the hallway and back to NavCom where she could lock the hatch. Not that a pissed cyborg couldn't tear open a locked hatch. Still, she made herself stay and stare defiantly up at him. She was the captain, damn it. She couldn't run off with her tail between her legs.

"You think the empire didn't use intimidation and cruelty to cow people?" she asked. "You're the fool if that's the case. Too busy kissing their asses to realize what terror the average person felt. Nobody dared speak their mind. If they did, they disappeared. You walked into the wrong place, talked to the wrong people, and you disappeared. You think we didn't all know what was happening? That those people were killed or brainwashed? Didn't any of your loyal cyborg cronies ever say the wrong thing and disappear?"

"Nobody makes a cyborg disappear."

"Must be nice to be so gods-damned special."

He was staring at her, far too close for her liking. She couldn't move back with the edge of the hatch digging between her shoulder blades, but she sure would have liked to. Fury burned in his eyes, and his fists had only tightened as she spoke. She saw for the first time the naked truth in his intense face, that she represented everything he hated. He probably blamed her for ruining his perfect life of being an imperial sycophant, of using his bare hands to kill anyone who dared defy the emperor.

With more audacity than she felt, she made herself lift her chin and ask, "You going to show me the map of the inside of this asteroid, or do I just get to grab my butt with both hands and let the autopilot steer us into a rock?"

Seconds passed without him moving, without him doing anything but staring into her eyes, as if he could make her pay for all the Alliance had done with the power of his mind. She almost told him that he wasn't a damned Starseer, but she sensed she had already pushed him far enough. She couldn't assume he wouldn't hurt her just because she was the pilot. A person could suffer a lot of pain and still be functional enough to fly.

Finally, he stepped back and turned toward the asteroid floating innocuously above the desk. He swiped an irritated finger through the display, and the map grew larger.

"It's rough, at best, and it may not be accurate," he said. "I advise that you save the butt grabbing for later and fly very slowly and very carefully. There *is* a way in, but it may be difficult to navigate."

"Into what?"

He glanced at her, his lips pressing together.

"If you don't tell me, how am I going to know when I get there?"

"It's a research station."

"For researching what?"

"You don't need to know that to find it."

She propped her fist on her hip and almost told him that the empire didn't need to worry about keeping confidences anymore, that the emperor was dead and there wasn't anyone left in the organization with the time to care about old secrets. But did she want to pick another fight with him? Next time, he might not keep control of his temper, and a pissed off cyborg would be a very dangerous thing.

"Fine," Alisa said. "You didn't answer my other question. Are we dropping you off there?"

He hesitated. "I may need a ride out again. If the person I seek isn't there or isn't—" He shook his head. "I may need a ride to Perun."

It occurred to Alisa that she might have the opportunity to strand him on this asteroid of his. If there weren't any ships and pilots docked at this research station, he could be stuck there for a very long time. One less cyborg to go back to Perun and help the empire try to reestablish itself. One less cyborg to get in her way.

An alarm blared, making her jump. She cracked her elbow on the hatch and scowled.

"What is it?" he asked.

"Proximity alarm. We've got company."

CHAPTER SEVEN

When Alisa reached NavCom, Mica was still there, though she was standing now, frowning as she looked back and forth from the sensor display to the view screen. Alisa turned off the alarm and slid into the pilot's seat. The asteroid field still stretched before them, but a massive ship had come into view in the distance, flying parallel to the edge of the belt. The huge craft stretched miles in length, with all manner of equipment protruding from its hull. It reminded Alisa of all the tools in a dentist's office, if they had tumbled from their drawers and stuck to a giant rectangular magnet. With an engine.

"Corporate mining ship," Alisa said. "We shouldn't be of any interest to them."

Mica waved at the view screen. "So, it's just a coincidence that they came out from the asteroid field and are heading straight toward us?"

"Uhm." Alisa peered at the sensor display, hitting a button so it would play in reverse.

"Perhaps it's attracted to the scrap potential of this freighter," the cyborg said, coming to stand in the hatchway.

Having him behind her made Alisa's shoulder blades itch.

"I hope you're not implying that all this ship is good for is scrap," she said, "or I might arrange to have it land on you once we've let you out to snoop around on your secret station."

"Snoop?" Mica glanced back at him.

"I get the impression from the vague directions I've been given that our cyborg friend here isn't an invited guest." Alisa grimaced as the sensor displayed the last fifteen minutes of readings, readings that showed the mining craft angling toward them until it was close enough to trigger the proximity alarm.

"I'm not *un*invited," the cyborg said.

"Just so long as we don't get shot at on the way in." Alisa lowered her voice to mutter, "I've gotten more than I bargained for on this trip already."

"It's possible there's no need to head for a secret base in an asteroid field to get shot," Mica said. "If that ship gets much closer, he'll be able to shoot us right here."

"Mining ships don't have weapons." Alisa was about to make a comment about her engineer's pessimism, but the cyborg spoke again.

"That one does." He stepped forward, leaning past them to point at some of the protrusions on the big ship that Alisa had assumed were mining equipment. "Torpedo launcher, mega blazer, e-cannons, and that's a new DZ-468-A, less than two years out of the factory."

"Asteroids must be getting feisty out here for a mining ship to need all that," Mica remarked.

Alisa slumped back in her seat. "I take it that pirates or something of that nature took over that ship."

"Pirates would be my guess." The cyborg lowered his arm and stepped back.

Alisa turned off the autopilot and grabbed the flight stick. "Mica, head down to engineering, will you? Just in case there's trouble."

"How can there *not* be trouble?" Mica slid out of her seat.

"Unless they've ratcheted up their engine in a big way, we'll be faster than them." Alisa angled them away from the mining ship and toward the asteroid field. They had to go in anyway, and there would be plenty of hiding spots among the rocks. Maybe they could even hide in the cyborg's secret research facility.

"They've ratcheted up their weapons," Mica said. "What makes you think they won't have put a new engine or six in there?"

Alisa shook her head and flicked their shields on, though she still hoped the pirates wouldn't bother with them. "We'll still be more maneuverable. Piloting that hulk must be like flying a planet."

"They're launching a torpedo," the cyborg said, watching the sensors. "Ship-rated."

"I see it."

Alisa dove, twisting the bulky freighter as if she were back in her one-man Striker. She headed toward a small asteroid on the periphery of the belt. The torpedo blew up behind them with a flash of white that lit the view screen. The *Nomad* shuddered, experiencing the shockwave even though they had evaded the explosion.

They could take a few direct hits to the shields, but Alisa would prefer not to—they might need that shielding when they were flying through the belt. There would be all manner of debris in there, some of it too small and densely packed to avoid, but dangerous to the integrity of the ship all the same.

A second torpedo shot after them as Alisa took them behind the asteroid. She thought it would act as a shield, but this time when the white light flashed, the explosion blew a new hole in the asteroid, and rock debris hurtled everywhere. Shards ranging from head-sized to shuttle-sized battered the *Nomad*. Even though they did not strike with the devastating force of a manmade weapon, the console lit up with complaints at the assault.

"Ship-rated," she muttered. "More like asteroid-rated." An alarm flashed to her right. "Mica, engineering is calling you."

"As always." Mica headed for the exit.

The cyborg and his big muscled torso had to turn sideways so she could pass. Alisa hoped he would leave right after Mica did—she didn't care for critics standing behind her as she flew, definitely not imperial cyborg critics. Instead, he eased into the vacated seat beside her.

Irritated, she hit the comm switch with more force than necessary to call upon the other craft. "Greetings, unidentified mining ship," she said. "This is Captain Marchenko of the *Star Nomad*, an *unarmed* and *peaceful* vessel on an expedition to gather interesting ore samples for a scientist among us who is seeking a better understanding of the universe. If we're heading toward your mining claim, we will gladly divert to another location. Please direct us as you wish. Violence isn't necessary."

Alisa glanced at the cyborg, half-expecting him to comment on her ruse. It wasn't as if she expected it to work, but now and then, she had come across men who hesitated to fire on women, some ancient Earth notion of being chivalrous, she supposed. Maybe whoever was at the weapons control console over there would feel that way.

"A better understanding of the universe?" the cyborg asked. "Is that what your female passenger is looking for when she chants to herself in her room?"

At least he wasn't making comments about Alisa's wild flying. That flying had kept her and her crew alive many times in the past when they shouldn't have survived. Only when the odds had been too astronomical, the numbers too great, had she lost battles.

Static spat from the comm. "Puny freighter," a woman's voice said, "you've entered territory claimed by the Fist of Darkness. Your ship is ours. Slow down and prepare to be boarded."

So much for finding a chivalrous man in charge of the other ship.

Alisa muted the comm. "Fist of Darkness?" she asked the cyborg. Maybe he had some knowledge of them.

He shook his head. "Must be a new one."

Alisa flicked the mute off. "If we've stumbled into your territory, Fist, we'll gladly leave."

"It's Fist of *Darkness*, and nobody leaves our territory alive."

"Charming." Alisa muted the comm again.

"Given how much trouble you get into," the cyborg said, "you might want to look into installing weapons on your ship."

"I'm sure my mother would have installed weapons long ago if the empire hadn't made it illegal for civilian ships to have them."

"Your mother?"

Alisa had forgotten that Mica was the only one who knew the history of this ship, that it belonged to her family, or it had before she had junked it. She felt a twinge of guilt for that, but reminded herself that the ship had betrayed *her* first, not the other way around.

"This used to be her ship," she said shortly. This wasn't the time to explain her background in great detail. "I grew up on it, running freight with her. And we ran into trouble back then too. Weapons would have been extremely useful. Too bad having them could get you thrown into jail. Or worse."

"The empire kept the shipping lanes safe. It wasn't necessary for civilians to have weapons."

"The shipping lanes, usually, but not always. And not everyone wanted their cargo picked up or delivered to places on the shipping lanes."

"If your mother was a smuggler, then—"

"She wasn't a smuggler," Alisa snapped. "Your empire wasn't as infallible or great as you seem to think it was."

"Nevertheless, I doubt the Alliance will have the infrastructure to maintain the same degree of order."

"Fine, I'll put in an order for cannons as soon as I can get ahold of a catalog from the weapons supply store." And as soon as she had the money to do so.

Pushing the ship to maximum speed, Alisa took them away from what remained of the asteroid—about half of it. The formerly roundish rock now looked like a cheese wheel that had been attacked by rats. The bulky mining ship turned to follow the *Nomad*. More asteroids loomed ahead, larger now on the viewing screen, a mix of giant rocks, some almost moon-sized and projectiles as small as a fist. Hit either one fast enough, and it would screw up a ship. Any sane pilot would slow down; Alisa tried to get even more juice from the engines.

Another torpedo chased them into the asteroid belt. It blew up just off their tail, and Alisa's hand tightened on the flight stick, the *Nomad* rocking as the force brushed the edge of the shields. The sound of chickens squawking in complaint drifted up from the cargo hold. Alisa sighed. At least her two human passengers weren't up here complaining. Yet.

The *Nomad* would already have outpaced a regular mining ship. As Mica had suggested, this one must have improved its engines. But Alisa held out hope. The asteroids would be more of an obstacle to the pirates as their big ship struggled to maneuver around them. Unless they just shot them into oblivion.

She glanced at the cyborg. His face was hard to read. Cyborgs probably weren't allowed to look afraid. "I don't suppose you'd like to hop on the vid-comm, flex your cyborg muscles, and tell those pirates that a platoon of your kind will be waiting in here in combat armor if they try to board us?"

"My *kind?*"

"You know, brawny and full of enhanced machine bits."

Three suns, he wasn't going to pick this moment to be offended by her irreverent streak, was he? She didn't like him, but it wasn't as if she intentionally wanted to irritate him, not now. If they did get caught and boarded, she would need his help.

"I'm just as human as you are, Marchenko," he said stiffly, then pushed himself to his feet. "I'll put on my combat armor, but I suggest you *not* mention I'm here. Let them think Beck is your only defender."

From the tone of his voice, she couldn't tell if that was a dig at Beck or not. It probably was.

"Cyborg?" she asked, glancing back, but only for an instant. They were deep within the asteroid field now, and she couldn't divert her attention for long.

"What?"

"You have a name?"

He grunted. "What do you care?"

A fair enough question, considering they had been on the ship together for more than a week, and she hadn't tried to get to know him.

"I don't," Alisa said, "but if they have cyborgs, too, it could get confusing when I'm yelling, 'Cyborg, shoot, shoot.'" She threw a smile over her shoulder, though she didn't know why she bothered. It wouldn't assuage his prickly feelings toward her.

Indeed, he was staring at her, his eyes hard. She expected him to turn and walk away without answering.

"Leonidas," he finally said.

Leonidas? What kind of name was that? Something out of Old Earth mythology? She wagered that whatever it was, he had made it up on the spot.

"Great," was all she said. "Can I call you Leo?"

"No." This time, he did turn and walk away.

Alisa hoped that seeing him in his big red suit of armor would make those pirates wet themselves if they managed to board her ship. *Not* that she intended to let that happen.

She dove between two huge reddish-brown rocks, hugging the curve of one and changing direction so that she could dart farther into the field while the asteroid blocked the pirates' view. She swooped left and right, up and down, putting as many rocks between herself and the mining ship as possible. She thanked the gods that they were a long ways from Opus and Rebus so the gravitational pull wasn't as much of a tangled mess as it was when flying between the three suns.

Asteroids skimmed past, near misses making her flinch, though her hand remained steady on the stick. A few not-so-near misses bounced off the shields, but they were rare. Alone in NavCom, with nobody's judging eyes upon her, she found the peaceful relaxed state of mind where her body reacted of its own accord, the ship like an extension of her own nervous system as her brain processed information without conscious effort on her part.

As she had predicted, the mining ship fell behind. Alisa eased back on her breakneck speed and was about to call back that the cyborg—Leonidas— wouldn't need to dress to kill after all. Before she could, a warning bleep came from the sensor panel. There was a ship ahead of her. No, three ships ahead of her.

"*Now* what?" she groaned.

CHAPTER EIGHT

The first ship that appeared, coming over the rim of an asteroid like a sun rising, made Alisa suck in a startled breath. It was a Striker-18, the exact spacecraft she had flown her last two years in the army, the spacecraft she had been flying in the final battle when she crashed. What was the Alliance doing out here?

Thrusters firing, the small but deadly vessel flew toward her. She was of half a mind to open the comm and try to talk to the pilot, but two more ships flew out from behind boulders ahead of and to either side of her. Those two were also one-man craft, but they were imperial bombers, not Alliance ships.

As Alisa dove under the asteroid the first ship had just appeared above, she realized that these all had to be stolen ships, not representative of either Alliance or imperial forces. She streaked downward and away from all three, immediately guessing from their positions that they were with the pirates and that they had been sent out here to cut her off. They either had orders to destroy her or to delay her so the mining ship could catch up. Well, *neither* was going to happen.

Unfortunately, the one-man ships not only outnumbered her, but they were faster and more maneuverable than the *Nomad*. They zipped after her, shooting a stream of blazer bolts, peppering her rear shields. The attacks weren't as powerful as those torpedoes the other ship had fired, but she knew from firsthand experience that a one-man craft could do enough damage to bring down a bigger ship eventually. Worse, the sensors showed the bombers readying torpedoes of their own.

She weaved and dove through the asteroids, her mind not as calm and her reflexes not as instantaneous as before. She was too busy trying to come up with a plan, with a way to outsmart those bastards. That was all she could do, since she had no weapons and no way to outrun them.

She *did* notice that they did not fly through the asteroids as quickly as she would have in those small, quick vessels. They might not be as experienced as she. She led them into a denser portion of the asteroid field, hoping she might get lucky and one would splat against the rocks. Too bad the pilot's shields would save him from utter destruction even if that happened.

"Bombers?" Leonidas asked, back in the hatchway, this time in his red armor, his helmet under his arm.

Even though she knew it was him, and that he was the same man—cyborg—he had been a few minutes ago, a jolt of fear ran through her at seeing that armor in her peripheral vision. Odd that memories of cyborgs storming her ship in the past could terrify her more than the attack that was going on right now.

"Yeah," she said, her voice dry. "Two of them are."

"You have a gauntlet you can lead them through?" He set his helmet on the co-pilot's seat and leaned over the back of it, too large to sit in it now that he was suited up.

She was heading into a gauntlet right now, the asteroids small and dense, dust turning the dark space ahead into a pale brown cloud. "I do. What are you doing?"

He had started typing commands on the keyboard nestled into the console amid the switches and buttons. She almost objected out of principle, irritated that he presumed to touch her controls, but she couldn't spare the attention to speak. Asteroids loomed in all directions, threatening to smash into their shields enough times to wear them out. Already the energy panel read half depleted, and she could feel the ship's core throbbing through the decking as it tried to create more power to fuel them.

"With luck, lowering their shields," he said, punching in a long string of numbers and symbols on the keyboard.

"How?"

Alisa banked around a giant asteroid, then dove as she spotted a field of large ones mixed with thousands and thousands of smaller ones. That ought to challenge any pilot. The two imperial bombers chased right behind her, side by side, weapons firing up her ass. Cheeky bastards.

"Command codes."

"What the hell are those?" Alisa had never heard of some remote code that could force a ship to lower its shields. If there had been such a thing during the war, her people would have been using them left and right.

"Codes designed to keep Alliance thieves from stealing our hardware." He eyed her out of the corner of his eyes, then tapped a button on his armor. Twin razor prongs popped up above his wrist in a spot where if he punched someone in the face, the follow-through would probably gouge his opponent's eyes out. "There are codes to lock up the controls on the various imperial ships and other ones to force them to drop shields. They're hardwired in at the factories."

"I don't suppose you can make their controls lock up now?" Though curious as to what the knives were for, Alisa couldn't focus on him. She banked and slid the *Nomad* under the belly of an asteroid, still having a notion of losing her pursuers. The Alliance ship had fallen behind, but those two bombers refused to be shaken.

"I don't remember those codes," he said dryly. "I've never had an occasion to use them. Where's the scanner? That thing?"

She was too busy flying as close as she could to the crater-filled body of the asteroid to respond. He must have answered his own question, because he used one of the razor prongs to cut his finger. He dribbled a drop of blood onto the scanner. It flashed blue in acknowledgment.

"*Now* what are you doing?" Alisa left the shelter of the one asteroid, weaved through a field of debris, and headed for two more giant asteroids, these almost hugging.

"Identifying myself." Leonidas typed something else on the keyboard, then held his finger over the transmit button. "I'm ready. Can you put them into a position where it will matter?"

"Trying."

Alisa veered straight for the narrow gap between the two massive asteroids. Even as she approached, it seemed to grow smaller, the rocky bodies drifting closer together. She flipped the *Nomad* sideways to make its profile narrower. The ship shuddered as the shields bumped against rock, and she felt the shimmy in the flight stick.

"Easy," she murmured. "Easy."

The two bombers followed right behind her. The gap widened slightly, and Alisa followed the curve of the bigger of the two lumpy asteroids. For a moment, its body hid the bombers from her and vice versa. She flew in a loop, flipping the *Nomad* and throwing all of the defensive power into the forward shields.

Leonidas sucked in a surprised breath as the bombers raced around the curvature of the asteroid, straight at them. Alisa held her course. The bombers split, one heading left and one right to keep from crashing into her.

"Now," she ordered, glancing at Leonidas.

He hit the transmit button. The bomber that had gone left steered straight at the astcroid, its pilot clearly flustered by the near miss. He tried to pull up, but not in time. A protrusion on the lumpy surface clipped the bottom half of his ship, and he blew up, a fiery ball leaping from the surface of the asteroid.

The second bomber veered in the other direction and was in no danger of crashing into the big asteroid, but his wing must have clipped one of the smaller rocks. With his shields up, it wouldn't have mattered, but his velocity made the impact forceful enough that it knocked him off his course. He spun in circles, thrusters flaring orange as he tried to stop himself. Before he managed to slow the craft, it smacked into another asteroid and exploded.

Alisa did not stick around to check for survivors. That Alliance craft was still out there, and she didn't know any codes that could make it lower its shields. At least the big mining ship had disappeared from her sensors. She had avoided the smaller vessels' attempts to drive her back toward it, and if it was still following them, it had fallen too far behind now to matter.

Leonidas stepped back, flicking his wrist so that his razor blades disappeared into his armor again. He picked up his helmet and tucked it under his arm. His expression was bland, as if this was all in a day's work. If he had been impressed at all by her flying, he didn't show it. Not that she cared one whit about impressing him.

He produced a handkerchief from a pocket inside the back of the helmet lining, spit on it, then wiped the scanner clean of his blood. Next, he put it away and produced the netdisc he had shown her in his cabin. When he activated the holodisplay, the map and coordinates appeared again.

"We may still be on their sensors," he said. "Take a circuitous route to get to our destination."

"I'm not an idiot," Alisa snapped, annoyed that he was presuming to give her orders, even if they made sense.

He turned his bland expression on her, then walked out without another word.

It occurred to her that she should have thanked him for his help. He'd proven himself the most useful member of her crew twice now, first with blowing up that ledge—nobody else could have climbed up to set those explosives, nor had anyone else possessed explosives in the first place—and now here. But, she reminded herself firmly, he *wasn't* a part of her crew. He wasn't on the docket, and he hadn't claimed any loyalty to her or anyone else here. If he had his way, he would be in charge. From the way he barked orders, he was used to that. Well, not on *her* ship.

Scowling, Alisa turned her attention back to flying—they were still deep within the asteroid belt, giving her plenty to worry about. Still, she found her gaze shifting over to that scanner. Had he cleaned it because he was polite and didn't want to leave a mess on her console? Or because he wanted to make sure she couldn't get a sample of his blood? It wasn't as if she had access to the imperial census archives that kept track of every subject by DNA and fingerprints.

But if she *did*...she wondered what she would find if she could look him up. It made sense that the command codes he had typed in wouldn't have been enough to order an imperial ship to lower its shields on their own. Their headquarters wouldn't have wanted to give any soldier who happened to get his hands on the codes the ability to do such a thing. Soldiers could be bought or blackmailed, the same as the next person. So, his blood had been part of the key to unlock those shields. Just how many people's blood had been programmed into those imperial ships for that purpose?

Not many, she guessed. Not many.

CHAPTER NINE

After a couple of hours without further sign of pursuit, everyone on the ship relaxed, and people started wandering into NavCom to look at the asteroid field and ask questions. Alisa thought about locking the hatch and keeping everyone out, but she owed her other two passengers an explanation. Soon after they had left Dustor, she'd explained that there would be a diversion before they headed to Perun, but she hadn't said anything that would lead them to believe they would be in danger. Of course, she couldn't have anticipated pirates haunting the T-belt, not when there wasn't anything out here except ore, and that was only for those with the patience and dedication to mine it out. Not to mention equipment. Still, this far away from the civilized planets, she couldn't say that running into trouble surprised her.

Yumi and Alejandro came to NavCom together.

"Everyone doing all right?" Alisa asked. Perhaps she should have gotten on the intercom and asked earlier, but she had been too busy navigating through the maze of rocks to leave her seat or worry overmuch about customer service.

"My chickens were alarmed by the battle," Yumi said. "Out of fear, they squabbled among themselves, and some blood was drawn. Fortunately, the good doctor here had some QuickSkin. While not rated for livestock, it did the job."

Alejandro inclined his head.

"The girls have quieted down now," Yumi said.

"That's good."

"There may not be eggs in the morning."

"There's plenty of oatmeal in the mess." Alisa admitted that the eggs had been a nice treat. Fresh food was a rarity out here unless one had recently left a planet or a moon.

Yumi leaned on the back of the co-pilot's chair and eyed the asteroid field. "May I sit at your sensor station? I've never been out here before. It would be interesting to take close-up readings of my own instead of relying on textbooks."

"Close-up? Should have been here two hours ago. I could have given you *very* close up."

Yumi tilted her head.

"Never mind." Alisa pointed her thumb behind her shoulder at the fold-out seat. "Read away."

"Excellent. I'll take some recordings to use in the classroom for my students."

"That's right—you said you're a teacher, didn't you?"

"A science teacher, yes. Though I am looking for work. I was a part of a program to start more schools on Dustor, but that was scrapped halfway through the war. Oddly, people aren't interested in sending their children out in the world to study when bombs are being dropped in the streets."

Alisa frowned, trying to decide if that was simply a wry observation or if there was a hint of condemnation in there, condemnation for an officer who had been a part of the force that had been behind the bombings. Not that they couldn't have been avoided had the empire simply accepted its fate and succumbed earlier. It had taken the death of the emperor himself before things had finally fallen apart, and white flags had been raised in surrender.

Yumi continued speaking, not noticing Alisa's frown. "After that, I found work and refuge in the Red River Sanctuary among the monks seeking a deeper understanding of themselves and of the universe through meditation."

Alisa resisted the urge to ask if it was hard to meditate with bombs going off in the nearby city.

"I'm surprised I didn't see you there," Yumi added, nodding to Alejandro's robe.

"It wasn't until after the war that I headed to Dustor for research and to seek a better understanding of the universe," he said.

"A planet habitually scoured by sandstorms and earthquakes and now run by the mafia being the natural place for those things," Alisa said, wondering what kind of *research* one could possibly do there.

"It is a place in need of guidance from the sun gods," Alejandro said. "I had intended to stay longer, but pressing business back on Perun has demanded my return." His lips thinned as he regarded the asteroid field. He'd been too polite or cultured to complain about the delay when she announced it, and this was the first glimpse she'd had that it irritated him. "Are we allowed to know why we've come to the T-belt and how long we'll be delayed here?" Despite the brief display of irritation, his tone was as calm and measured as ever. Almost melodious. She wondered if he was a good singer.

"You'll have to ask Leonidas. This is his mission. Trust me, I didn't want to come." Alisa waved to the co-pilot's seat in case Alejandro wanted to sit down. She would rather have everyone seated than anyone looming over her shoulder.

He lifted his fingers, declining the offer. "Leonidas?"

"The cyborg."

"Interesting choice," he murmured so softly Alisa almost missed the words.

"I assume it's not his real name," she said, fishing. She recalled that Alejandro had seemed to recognize something about Leonidas when they first saw each other in the cargo hold.

"Likely not."

Disappointed, she guided them around another asteroid. Was that all she would get from him?

"I figure there are some people who might want him dead if they knew who he was," Alisa tried, though she hadn't figured any such thing.

"I'm certain there are many people who want cyborgs dead." Alejandro clasped his hands behind his back and watched the asteroid field.

They flew past a big one with a refining station taking up a third of the real estate. It wasn't the first sign they had seen of mining operations as they had passed through. After their run-in with the pirates, Alisa was glad they had all appeared automated thus far. At the least, nobody had hailed them and asked them what they were doing.

"Leonidas?" Yumi lifted her head. She'd had her nose to the sensor display, tinkering with the controls. "That was one of the Spartan kings, yes? The one who died at Thermopylae."

Alejandro regarded her through his eyelashes. "I thought you taught science, not history."

"A science teacher can't read a history book now and then?"

Alisa wished she knew what they were talking about, especially if there was a hint to the cyborg's identity in it. But her education hadn't been thorough when it came to history, at least Old Earth history. She knew about the Foundation, of course, and about the colonies, the Starseer attempt to conquer the system, the Order Wars, and the eventual establishment of the Sarellian Empire, but her mother had been more interested in teaching her how to survive flights through the system than about ancient history, and at the university, most of her courses had revolved around mathematics and astronautics. She supposed the cyborg's past didn't matter much to her. She was just going to drop him off as soon as she got the chance. Besides, seeing his blood work to lower the shields of an imperial ship told her enough. He'd likely been someone fairly high up in the military command structure. He might even have been someone she had faced in battle before. That thought made her shudder.

She focused on her controls, checking their current location against the coordinates Leonidas had given her. They ought to be getting close.

"Leonidas belonged to the Agiad dynasty, if I recall correctly," Yumi said, "and they claimed descent from the divine hero Heracles." She chuckled. "I suppose I could see why a cyborg might wish to be associated with such a representative of masculinity."

"I will be in my cabin if there is further need of a doctor," Alejandro said and walked out.

Yumi peered after him. "Did I offend him?"

"He was an imperial. They get offended easily these days." Losing a war would do that to a person.

"Was he? He didn't say."

"I'm just assuming. Most rich and well-educated people are beholden to the system they're born into and aren't real appreciative when things get changed and they lose their status."

"How do you know he's rich? Your fare wasn't *that* extravagant."

Alisa lifted a shoulder. In truth, it was just a hunch. His robe certainly didn't denote great wealth, but he had a manner about him, one that spoke of education and being raised in a genteel environment. Maybe because she'd been raised out in the scruff of the system on the battered old freighter, she could sniff out the privileged, even when they hid under monastic robes.

As they skimmed past a red asteroid with a bluish layer carved off the end, a new thought popped into Alisa's mind. "Say, Yumi, do you want to do me a favor? Can you take some readings and get an idea of what minerals are in the asteroids out here? Especially if there's anything unusual or rare?"

"I can try. We would need core samples to truly analyze them. Why do you ask?"

Alisa glanced at the hatchway, making sure Leonidas hadn't strolled up to observe again. He moved quietly for such a big man. Even in combat armor, he hadn't clomped as much as one would expect.

"Just wondering what kind of research station someone might set up out here," she said quietly.

"Is that where we're going? A research station?"

"That's what I was led to believe." She looked toward the holodisplay where the oblong asteroid still floated.

"Give me a few minutes, and I'll see if the rocks themselves have any clues. The area might simply have been chosen for its remoteness. Without directions, you'd never find a particular asteroid in this maze. Even *with* directions, you would have to take into account the orbit of the asteroids and the Yarkovsky effect, among other things."

Alisa eyed the holodisplay again. Had Leonidas gotten the map from someone else, perhaps through trade—or force? Or had he figured it out for himself?

"The T-belt is known for containing asteroids rich in gold, platinum, cobalt, iron, nickel, osmium, and ahridium," Yumi said, her nose to the sensor display. "I see nothing to contradict that so far. As for rare ore, I don't know. Do you want to stop and take a core sample? I would be happy to examine it."

"No stopping," came Leonidas's voice from the corridor. He walked into NavCom, still wearing his combat armor, and gave cool looks to Alisa and Yumi. "We're almost there."

Alisa thought about telling him that it was her ship, and she would stop to be a tourist—or a geologist—whenever she wished, but the truth was that even though she was curious about their destination, she did not want to delay out here. Those pirates could still be looking for them, and who knew what other nefarious entities were lurking out here? Besides, she could have Mica figure out a way to grab samples of the asteroid they landed on—or in—while Leonidas was exploring.

"Your wish is my command, Sir Cyborg," Alisa said with a smile.

"So glad you asked for my name," he muttered.

As Alisa piloted them along the curvature of a slowly spinning asteroid, an oblong one came into view, its surface dotted with so many craters that it looked like a block of Boracan eye cheese.

"That's it," Leonidas said, his voice calm, though he had to be excited inside. Assuming cyborgs could get excited inside. "Take us to the far side." He poked at the holodisplay and produced a close-up of a set of three craters. "We're looking for that configuration."

"Anything on the sensors, Yumi?" Alisa wanted to make sure there weren't any ships around to see them slip into the crater. She could easily imagine getting trapped in a dead end.

"Iridium, cobalt, aluminum, nickel…"

"I meant ships. Are there any ships on the sensors?" Alisa leaned back and slapped the button to widen the scan to the field rather than a specific asteroid.

"Ah. Nothing within range."

Alisa reduced their speed and flew slowly over the surface. The asteroid was about ten kilometers on its longest axis and less than half that wide. A sizable research facility could be maintained inside. She looked for signs on the surface that it had been mined, but did not see any obvious clues.

"There." Leonidas pointed, the configuration of three craters coming into view, exactly as they appeared on his map.

"Which one do I enter?" Alisa eyed them without pleasure. They weren't wide, and the spin and the gravitational force of the asteroid could add challenges.

"Any of them. They're supposed to connect at one central tunnel."

"Supposed to. Words like that fill a pilot with confidence."

He grunted. "I haven't noticed that your confidence is lacking."

"I'm going to take that as a compliment, though I doubt you meant it as one."

One of his eyebrows twitched, but he did not disagree.

Alisa chose the upper crater, reversing the thrusters to slow them as they approached it. Already, she could feel the gravitational pull of the massive rock. The dark hole yawned, no hint of manmade influence inside. She flicked on the ship's searchlight, and a strong white beam illuminated the way. Around the edges, the crater appeared natural, a deep pockmark that extended hundreds of meters into the surface where something had struck the asteroid long ago. Farther in, it narrowed and the walls grew less natural. What should have been the pit of the crater turned into a tunnel, a manmade tunnel. The sides appeared to have been chiseled out by robots, much like one would expect to see in a mining complex.

Leonidas leaned forward, gripping the back of the empty co-pilot's seat, the first indication that he was excited.

The darkness grew absolute as they flew deeper, the light from the stars and the suns fading behind them. Even though Alisa knew nothing lived out here in the vacuum of space, she half expected a bevy of bats to flap out of the black depths, battering them with their wings.

"Fly carefully," Leonidas said. "There may be traps."

"*What?*" Alisa shot him her best incredulous look. "You didn't think to mention that earlier?"

"I deem the likelihood low. I heard nothing about traps when I was researching this place. I simply thought it advisable to mention the possibility."

Alisa would have preferred if he hadn't.

"This is quite fascinating," Yumi said, glancing from the view screen to the sensor display. "Had I known the trip would include a tour of the Trajean Asteroid Belt, I wouldn't have balked at the price."

"You didn't balk at it, anyway."

"In my mind, I did."

Alisa nudged the flight stick. "Is this asteroid spinning on us, or was this tunnel carved out by a miner high on glowrum?"

"Small asteroids may spin a complete rotation once every few minutes," Yumi said, "but the large ones spin much more slowly, generally taking many hours to complete a rotation."

"Glowrum it is," Alisa said, nudging the stick again. None of the rear cameras showed a view of the exit hole anymore.

Two other tunnels melded into theirs, like streams joining a larger river. Alisa wondered if there was anything in those other tunnels. It seemed strange to dig three entrances to a secret research base. Unless psychedelic alcohol truly had been involved.

"I'm reading an energy source up ahead," Yumi said.

"A fission reactor will be providing electricity for life support and basic operations," Leonidas said.

The search beam bounced off metal up ahead. Massive cylindrical tanks—water tanks?—were embedded in the rock to either side of the tunnel, leaving only a tight space to pass through. There wouldn't have been room for a ship much larger than this one.

Thinking of Leonidas's mention of traps, Alisa slowed them further, easing toward the gap, her fingers on the maneuvering thrusters.

Yumi stirred. "There's a surge of power. We—"

Blue light flashed, and Alisa cursed. The harsh light wasn't just outside, but filled her ship, reminding her of the X-ray search beams she'd had to walk through when entering campus back on Perun. Those had been scanners. She hoped that was all these were.

Even as she had the thought, the ship lurched, as if a hand had reached out and grabbed it. They halted abruptly, hanging in the space between the two tanks.

"Uh, Leonidas?" Alisa prompted.

"Unauthorized personnel," a mechanical voice announced over the comm. "This is an imperial research station. If you cannot identify yourself as an authorized visitor, you will be destroyed."

"Uh," Alisa said again, reaching for the thruster controls, worried she wouldn't be able to reverse the ship.

Leonidas caught her wrist. "Touch nothing."

"I sure hope you're authorized."

Leonidas hit the comm button with his free hand. "Research Station Blackstar, check again for authorized personnel."

The wave of blue light washed through the ship again, highlighting their faces as it drove every shadow from the cabin. Alisa spotted dust bunnies under the co-pilot's seat and told herself to clean that later—if they survived until later.

A red light appeared ahead, seemingly springing out of the side walls. What was that? Some kind of ray of energy that was going to irradiate them all?

Leonidas frowned. Had he expected to be recognized and let in?

The red light increased in brightness in front of them, and an alarm beeped on the console.

"The temperature is rising out there," Yumi said, her earlier curiosity and enthusiasm for this "tour" replaced by concern as her words came out rapidly. "Quickly. If it continues at its current rate, it'll reach the melt point for most metals."

"The shields are up," Alisa said.

"They won't hold indefinitely."

Alisa pulled her wrist away from Leonidas. He let her—she wouldn't have been a match for his strength otherwise. He wore a puzzled expression, the first one she had seen from him.

"Unauthorized personnel," the mechanical voice announced. "Prepare to be incinerated."

Alisa hit the thrusters with the side of her fist. Time to get out of here.

A good idea, but the ship did not move. Whatever was keeping them from continuing farther also kept them from retreating. The red light grew so intense that Alisa couldn't look at the view screen. Sweat broke out along her brow. She wasn't sure if it was because the heat was already making itself felt through the shields and the hull, or if she was just panicking. Squawks from terrified chickens floated up from the cargo hold. She wasn't the only one panicking.

Deep nasal-sounding breaths came from behind her seat.

"What are you doing, Yumi?"

"Placing myself in a state of optimal heart rate variability to reduce my body's stress response and induce calmness," Yumi said slowly, her eyes closed to slits. "The Starkowatz Philosophy teaches us to feel less anxious about death through altering our consciousness, but sometimes, it can be difficult to get the mind to cooperate." She closed her eyes all the way and went back to her breathing.

"I have trouble getting my mind to cooperate all the time. Leo, buddy, last chance to do something, or we're about to find out what the melt point is for cyborg sprockets."

Leonidas gave her one of the flat looks he was exceedingly good at, then leaned closer to the comm. "Research Station Blackstar, check for delivery of authorized *cargo*," he said, forgoing the mention of personnel this time.

The blue light flashed, scanning them again.

Alisa tried again to move the *Nomad*. The thrusters activated without a problem—they just couldn't generate enough of a push to send them anywhere.

Abruptly, the blue light disappeared, and so did the red light outside. The view screen dimmed, though it had been so bright that the red rectangle remained in Alisa's vision, as if burned there for all eternity. A small price to pay for the cessation of that heat. She might have slumped down in her seat, but the field holding them released them. She nudged the thrusters, and the *Nomad* ambled forward, as if it had never been held.

Leonidas wore a dyspeptic expression, not looking nearly as relieved as Alisa felt over escaping death.

"Is that you?" she asked, the pieces of the puzzle clicking together. Unless one counted Yumi's chickens, she didn't have any other "cargo," certainly nothing that would have pleased an imperial security checkpoint. "The authorized cargo?"

Leonidas smoothed his expression, ignoring her question. "There's a docking station. Find a spot for us, then join me in the cargo hold." He shifted his helmet out from under his arm, gripping it with both hands. "Have your new science officer check and see if there's oxygen and gravity inside of the station." He turned, plopping the helmet onto his head as he walked out.

"Anyone tell you that you're not the captain here?" Alisa called after him.

She wasn't surprised when he didn't respond. He'd been irked when she had referred to him as *your kind*. Being classified as the cargo probably irritated him even more.

CHAPTER TEN

At the end of the tunnel, Alisa found only two docking ports, tubes and connectors dangling out of the wall as if someone had left in a hurry. Maneuvering the *Nomad* into the cramped spot took a lot of care. She couldn't imagine that two ships could ever dock at once.

"Guess they don't invite a lot of people over for game night," she said to Yumi, who still sat behind her.

One of those tubes looked like it might be for replenishing water tanks and thus, through electrolysis, a ship's oxygen supplies. Alisa would have to check to see if it was operable. She felt like fate, if not Leonidas, owed her something for what had been a harrowing trip out here.

Near-death experiences hadn't been uncommon during the war, but she had been fighting for something noble then. To die out here for nothing, with Jelena never knowing what happened to her mother, that would be intolerable.

"Are you going to get out and look around in there?" Yumi asked. "Or is he going in alone?" Her voice was steady. She seemed to have recovered from their close call with that security system. Maybe the noisy breathing had worked to calm her down.

"Oh, he's *definitely* going in alone," Alisa said as she let the autopilot complete the docking procedure. She took the helm when they were cruising through asteroid fields and dodging enemies, but preferred to let the computer line the tabs up with the slots. Besides, she had a headache after the intensity of the last few hours. "I wouldn't mind exploring a bit on my own though."

In truth, she wouldn't mind poking around to see if there might be anything they could salvage and sell. With the empire gone, this research station might be abandoned. A few years ago, she had never imagined herself poking around in wrecks or abandoned facilities, scavenging for parts, but the reality was that she didn't know what awaited her back on Perun or if her bank account even existed anymore. If she could find a few valuable items to sell, she might be able to replace the parts Mica had mentioned, and she would be in a less desperate situation going forward. She did not want to take custody of Jelena if she couldn't afford to keep her fed and clothed. Further, for all she knew, it might take a bribe to get onto Perun and find her in the first place. She had no idea if she would be able to communicate with her sister-in-law, or even if she was in the same place as she had been months earlier, when she had mailed that letter.

"It will depend on the atmosphere," Alisa said as a hiss sounded, the airlock connecting and sealing with the station. "Leonidas has a suit, so he can go in, regardless. Beck should be able to go in too. Though if I send those two in together, I'm not sure both of them will come out."

No, if Beck went in, she wanted to go in too. It was annoying not to have a spacesuit—not to mention unsafe. If some maintenance issue popped up that required a space walk, Mica would have to send Beck out to do the fixing, something he might not have any experience with. Alisa supposed she should be happy they at least had two people capable of going out, but spacesuits would definitely go on the list of things she would buy if she could find some valuables here that were worth selling.

"I can't tell from here what the atmosphere is like inside the station." Yumi waved at the sensor display.

"You might be able to get a reading once the airlock is open. If the men have good combat armor, their suits will also be able to scan the air, see if it's breathable. They might be able to tell if anyone is home too."

Her hopes of salvaging would go up in smoke if there were residents. It would be one thing to acquire a few items from an abandoned station, but what if Leonidas expected to find people here? As much as she would like new equipment for her ship, she wasn't going to steal for it.

"Uhh, Captain?" came Mica's voice over the intercom. "Could you come down to the cargo hold? We have a problem. Specifically, *I* have a problem."

The ship was sealed in, so Alisa pushed herself out of her seat and headed toward the lower deck. Her legs felt wobbly after sitting for so long—sitting and facing death.

She found Leonidas standing near the airlock in his crimson armor, his helmet fastened and a rifle and a bag slung over his shoulder. Though Alisa had not asked him to, Beck had suited up too. His armor was white with silver accents, and he also carried an assault rifle. Mica stood near the airlock, too, but as Alisa walked down the stairs, she assumed that whatever problem she had called about was between the two men.

Mica folded her arms over her chest and scowled at Alisa, making her rethink that assumption.

The chickens jittered and squawked at her as she left the stairs. A lot of feathers dusted the decking over in the corner that Alisa had given Yumi, feathers that had managed to fly impressively far from the temporary fencing that kept the birds secured. The poor things probably hadn't appreciated the heat wave any more than the crew had.

"What's the problem here?" Alisa asked.

"Your cyborg thinks he's taking me on a date," Mica said.

Her cyborg? When had she been given ownership over Leonidas?

"What's the matter?" Alisa asked. "He's not cute enough for you?"

Leonidas's eyebrows twitched behind the faceplate of his armor. They liked to do that even when he offered no other reaction. Tiny rebellious body parts that would not be sublimated.

"Not funny," Mica said. "I don't even know what the atmosphere looks like over there. I'm not leaving the ship. Engineers don't leave the ship. We stay in our engine rooms and cuddle with our machinery. There are centuries and centuries worth of precedents to back me up."

"You won't go anywhere you don't want to go," Beck said, tapping the barrel of his rifle and eyeing Leonidas, who was standing close enough to him that he could probably knock that rifle out of his hands before Beck could aim it at him.

Alisa looked at Leonidas, his face hard to read—his eyebrows weren't doing anything now. "Care to explain?"

"You won't leave without your engineer," he said, his voice sounding hollow through the helmet's speaker.

Alisa mouthed the words, trying to understand what he meant. It took her a moment to piece it together.

"You think we'll strand you here?" she asked.

"I'm certain you've considered it."

Yes, but *he* wasn't supposed to know that.

"I would be a fool to leave our best fighter here when there are pirates swarming around out there, probably waiting for the *Nomad* to leave the belt." Not that Alisa had any intention of flying out of the belt in the same spot that she had come in, but it seemed a reasonable argument to sway him.

He gazed back at her through the faceplate, not noticeably moved by her argument. Maybe he thought she *was* a fool.

"She comes with me," he said.

"I'm not going anywhere, Muscles," Mica said, taking a few steps away from him to stand beside Alisa.

As if *she* could do something to stop Leonidas if he decided to grab her. She wasn't even carrying her Etcher, not that the bullets would do more than bounce off the hard shell of his armor.

"Besides, I don't have a spacesuit," Mica said. "Who even knows if there will be air over there?"

Alisa glanced toward the control panel next to the airlock. They could check that now that they were attached.

"The air will be fine," Leonidas said without turning to check.

"How can you know?" Beck asked, still tapping a beat on his rifle. "You been here before? Whatever your little quest is here, it has nothing to do with them." He waved toward Mica and Alisa.

Leonidas hesitated. Because he knew it was true? That it was unfair of him to ask for a hostage?

"At least one person lives inside here doing research," he said, then repeated, "The air will be fine."

"Then why did you get all suited up?" Mica asked.

"It's combat armor," Leonidas said.

Mica's brow furrowed. "Yes…"

"You're expecting trouble?" Alisa asked. "From the one person you think is in there? Or from something else?"

"Back before the war ended," Leonidas said, "this station hadn't been heard from for months. There were plans to send someone out to check on it, but all of the empire's resources were otherwise occupied." His words came out clipped, annoyed. Probably because he was talking to some of the people who had been occupying those resources. "I don't know what's been happening since the war ended, and yes, I am prepared for trouble if it should arise."

Right. He had been busy squatting in her ship in a junkyard full of crazies since the war ended. For the first time, it occurred to her to wonder how he had gotten down there in the first place. *She* had been left behind because she needed medical attention. What was his story? Had his people simply forgotten to take him home? Or had he volunteered to stay behind when things had fallen apart and the imperial forces had retreated? Had he failed them and been left as a punishment?

"Well, if there's going to be trouble, how about I go with you?" Beck asked. "I wouldn't mind a walk to stretch my legs, and I'm suited up. I'm the logical one."

"You're not integral to the operation of the ship," Leonidas said.

"What does that mean?"

"You're expendable."

Beck glowered at him. "I really hate you, mech."

"The engineer comes with me," Leonidas said.

Alisa sighed. This was ridiculous. Hadn't she risked the ship in that battle with the White Dragon rather than leaving Beck behind? Did Leonidas truly trust her so little that he thought she would go to extremes to get rid of him? It was true that she had not given him a reason to trust her, and she certainly didn't trust him, but she still felt disgruntled by the situation. It didn't help that she *had* been considering leaving him. It made her feel like she had been caught doing something naughty.

"If the air is acceptable, *I'll* go with you," Alisa said. "The ship isn't going anywhere without a pilot."

She expected him to object, since he'd objected to everyone else's attempts to alter his plans. Instead, he nodded and said, "That would be acceptable."

"What? No, it wouldn't," Mica said, gripping Alisa's arm. "What if something happens to you? He just said there might be danger waiting in there. You think *I* can fly this rusty relic? It doesn't even have gravitational calculation computers. I'm surprised there isn't an abacus hanging in NavCom next to the plush spider."

"She won't be in danger," Leonidas said. "I'll protect her."

Alisa grimaced. She didn't need a damned protector, certainly not when that protector was basically kidnapping her from her own ship.

"That's ridiculous," Mica said. "You know what happens when non-expendable crew get sent out on stupid missions that have nothing to do with them? They get expended. What are we going to do without a pilot? Besides, the captain is…" Mica seemed to grope for the words, turning a distressed expression on Alisa.

Alisa hoped that meant that her engineer would object to her death for more reasons than the logistical.

"What's going on?" Yumi asked from the walkway over the cargo hold.

"A discussion," Alisa said, sighing again. She didn't want to involve the passengers.

"Have you decided whether we can go out there with you? I would be curious to look around."

Leonidas looked up at her, and Alisa assumed he would reject the notion, but he didn't say anything.

"Well, *I'm* certainly going," Beck said. "Whether the mech wants me or not." He came to stand beside Alisa, on the opposite side from Mica.

Having people who wanted to watch out for Alisa made her feel appreciated, but she still wished this had played out another way. Going out to explore meant she could keep an eye out for salvageable material, but how was she supposed to gather it with Leonidas hovering over her? He seemed like the type to object to the looting of an imperial station, abandoned or not. Of course, if he expected to find someone here, diligently working along and perhaps not realizing that the war was over, her plans for salvage might be moot.

"I wouldn't mind having the science officer along," Leonidas said, ignoring Beck.

"Science officer?" Mica frowned up at Yumi, who smiled and waved back.

"Remember how I said she was a science teacher?" Alisa asked. "It seems Leonidas has promoted her."

"Leonidas?"

"Yes, we've named our cyborg."

"I miss so much being buried in engineering."

"I'll start sending out memos to keep you apprised of these cataclysmic events."

Leonidas turned toward the airlock, where a green light proclaimed the passage ready for use. Apparently, discussion time was over.

"Let me get my gun and my bag, and we'll go," Alisa said.

CHAPTER ELEVEN

Alisa stepped out of the airlock behind Leonidas, taking a few tentative sniffs of the air. The sensors on the ship's panel had proclaimed the mix to be adequate and for gravity to exist inside of the station, but the place was utterly dark and had a definite creepiness to it. The air smelled stale, and the temperature couldn't have been more than a degree or two above freezing, but her lungs did not object to the substance she inhaled.

"Should have brought a parka," Alisa said, not that she had anything heavier than her flight jacket.

Not commenting, Leonidas moved away from the airlock, not hampered by the darkness. He held his rifle in the ready position as he walked a large semicircle, looking out into the gloom of a large room with crates littering the floor in a random mess.

Alisa could barely make them out and pulled her multitool off her belt, thumbing on the tiny flashlight embedded in the tip. The haphazard arrangement of the crates made her suspect the gravity had gone out at some point before being restored.

"Can cyborgs see in the dark?" Beck asked, stepping out of the airlock beside her. "Or does he just have a better model suit than I do? I couldn't afford the night vision upgrade."

Alisa would have guessed that the fleet-issued suits were top-of-the-line with every upgrade imaginable, but Yumi offered another possibility.

"They usually can see in the dark," she said brightly, joining them. She produced a handheld flashlight and shined the beam around the chamber, including the walls and the ceiling. Her light paused on a panel next to large double doors on the far side. They were closed. "In addition to numerous enhancements to their skeletal, nervous, and musculature systems, the imperial military cyborgs often received optical, nasal, ear, and tongue implants to improve their senses."

"Tongue?" Beck asked. "It's important that they taste well?"

"To better detect poisons," Leonidas said, his helmet swiveling back toward them.

Alisa wished he would take it off. He looked too much like an enemy she should be shooting in that crimson armor. An enemy who might shoot back at any moment.

"Maybe he'll be better able to appreciate your culinary offerings when you get around to grilling something for us," Alisa said.

"Something I'm planning to do as soon as I can get some fresh meat. Ms. Moon has informed me that the chickens are off limits."

"We might be able to find you something here," Yumi said, shining her flashlight over some small animal droppings.

"I have been known to create wonders, even with subpar ingredients," Beck said.

"I'm not eating space rats," Alisa said. "I don't care how amazing the sauce is."

"The secret is in the marinade. You can tenderize anything with enough acid."

"Marchenko," Leonidas said, his voice cutting through their conversation like a knife.

"Yes?" Alisa asked.

He had walked over to the door with the control panel. He pointed to the floor next to him.

"She's not your dog, mech," Beck said.

Leonidas ignored him and kept pointing at the spot.

"Guess he thinks he can't protect me from across the room," Alisa said, hoping that was the only reason he was presuming to order her around. Since they had been the only ship in the dock, that meant that the *Nomad* was his only option for getting off this asteroid, so he *ought* to be invested in keeping her alive.

"Captain," Beck said softly. "Here." He pulled a double-barreled blazer pistol from his pack and handed it to her. "I've got my rifle and onboard weapons. You keep this. It's got a lot more kick than your Etcher, and it'll fire five hundred times before needing a reload."

Alisa was tempted to ask if it would cut through combat armor, but Yumi's implication that Leonidas had enhanced hearing made her keep her mouth shut. She tapped the tiny comm unit embedded in her multitool, missing her earstar, which would have allowed her to have a private subvocal conversation with the recipient. A new earstar was definitely on the wish list of things to purchase once she had some money.

"Mica, do you read me?" Alisa asked.

"Yes, Captain."

"Everything all right in the ship?"

"Fine so far. The doctor and I are having a chat up here in NavCom."

"Don't tinker with my controls. I've got my equipment set up the way I like it."

"Yes, he was just commenting on your stuffed animal."

Alisa snorted. "We're heading in. Stay in contact."

"Will do."

As she finished the conversation, Alisa walked across the room to join Leonidas. She tried to decide if he was irritated that she had taken her time in doing so, but he watched her approach without comment or eyebrow twitches. Beck strode after her, sticking close. Yumi came more slowly, pausing here and there to read the labels on the crates.

When Alisa joined him, Leonidas tapped the control panel with one gauntleted finger. The door beeped and slid aside. He walked into a wide corridor lined with machinery, with wires and tubes disappearing into the walls. Alisa couldn't tell if it was mining equipment or something to do with life support. Perhaps a mix of both. The equipment appeared eerie and skeletal under the wan illumination of her flashlight. Some of it might have been valuable, but everything was too large to consider unhooking and dragging back to the ship.

Something scurried past a dark corner.

Just a rat, Alisa told herself, or some other small scavenger. Such creatures always seemed to find their way aboard ships and ended up anywhere humans settled, even stations in the depths of space. Or the depths of an asteroid.

Leonidas walked through the wide corridor, pausing to wait when Alisa dawdled. His intention might be to stay close to protect her, but she felt like she had a keeper. She wondered if he knew she had scavenging in mind. If so, he would probably be affronted. He seemed so loyal to the empire. Maybe that had been indoctrinated into him at the same time as he had received his implants. There were many stories about how the empire had manipulated people's minds. She wouldn't be surprised if they had done it to their own soldiers.

"Did it hurt?" Alisa asked as she and Leonidas headed for another door.

"What?" he asked.

Behind them, Beck had stopped next to Yumi, who was bent over by the wall, her long black braids falling over her shoulder as she shined her light into a low alcove. Maybe Alisa should tell her to look for valuable materials while she kept Leonidas occupied.

"Getting all those things implanted and enhanced," she said, not quite sure why she was asking. This probably wasn't the time for idle chitchat.

"It was a long time ago." Leonidas hit the controls to open the door, then stepped inside first, once again pausing to scan the new area, his rifle at the ready.

"I guess that's a yes."

"I was sedated for a lot of it."

"But not all of it?" Alisa could not imagine lying on some surgeon's table—or maybe it had been an engineer's table—letting someone cut all over her body to stick things in. If his bones had been enhanced, did that mean they'd had some way of doing that with shots? By injecting something? Or had they cut down and removed his organic bones and replaced them with non-organic ones? If the latter, that *had* to have hurt. Being unconscious for a surgery didn't help with the pain afterward.

"What made you sign up for that?" she asked. "Bonus?"

She knew the imperial military had offered signing bonuses to people willing to go into high-demand or highly dangerous fields. Turning oneself into a cyborg seemed like it should qualify.

"I'm not reading any life forms in this part of the station, aside from a few rats," Leonidas said, touching the side of his helmet. "But the walls are thick, with a lot of dense rock behind them, so my sensors are limited with how far they can detect."

"But you're expecting someone to be alive here?" she asked, taking the hint that he didn't want to talk about his past or admit to having experienced pain in his life.

"Ideally."

"Is that what you're here for? To talk to someone? Or to take that some-one off the station?"

They walked into another room full of crates. They were stacked in neat piles along the walls. These crates were either magnetized, or the gravity hadn't gone out here, as it had in the other room.

"This isn't a kidnapping mission, is it?" Alisa asked. "Aside from the kidnapping you're doing right now in parting me from my ship, that is."

"Do Alliance pilots always talk this much on missions?" Leonidas strode through the room, barely glancing at the crates.

"Oh, yes. We're a chatty bunch."

Beck and Yumi were discussing something behind her, and Alisa was tempted to fall back to walk with them. They wouldn't mind her chatter. But Leonidas would probably say her name and order her to heel if she slowed down.

A few passages opened up to the sides, barely noticeable in the dark-ness. Since the station had gravity and life support, Alisa wondered why the lights were out and if it would be possible to turn them back on. She would prefer fewer shadows about.

She shined her flashlight into the corridors and along the ceilings, pick-ing up cobwebs dangling in the corners. A layer of dust coated the crates. If anyone was still working here, it had been a while since they ran the cleaning robots through the place.

Ignoring the side tunnels, Leonidas opened the door at the far end of the room. He stepped in, but then halted. Alisa almost bumped into him.

"What is it?" she whispered, steadying herself with a hand on the back of his armor.

Though curious, she didn't try to look past him, not yet. If something was in the next room, he had the better means to deal with it.

Leonidas took a couple of steps, scanning this new room as he had done with the others. Alisa shined her flashlight across the room—it was another space filled with crates, boxes, barrels, and bags of materials. A few of the bags had been cut open, with fine powder spilled out onto the floor. Cement mix, or something like it? If so, someone had not been careful unloading it. A few crates were scattered in the middle of the room, knocked on their sides. Maybe something had happened to the gravity in here too.

Leonidas let his rifle dangle from its strap and lifted his hands to remove his helmet. It came off with a soft hiss of escaping air. After tucking it under his arm, he looked around again. No, he was sniffing the air in short quick breaths, like a hound.

"It smells like some animal's den," he said.

Alisa followed his example, sniffing gingerly. There might have been something more than the scent of stale, recycled air, but she couldn't identify it.

"Rat droppings?" she guessed.

"No. And it's from more than that," Leonidas said, pointing at the floor. "Something big and with a strong musky scent has been in here. Recently." He looked toward a corridor that opened from the side of the room, the dark tunnel uninviting.

"Not that strong," Alisa muttered, barely noticing a scent.

She pointed her flashlight at the floor, not sure what he'd been talking about when he'd said *that*. Under the light layer of dust, a stain darkened the gray metal. A puddle shape, a couple of feet across.

"What is it?" she asked. Could he tell? Just from looking?

He looked at her, his face not much more telling with the helmet off. But he did look…grim.

Without putting the helmet back on, he walked about the room slowly, his rifle in one hand again, aiming toward the shadows.

"Is that blood?" Beck asked, coming through the door behind Alisa.

Her stomach flip-flopped as he bent over for a closer look at the stain. It *did* look like dried blood. Yumi squeezed in, too, also looking down.

"I don't know," Alisa said, trying to sound calm and not disturbed by the eeriness of the station, even if she was wishing she had stood her ground back on the ship and told Leonidas to go explore on his own.

He was now looking down at something between two crates. Alisa debated if she wanted to know what he had found. It wasn't until he crouched down and poked at something with his rifle that she walked over to join him.

"Might be something valuable," she muttered, though she knew she was only trying to fool herself.

She saw the ripped shreds of cloth first, the remains of a curtain or tablecloth in a garish floral pattern. No, she realized with a jolt, glimpsing more of it. Not a curtain. A dress. There was the sleeve. It was bloodstained, the same as the floor.

Leonidas held up a single boot with punctures in it. Teeth marks? Claws? Alisa didn't know if her mind was traveling to ridiculous places— how would some big predator have found its way onto a research station? Still, the punctures did not look like bullet holes or laser burns.

She shone her flashlight around on the damaged items, then farther into the darkness beyond them. The beam caught on something white. She swallowed. A broken bone.

Leonidas walked over and picked it up, then held it toward the light so she could see. "A human femur."

Alisa had already recognized it. "Broken in half."

She slid her beam along the floor, wondering where the other half had gone. Maybe she didn't want to know.

"Not by a rat." He walked closer, holding it out toward her. As if she wanted it. But all he did was point to gouges in the bone. Teeth marks.

"No," she agreed. "Not unless a giant mutated space rat did it."

He looked at her, once again no hint in his gaze that he appreciated her humor.

"Sorry," she said. "Was it someone you knew?"

"No." He laid the bone on top of the closest crate. "The person I seek is a man."

"I've noticed all of the doors are opening for you. Is there a comm? Could you try calling him to see if he's here?"

"I suspect that if he were here, he would have taken care of this." He spread a hand, whether to indicate the bloodstains and bones or the mess in general, Alisa did not know.

"You sure? If there was something roaming around killing people in my research station, I'd hide in my lab with a box of ration bars and something heavy in front of the door."

"This happened a while ago." Leonidas touched the bone again—it had been completely cleaned of muscle and tendon. "Months ago, likely."

"A box of ration bars can get you far. So long as you're bright and don't open the door when something with claws knocks."

His eyes narrowed as he looked at her again. "You should get your own set of combat armor if you'll be out in the system on your own."

She blinked at the non sequitur. What had prompted that?

"My armor is my ship," she said.

Much like engineers, pilots weren't supposed to go tramping around in dangerous places outside of their ships.

"With your mouth, that won't be enough."

"Oh, you're very charming," Alisa said, understanding his comment now. "How is it there wasn't a Mrs. Cyborg squatting in my ship with you?"

His jaw clenched, his expression growing frostier than she thought the joke warranted. Unless maybe there had *been* a Mrs. Cyborg once and he had lost her.

She opened her mouth, intending to apologize, but he spoke first.

"You're quick to claim ownership of a freighter that was registered to a junk man."

"You looked up who owned it before squatting in it?"

"To see if the owner was alive and if anyone would come for it, yes. You were unforeseen."

"Sorry to get in the way of your plans." Alisa was on the verge of reminding him that he would still be sitting on that dustball if it hadn't been for her, but Yumi joined them first, Beck walking behind her protectively.

"Do we know who these people were?" Yumi asked.

"*People?*" Alisa asked. "Is there more than one, or did you just find..." She kept herself from finishing the thought aloud, that Yumi might simply have found more pieces of the dress wearer. It was too bleak to bring up—everything here was bleak.

"There are some more bones over there. A skull." Beck pointed toward some crates stacked by the entrance to the side corridor. "And a man's clothing that's been ripped up. Also found this." He held up an Etcher, similar to Alisa's. "It's out of bullets."

"Typical armament for imperial scientists manning a research station?" Alisa asked Leonidas.

"No." Again bypassing the side corridors, he headed for a door at the end of the room. "According to my map, the labs start in here."

"It might be a good idea to take the women back to the ship," Beck said before Alisa and Yumi could move off.

"Oh, that sounds like an excellent idea to me," Alisa said, "but I doubt he'll allow it." She waved at Leonidas.

Beck glowered in that direction, his hands tight on his rifle. Leonidas had moved far enough away that Beck might get a shot off before he raced back here to attack him. Of course, Leonidas had his helmet off. One shot might be all it would take to blow his head off. Assuming Leonidas didn't sense it coming and dodge in time.

Alisa laid her hand on Beck's armored forearm on the chance similar thoughts were going through his head.

"Let's just see what's here," she said quietly, turning her back so Leonidas would not hear. "If the station has been abandoned by everyone except—" she glanced at the bones, "—rats, we might be able to salvage valuables without incurring anyone's wrath."

"That's probably why *they* were here," Beck said, waving his gun at the remains of the dead. "Something sure got wrathful."

With that feeling of bleakness growing heavier within her, Alisa only shook her head and walked toward Leonidas. If they were close to the labs, this little quest might be over soon. And the labs would be a likely spot for valuables. Probably. She had no idea what kind of research had been going on in them.

Leonidas hadn't opened the door yet. He was looking at the control panel beside it. *Most* of the control panel. The face of it hung askew, the screws missing and wires dangling out from inside of the wall.

"Someone tried to hack their way through a locked door?" Alisa asked.

"Hacked may be an apt word." Leonidas stepped aside so she could study the door itself.

Her flashlight beam highlighted cuts and scorch marks in the door, along with some dents that might represent someone's attempt to open it with bullets. A couple of dents marred the front of the control panel too. Leonidas looked back the way they had come, waving for Beck and Yumi to step aside.

He startled Alisa by taking her hand, his cool gauntleted fingers wrapping around hers.

"What are you doing?" she asked as he directed her multitool so that the flashlight beam pierced the darkness, landing on the door they had come in, one that had slid shut as soon as they all entered. She hadn't noticed it when they came in since it had been behind her, but the control panel there had also been shot up.

Once they had all seen it, Leonidas let go of her.

"Next time you want to hold my hand, you should ask," Alisa said. "I have high standards as to who I let fondle my fingers." The joke came out of habit more than because she thought there was anything funny about the situation. Quite the contrary. Her unease over everything was growing by the second. But she always found it preferable to make jokes than to admit to fear, to vulnerability. Especially now that she was a captain.

As usual, Leonidas ignored her humor. "I'll see if I can open this one."

He turned back to the door, lifting the dangling panel and poking at the wires inside. The consummate professional.

"Someone got trapped in here?" Beck said, looking back and forth from door to door. Alisa hadn't moved her arm, so her flashlight still shone on the damaged panel on the other side of the room.

"And wanted badly to get out, it looks like," Yumi said quietly. She stood close to Beck, having perhaps lost some of her interest in wandering off to explore.

"Why wouldn't they have gone that way?" Beck pointed toward the yawning corridor leaving from the side of the room. There was a door on it.

"Maybe that's where *it* came from," Yumi said.

"You have any idea what *it* was?" Alisa asked.

"Is," Yumi whispered.

"Pardon?"

"What it is. There aren't any animals that can pilot spaceships, so unless someone came and picked it up, it's still here."

"Well, that's comforting," Alisa said.

Leonidas stepped back from the control panel and considered the door again.

"No luck?" Alisa asked. "Guess we'll have to leave."

She was willing to give up her chance at salvage to avoid being eaten by whatever had munched on these people. If they *could* still leave. The doors had opened to let her team walk into the station, so why had they locked when these people had wanted to leave? Had this all happened at the same time as the gravity failed? Maybe the power had failed on the whole station. Or maybe someone had deliberately turned off the power so that the doors wouldn't work. But who would do that? Not some animal, certainly.

Leonidas shifted his weight so he could lay both of his palms against the door. Metal squealed as his shoulders flexed. The door slid open a couple of inches, and he let go with one hand, lunging to slip his fingers into the gap. From there, he heaved it open with more squeals of metal. It did not retract all the way flush with the jamb, instead hanging crookedly, a few inches still tilted outward on the top, but when he let it go, the door stayed open like that.

"Guess these people didn't have a cyborg with them to help them escape," Alisa said.

"I could have done that with a little help from my armor," Beck said with a sniff.

Leonidas ignored him and walked into a new room. This time, the lights flickered on, gleaming on the shoulders of his crimson armor.

Alisa turned off her flashlight, relieved that they would not have to deal with more shadows. Before putting the multitool away, she commed the ship.

"Marchenko checking in. Anything interesting happening back there?"

"Aren't you supposed to say more official things than that?" came Mica's voice in response. "Like, this is the captain. Status report, crew."

"You're thinking of the military. I don't think things have to be that official on a freighter."

"The doctor and I got bored in NavCom and are playing video games in the rec room."

"I'll assume that's a no, then. You have nothing of interest to report."

"I'm close to getting the high score on Space Avenger."

Alisa snorted. She was amazed Finnegan hadn't ripped the game console out of the table and sold it, though maybe it was so old that it would have cost him more money to tote it out of the junkyard than he would have gotten for it.

"That's the shooter game, right?" Alisa asked. "You'll never touch my score on the piloting one."

"Probably not, but I'm doing well here. The doctor keeps losing his man in the practice area before you board the ship and try to take it back from smugglers," Mica said. "I didn't know you could actually die before you got to Level One."

"It's not necessary to report *that*," Alejandro's voice sounded in the background, extremely dry.

"She asked what was interesting. I found that interesting. And amusing."

"It wasn't that funny."

"No? Then why did I laugh so hard that tea came out of my nose?"

"Sounds like a problem with a deviated septum. You should have a doctor look at that."

"My nostrils aren't available for study."

"We're fine in here," Alisa said, rolling her eyes. "Thanks for asking."

"You're welcome, Captain," Mica said.

Alisa turned off the comm. Yumi and Beck were looking at her, eyebrows raised.

"The others are fine," she told them.

"Clearly," Beck said.

Alisa headed through the doorway and into a rectangular room. Three of the walls held shelves and cabinets, many of them broken. Carbon had scorched the floor, leaving giant black marks, as if someone had set off an explosion in here. The fourth wall was mostly made of glass and had survived whatever bomb had been detonated. Another room stood behind it, one full of desks and workstations and equipment. One of the labs, presumably. It appeared to be mostly intact.

Relieved by the lack of bones and bloodstains on the floor, even if the carbon was puzzling, Alisa walked toward the closest set of shelves that wasn't mangled. She had to walk around a broken grid in the floor, metal bars warped or completely blown away. Water trickled past down below. She almost pulled out her flashlight again to investigate, but the shelves were far more of a pull.

She did not know what she had expected the lab to hold, but the rows of strangely shaped molds were not it. She stared at a shelf full of pieces of a puzzle that looked like they could be assembled to form a forearm. Another shelf held kneecaps. Another squishy, gelatinous implant of some sort. Her first thought was that they had come to a plant for assembling androids, but she had seen prosthetic limbs before, and this was something different. These looked more like they would be inserted in—

It struck her like a hammer on a gong.

"Cyborg parts," she blurted, turning toward Leonidas.

He had already opened a door in the glass wall and entered the lab. Beck and Yumi were talking quietly in the other doorway and had not yet entered the room.

It might not be noble or wise to think of scavenging when there were dead people twenty feet away, and their own safety was in question, but Alisa couldn't help but realize she might have found her moment—and her prize. Cyborg implants ought to be worth quite a bit on the black market. She had no idea how to sell things on the black market, but she could learn.

She slipped her hand into her satchel and pulled out an empty sack. Leonidas had his back to her. Good. He would object to the theft. No, not theft, she told herself. *Scavenging.* She wasn't a thief, damn it. She was an opportunist, and there was nothing wrong with that. This place had been empty for months, and the empire wasn't around anymore, not in anything like its previous incarnation, so it was highly doubtful anyone was going to come out here to claim these items. The cyborg assembly line would probably be on hold indefinitely. Not a bad thing, in her opinion.

Looking for the least damaged items, Alisa turned her back to the lab—and Leonidas—so she could surreptitiously slide some of the implants into her bag.

A soft splash came from behind her, from below that broken grid in the floor. She paused and looked toward it, not certain if it was something to do with the station's water filtration and plumbing system or if some of the cyborg parts needed to be tested in liquid for some reason.

Another splash sounded. Were those noises a result of the way the water was running through the channel? Or—she swallowed—was something down there?

Her gaze shifted toward the lab, as she wondered if Leonidas and his superior cyborg hearing had detected anything. Her hand shifted toward the blazer Beck had lent her. He and Yumi were still arguing about something by the doorway.

"Beck?" she started to ask.

A thump and a big splash from below made her stop, dropping into a crouch. Something dark and huge flew up through the opening in the grid. It whirled and jumped straight at her.

CHAPTER TWELVE

Alisa had the impression of fur, fangs, and at least four hundred pounds of muscled bulk before the creature was in the air, springing toward her, and all she could see was her death in its yellow eyes. She fired, shooting it in the chest, and dropped to the floor at the same time, doubting that even Beck's powerful blazer pistol would slow its momentum.

She meant to roll, to scramble out of the way as fast as she could, but she was too slow. The massive creature slammed into her, smashing her against the shelves.

Its bulk crushed her, and pain exploded from both sides of her body. Shelves and implants tumbled down as fur filled her eyes. She sensed it raising a paw to strike with deadly claws. She shot again, point blank this time, then tried to fling herself to the side. Half-pinned against the broken shelves, she could not go far. She glimpsed light and pushed toward it, trying to escape, but it only spun to follow her. It raised its paw again, as if those blasts had not hurt it at all. She tried to fire again, but the heavy paw smashed against her wrist, thwarting her aim. The blast of energy flew harmlessly wide, slamming into the ceiling.

She dove away, not caring which direction she went, just needing space between her and the monster so she could think, figure out something. Before she could think of anything, the ground disappeared beneath her. The stupid broken grid. She had been too busy fleeing to notice it.

A bar gouged her ribs as she tumbled down, flailing, unable to find anything to grab onto. She splashed into two feet of water.

Afraid the creature would be right behind her, she yanked out her Etcher, ignoring the fresh wounds that shouted out for attention. She'd dropped Beck's blazer somewhere, so this would have to do.

Shouts came from above. With water rushing past around her legs and blood roaring in her ears, she couldn't understand them, but she couldn't see the creature, and that was a good thing. A dark furry paw flopped down onto the grid. She flinched but aimed her gun at it. She almost shot, but it wasn't moving. The shouts had died down too.

A crimson suit of armor came into view. Leonidas knelt next to the hole and peered into her oubliette.

"You all right, Marchenko?" he asked.

Alisa lowered her Etcher. "I'm alive. Things hurt. I hope our semi-retired doctor doesn't have cold hands. I hate being worked on by doctors with cold hands." She clamped down on the stream of words, barely conscious of what she was babbling.

Worrying about cold hands was ridiculous right now, but being hurt and thinking of medics made her flash back to those months in the hospital, those first weeks she had been awake and when she hadn't been sure if she would live or die. Too many bad memories flooded her brain, threatening to take her over the edge.

She took several deep breaths, struggling to calm herself. Pain came with those breaths, but she welcomed it. Pain was grounding. It meant she was alive, that her body was working as it should. Thankfully, she did not think she had broken any bones. Not this time.

"Can you give me your hand?" Leonidas lowered his gauntleted hand, the red of his armor making her think of blood, of the fact that he was a cyborg, the enemy.

Alisa eyed the dark depths from which the water was flowing. From which that monster had come. What the hell had that thing been? And were there more of them? What if there were more coming right now?

"Yes," she said, reaching up and clasping his hand. Enemy or not, he was a lot more appealing than that monster had been.

Leonidas lifted her as easily as if lifting a feather, rising to his feet and wrapping his other arm around her waist, so he could pull her away from the broken grid. A piece of her jacket hung from the jagged bar that had snagged her on the way down.

Alisa glowered at it, then at the dead monster. Animal. Creature. Whatever it was. It lay between the grid and the broken shelves, cyborg implants littering its body like dead leaves.

Beck leaned against the shelves, catching his breath. Blood spattered his white armor.

"I don't know who thought it would be a good idea to put an oubliette in the middle of a lab, but I think they should be flogged. I know the empire was more into mental manipulation than flogging people, but there really should be an exception." Her voice sounded squeaky in her ears, and she forced herself to go back to breathing. She was fine. A few scratches, but she'd had much worse. Funny, though, how much more terrifying it was when her fate wasn't in her own hands. She *much* preferred facing death from the pilot's seat, the flight stick firmly in her grasp.

"I apologize," Leonidas said, releasing her and stepping back, though he kept a hand close, maybe not certain she wouldn't fall over.

Considering the blood dripping down her sleeve from somewhere, that was a possibility.

"For the lack of flogging?" she asked.

He wore a serious expression, and she immediately regretted her sarcasm. It had sounded like a heartfelt apology, even though she wasn't sure what had prompted him to make it. He—and Beck, too, it looked like—had killed the creature that had been intent on killing *her*. He didn't owe her an apology. She ought to be thanking him.

Instead of ignoring her joke, or giving her one of his irritated narrow-eyed looks, Leonidas actually smiled faintly. The gesture disappeared so quickly she wondered if she'd imagined it.

"For letting myself be distracted," he said quietly, his gaze flicking toward Beck. But Beck wasn't looking at them. He'd knelt down to lift the head of the creature, scrutinizing it. Yumi stood by the wall, her hand to her chest, a woman who, like Alisa, had gotten more on this trip than she bargained for. "I promised I'd protect you," he added.

His jaw clenched, some of that irritation springing into his eyes. For once, it did not seem to be directed at her, but inward, at himself.

Feeling uncomfortable at seeing that he actually cared about keeping her alive—or at least about keeping his word regarding keeping her alive—Alisa shrugged and looked away.

"The creature is dead," she said. "That's all that matters, right?"

It also mattered if there were more of them around. She wondered if there was a way to tell.

"I think it's an Octarian Blood Bear," Beck said.

"It is," Leonidas said. "We had training missions where we had to hunt and kill them with only a knife when I was a young soldier."

"Guess that's why you were so quick and efficient at killing it now, eh?" Alisa asked.

"Not that quick," Leonidas muttered.

"But I helped, right?" Beck smiled at Alisa and stuck one of his boots up on the bear's shaggy backside. Or maybe that was its butt. If man-eating bears had butts. "You saw me, mech. I hacked the hells out of that back leg and shot it twice."

"After Marchenko shot it in the chest twice," Leonidas said dryly. "It would have died from those wounds."

Maybe, but not before it flattened her. What if it had followed her down through that grid? All it would have had to do was land on her with those four hundred pounds, and she would have been crushed and drowned. She shuddered, glad the men had jumped in.

"Don't take my victory away from me, mech," Beck said. "There have been precious few of them this week."

Leonidas sighed. "Call me Leonidas."

Beck's mouth twisted, like he wasn't sure about that.

Leonidas walked over to the other side of the bear—such an innocuous sounding name for something that had been eating people here for months—and picked up the blazer Alisa had dropped. He thumbed on the safety and tossed it to her.

"Thanks," she said.

She was on the verge of also thanking him—and Beck—for helping, but stopped when he noticed the bag she had been filling. The bear had half-buried it when it fell, but the top half stuck out from under its body. Not wanting everyone to know she had been pillaging, Alisa hoped the dead bear would be too heavy, and that nobody would be able to extract her bag.

But Leonidas lifted the side of the bear as if it weighed nothing and withdrew it.

"That's nothing," Alisa said, reaching for it.

He looked inside.

She winced.

"You planning to make your own cyborg?" he asked, arching an eyebrow.

Three suns, would he believe that if she claimed it? No, he was being wry. She could see it in his eyes. He knew exactly what she had been doing.

"Sell the parts." She walked over, her stiff and aching body not keeping her from snatching the bag from him. "How else am I supposed to pay for that combat armor?"

He didn't say anything, and he didn't try to keep the bag from her. Maybe it was only in her imagination that his eyes seemed to judge her, but she couldn't keep from defending herself.

"You dragged me here," she blurted. "Isn't it fair that I get some compensation for my time?"

Leonidas said nothing, merely looked back toward the lab. Because she wasn't worth looking at? A sick feeling of disgust welled inside of her. She wanted to be mad at him, but she knew that the problem was within her, not with him. She dropped the bag, though she hadn't decided yet if she would leave it. Taking things she could sell was logical, damn it. This place was a desecrated mess. The empire was gone. Whoever had done this research was gone. Eaten, probably. If she didn't take these things, some other scavenger would be along to do the same thing.

"Stay close to me," Leonidas said, and headed into the lab again.

She followed him. Even if she hated being ordered around by someone who wasn't a superior officer in her army, and even if she resented being told what to do under the best of circumstances, she did not want to get hurt again, more because he would blame himself than because of the actual risk to her person. She did not know what that meant. Probably that she was going crazy, caring what a cyborg thought and felt. But he had said himself that he was human. It seemed strange to think of him that way when cyborgs had been nothing but superhuman enemies to her during the war, but he clearly believed it. He admittedly acted as human as the next person.

Yumi pushed away from the wall, gave the dead bear a wide berth, and headed for Alisa's discarded bag. She opened it and peeked inside.

Alisa paused in the glass doorway of the lab—Leonidas had already gone back inside. She was still waffling over what to do with the parts she had grabbed, but she didn't want someone else to presume to take them while she was deciding. Was Yumi thinking that she could buy a lot of chicken feed with the latest and greatest in cyborg bits?

Yumi dropped the bag. "You should look for eyes."

"Uh, pardon?"

"The optical implants. You could fit hundreds of them in your bag, and I bet they're worth even more than the muscle augmentations. My understanding is that the optical technology was born out of scientists creating new eyes for the blind—if you remember your history, you know that many people went blind when first colonizing Dravon. The human eye didn't do well there, until the domes were erected. Anyway, replacement eyes are not inexpensive, and there are many who could use them, not to enhance anything necessarily, but for quality of life issues."

"Have you seen any eyes?" Alisa asked, her interest piqued despite her moral dilemma.

"Not in here." Yumi shrugged. "Maybe there's another room."

Alisa looked toward Leonidas, though she did not expect him to help her shop for items to loot. Still, he was the expert on this place, the one with the map. He was hunched over a computer console facing the glass, his netdisc out again. Planning to copy some files?

"It's not a QuickMart," Leonidas growled, not looking at either of them. "I'm not going to look up the inventory to help with your theft."

No, he wasn't happy about having this place pillaged. Or maybe he wasn't happy he had not found the person he'd hoped to find, and that was making him cranky. She almost pointed out that he was being cranky, but she had not forgotten that he had saved her life. She resolved to tamp down her lippy streak. At the least, she wouldn't snap a retort about theft. Besides, she probably deserved his comment.

She stepped around a workstation, curious about what he was looking up. Would he let her see?

She almost tripped over the torn up remains of another body. More of the bones remained with this one, but they were equally gnawed and scattered about. A shredded white lab coat lay beside what was left of the ribcage.

The sight sobered Alisa, stealing all thoughts of comebacks and lippiness.

"That's not a thief," she said, then gave herself a mental kick. A nice stating of the obvious.

"No," Leonidas said, not taking his eyes from the holodisplay. Columns of text drifted in the air before him, the words too far away for Alisa to read. The little red light flashed on his netdisc. Yes, he was copying files. He opened a second display above another console, and video imagery of the station came up.

"Do you think it's…the person you were looking for?" Alisa asked.

He did not answer. Perhaps his silence was answer enough. He could have said no without revealing anything to her. But saying yes might mean revealing that they had come all this way and risked their lives for nothing.

Though she was curious as to what he was looking up, she opted to give him his privacy. Everything on that screen would probably go over her head anyway.

But as she backed toward the door, he looked up, pinning her with his gaze.

"Stay," he said.

"Because you've grown to appreciate my company, and you'd be lonely without me?" She hadn't managed to tame that lippy streak for long.

"Because there may be more of those bears on the station."

"What makes you think that?" She'd had the thought herself but wondered if his sensors had shown him something. He had not put his helmet back on.

Leonidas held up a finger, his gaze drawn back to one of the displays.

A clang came from the room with the shelves. Alisa jumped, spinning toward the noise and reaching for Beck's blazer again.

"Sorry." Beck waved a bloody knife. He had removed his helmet and was kneeling beside the dead animal. "That was just me."

Alisa curled a lip. "What are you doing?"

"Told you—I've been looking for fresh meat." Beck winked at her.

"I…you're joking, right?" Alisa leaned out the door and found Yumi. "He's joking, isn't he?"

"I'm not sure. He has carved a large sample."

"If there are more of those around, is it wise to fling blood all over the place?" Alisa asked. "Won't the others smell it?" She touched her side, aware that she was leaking blood of her own.

"These bears are top-level predators on Octaria," Beck said. "Each with a large range, a range they keep the competition out of—I doubt there are multiple ones in here. Even if they started out that way, they would have likely killed each other, especially since, ah, food supplies apparently got scarce here after a while."

Food supplies? Alisa did not want to think about that.

"Are they omnivores?" Yumi asked. "They may have been able to subsist on whatever supplies were here for humans. They may have also hibernated to slow their metabolisms and food requirements."

"I really don't want to know about their metabolic needs," Alisa said. "Leonidas, how much longer do you need? I think we're all ready to get back to the ship."

Leonidas was staring intently at one of the displays in front of him. Alisa walked back around the workstation. He'd closed down the one with the text on it and put away his netdisc, but the video display was running, showing footage on cameras around the station. Something moved on one of them, something big with black fur, and Alisa jumped.

"Is that live footage?"

Leonidas enlarged the image, and two more of the great fanged beasts came into view, all three of them shambling along on all fours, passing through the familiar chambers of the research station, rooms Alisa and the others had just passed through. In the video, the crates were neatly stacked, and there weren't any bones on the floor. That let her relax an iota. She leaned forward and checked the date stamp in the corner.

"Two months ago?" she asked.

"Yes, we're two months too late," Leonidas said, cupping his chin with his hand as he continued to watch.

"What brought them here? Can you tell?"

"Not what. Who."

He poked his finger through the display, and the footage started playing in reverse, the giant bears heading butt first in the direction of the airlocks. In that first room, a person came into view, someone wearing a black robe with a cowl pulled over the head. Leonidas scrolled back further, then let the video play, showing the person—it was impossible to tell if it was a man or a woman—coming out of the airlock behind the three giant bears.

"That's the one we killed," Leonidas said, pointing to the bear in the middle.

Alisa had no idea how he could tell. The big shaggy creatures all looked the same to her, the same and terrifying. But she was more curious about the person walking behind them, as if they were domesticated livestock rather than man-eating predators. The bears ambled in front of the cloaked figure without showing any inclination toward spinning around and taking a chomp. Even on all fours, they were as tall as the person's shoulder, and he or she appeared thin and insignificant next to their bulk.

Leonidas zoomed in on the robed figure's chest, showing a pendant with a red moon on a silver star background.

"Starseer," Alisa breathed.

She had only ever seen one in real life before, when she had been a girl walking through a busy concourse on a space station with her mother, but she remembered the dark robe, the cowl pulled over the head, and the pendant. Even though she hadn't seen the person do anything indicative of mind powers, simply walking along with a metallic staff like some monk of old, she hadn't forgotten the way people muttered and moved away. Even though Starseers were rare sights in the system anymore, everyone knew their history and what they could do.

As she and Leonidas watched, the cloaked figure opened doors without touching the panels, leading the bears into the room outside of this first lab. He or she waved a hand, and the creatures raced into the corridor, heading deeper into the station—to hunt. That done, the Starseer turned and walked out, the black robe sweeping the floor as he or she returned to the airlock and disappeared from the station's cameras.

Leonidas's fingers curled around the edge of the workstation, and a crunching sound came as they dug into the hard material. He glanced down, made an irritated noise, and let go. Alisa backed up when he turned his sour expression toward her.

"The Alliance have any Starseers on the payroll?" he asked, the words sounding like an accusation.

"Not that I know of."

Admittedly, she wasn't in the know when it came to decisions from the First Governor and senior military officers. She had been a lowly lieutenant for most of the war, and even when she'd made captain, she had only been in command of a squadron of Striker pilots. Who knew what had been going on among the leadership? Nevertheless, she doubted they had allied with Starseers.

"The Starseers have always been associated with the empire, haven't they?" she added.

"I heard rumors that some were working with the Alliance. It's unlikely you people could have overthrown the empire without help."

Alisa bristled at the implication that normal human beings couldn't have any effect on a bloated government so full of itself that it hadn't seen the threat coming until it was too late for them to do anything. "Of course. We people were so inept. How could we have possibly beaten the mighty empire and its cyborg armies?"

"I didn't say you were inept, but you were outnumbered twenty to one, if not more. We had superior forces, supplies, and the infrastructure for delivering them. If you hadn't resorted to despicable guerrilla tactics—"

"Tactics aren't despicable if they're your only chance for freedom. You think we didn't know we were outnumbered? That the odds were against us? What were we supposed to do? Toss our infantry soldiers out on a battle-field to face your superior forces in open combat?"

Leonidas stepped toward her, huge and intimidating in that armor, and it was all she could do not to scramble backward. "You were supposed to fight with *honor*, not bombing civilian buildings and destroying resources that all of humankind relies upon."

"I never bombed any civilians. I served on the *Merciless* and the *Silver Striker*. We were in space, transporting people and engaging in battle to defend our resources. Your warships were the ones that wanted to annihilate us, wipe our rebellion from the system. And don't act like the empire never did anything morally reprehensible. You think I've never heard of what the Cyborg Corps were responsible for? The assassinations you carried out during the war? The way you made powerful people disappear before the war ever started? Everybody knows what that red armor stands for." She poked him in the chest. She might as well have poked a steel wall—all it did was hurt her finger.

"Everybody knows *nothing*. I've never assassinated anyone. I've always fought with honor. The stories you people make up to justify your actions are ridiculous."

"Stories? Sure, me and millions of other people. We're just sitting around and making up stories about cyborgs."

"I have always acted honorably," he repeated, his nostrils flaring.

"So. Have. I."

"Yes, you're a very honorable thief, shoveling imperial goods into your bag."

"Oh screw you, mech." Alisa bumped her hip on the workstation as she stalked toward the door, but she barely noticed. She almost crashed into Beck, who had come over to peek inside.

"Problem?" he asked, looking at the two of them.

"No," Alisa said at the same time as Leonidas. It came out with the fury of a curse word. For both of them.

"That's good." Beck gave Yumi one of those long looks of concern. "I've got some meat for tomorrow. Just got to do some research and figure out what kind of marinade I need to soften it up a touch. How about we head back to the ship, so I can do that?"

"Fine with me." Alisa didn't bother looking at Leonidas to see if he was done with his research. She didn't particularly care. Instead, she tapped the comm button on her multitool. "Mica, how's that game going? You beat my high score yet?"

A hiss of static came from the comm, then silence.

"Mica? Dr. Dominguez?" she asked, a sinking feeling spreading through her stomach. She looked toward the dead bear, remembering the two others in the video. They couldn't have gotten through the airlock and onto the ship, could they? If they had, there was no cyborg on board to make short work of them.

"We have to get back to the ship," Alisa said. "*Now.*"

CHAPTER THIRTEEN

Alisa was about to step into the airlock, both Beck's borrowed blazer and her Etcher in her hands, but Leonidas caught up then and stretched out a hand to stop her. She opened her mouth, intending to bark at him to get out of the way, but he only held her up long enough to step in front of her. He strode into the airlock tube, his own rifle pointing down it.

"Stay between us," Beck whispered from behind her. He shooed Yumi toward Alisa, and they followed Leonidas into the tube.

As soon as she could, Alisa hustled into the cargo hold, searching in all directions, afraid she would spot blood—or worse. The chickens were still there, squawking plaintively. If a bear had stormed onto the ship, would it have gone for them first? Or would it have been drawn by larger prey?

Leonidas must have felt some of Alisa's worry, her urgency, because he broke into a run, heading for the stairs. With the cargo hold empty, it did not take long to verify that there weren't any bodies in it, so Alisa hurried after him. She prayed that they would find Mica and Alejandro in the rec room, still playing that game. Maybe something had simply happened to short out the comm system.

They reached the small kitchen and mess hall, and Alisa peeked into the rec room off to the side. The asteroid game hovered in the air over the table, the back of a character's head and gun in view as he stood in a spaceship, ready to clear more enemies from the level. The game was a little too apt at the moment.

Leonidas continued toward NavCom, but Alisa headed toward the game station. Dread curdled in her stomach as she worried she would find one or more bodies in the back. Nobody was there. The chairs and table were locked to the deck, so they couldn't be knocked over. Too bad. That might have been a clue to suggest a fight or that Mica and Alejandro had gotten up in a hurry to run and hide.

Clangs sounded as someone checked the sleep quarters. As Alisa finished her circuit of the rec room, something caught her eye. A necklace with a broken chain. She knelt and picked it up—it was the three-starred pendant that Alejandro wore outside of his robe.

Leonidas appeared in the hatchway, his armored shoulders brushing the jamb. "NavCom is empty, as are the cabins. If they're here, they're hiding."

"I don't think they're here," Alisa said quietly, spreading her palm to show him the pendant.

"There's no hint of the animal den smell I detected on the station, nor did I see any blood."

"So, it wasn't the bears." Alisa felt a modicum of relief at that, but their people were still missing. Mica was the closest thing she had to a friend here, the only person she had any history with. "Then what got them?"

"The pirates, I'd wager."

Alisa stood up, clenching her jaw. "No, they couldn't have. I did what you said. I took a circuitous route here. I checked to make sure there weren't any ships within sensor range before veering into the asteroid. There's no way they followed us here."

"I didn't say that they did. They were here before. Somehow, they knew about the station."

"How do you know…" Alisa halted the question in the middle, remembering the shredded clothing. "The people who were killed in those storage rooms. You think those were the same pirates from the mining ship? That they came to loot the station?"

"As you and your science officer have noted, cybernetic implants are valuable."

"But why take my engineer and a passenger?" Alisa looked down at the pendant. "If they're just thieves trying to get everything they can, why not take my whole ship?"

Before he could answer, the *Nomad's* tinny computerized voice spoke, echoing throughout the ship. "Self-destruct will commence in fifteen minutes."

Leonidas's eyebrows rose.

"Uh, Captain?" Beck called from the kitchen. "Should that be concerning us?"

Alisa shook her head, confusion swarming her. "There's no self-destruct option on the *Nomad*. It's a freighter, not some warship full of military secrets. There's no need to sacrifice it if enemies board."

"Are you sure your engineer couldn't have rigged something?"

"How could she have had time to do that? They didn't even have time to call us on the comm. They had to have been taken by surprise. Even if they *did* have time, all she would have done was set explosives in engineering. I don't see how she could have tied in the ship's computer to make announcements."

"Self-destruct will commence in fourteen minutes," the computer announced cheerfully.

Great, it must have reached the point where it would warn them on the minute, every minute.

"I'm going to search for explosives," Beck said.

"Maybe we should just get off the ship," Yumi said. "How badly will the station be damaged if the ship blows up while in its dock?"

"I don't know," Beck said, "but I'm not in a hurry to go back inside and fight two more of those creatures. I've got plenty of meat to grill already."

"Not to mention that we could be stranded in there for a long time if we didn't have a ship." Alisa waved Leonidas aside and headed toward NavCom. "I'm going to scan through the camera footage, see what happened."

"Better scan quickly," Leonidas said, running after Beck, apparently believing that Mica could have jury-rigged something.

In NavCom, none of the alarms were flashing. The console waited quietly. If there were a self-destruct sequence, there should have been a warning up here.

Alisa found the video footage and scanned back for the last half hour on both the internal and exterior cameras. She groaned, catching something right away. A combat ship about a third of the size of the *Nomad*. It had docked next to them in the adjoining airlock.

If Mica had been up here in NavCom, she would have seen them coming on the cameras, but the ship's proximity alarm would not have gone off, not when they were docked. Being docked usually meant they were on a space station or spaceport with all manner of ships around. Nothing to be worried about.

Alisa cursed herself. She should have thought to set some kind of alarm or at least ordered Mica to stay up here instead of wandering around the rest of the ship, looking for games to play.

She checked the time stamps as the footage continued in reverse, showing the pirate ship's approach. It had only been docked for eight minutes. Long enough for the pirates to get off their ship, storm onto the *Nomad*, and kidnap Mica and Alejandro. But, as Alisa had already asked, why had they only taken the people instead of stealing the entire ship? NavCom had been wide open. They could have easily come up here, and a halfway decent pilot could have figured out how to steer her out. That big mining ship surely had a landing bay large enough to hold her.

"Self-destruct will commence in eleven minutes," the ship announced.

"Oh," Alisa said with new understanding. "Right. They must have heard that and figured they had better get away from this ship and the station while they still had time."

"Who are you talking to?" Leonidas asked, striding up the corridor and into NavCom, glancing toward the comm panel.

"Myself. I'm an excellent conversationalist."

"Beck and Moon are still looking, but we've seen no sign of explosives yet. We should leave soon and get to the far side of the station. If your ship blows up, it will affect the integrity of Blackstar." He grimaced. "It may destroy the whole station."

"That's one way to get rid of the bears."

"Your humor is—"

"Inappropriate, I know."

His eyebrow twitched.

"It's how I distract myself when I'm scared for my life. Or the lives of others. Especially others that I talked into coming along on this trip. Hells, I even *charged* Alejandro to come along. He just wanted to go to Perun." Alisa took a deep breath, immediately regretting her outpouring of honesty. Leonidas was not a confidant.

She turned her back toward him and pulled up the internal camera footage. It did not cover every inch of the ship, but it would show her if people had, indeed, come onboard.

"The responsibility for this situation is more mine than yours," Leonidas said, coming to stand beside her and look down at the footage. "I will get them back."

She wasn't sure how comfortable she felt standing shoulder to shoulder with him, but she did appreciate that he wasn't dismissing the others as unimportant. She could have imagined him waving his hand at their loss and insisting they continue on to…wherever he planned to go next. Perun, she supposed. She hadn't agreed to transport him farther.

"All by yourself?" she asked, enlarging the footage of the rec room—only twenty minutes earlier, Alejandro and Mica had been sitting at the table in there, playing the video game.

"If need be."

"You don't want Beck? Didn't he say he was integral in defeating that bear?"

"He was integral in defeating its rear left haunch." Leonidas pointed at the footage from the cargo hold, of eight armed men storming through the airlock, wearing unmatched collections of combat armor and carrying an assortment of deadly weapons, everything from shotguns to laser rifles to swords.

"Self-destruct will commence in eight minutes," the ship said.

Alisa had been busy concentrating and had barely noticed the last couple of announcements. Eight minutes was not long, especially if they needed to run to the other side of the station. She brought the footage for the cargo hold and the rec room to the forefront, running them forward in sync while minimizing everything else.

The pirates must have made a sound, because Mica looked toward the entrance to the rec room. She reached for her pocket where she should have had her comm unit. She'd been about to pull it out, but Alejandro raised a finger to his lips. He said something—the cameras did not pick up audio—then ran out of the room.

Mica started after him, but paused, her gaze snagging on the game. To Alisa's surprise she turned back to it, lifting her hands to touch the holo-controls that hovered below the main video. She glanced toward the exit several times as she maneuvered the avatar forward to kill a virtual enemy, then flick something on a control console within the game. Mica dropped to her knees, pulling open the control panel under the table. From the angle of the security camera, Alisa could not see what wires she was tinkering with, but she knelt back and glanced toward a corner of the rec room up near the ceiling. That spot held a speaker.

"It's in the game," Alisa realized.

"What?" Leonidas asked.

On the video, Alejandro ran into the rec room, a baton and a blazer in his hands, weapons Alisa would not have guessed he had. He whirled to push the hatch shut, but was too late. The pirates charged into the room. He raised the blazer and fired, but the crimson bolt splashed uselessly off an armored man's shoulder. The pirates did not slow down. Alejandro tried to fight, to protect Mica, but there were too many enemies. One armored pirate thrust him to the side, hurling him against the wall. He landed hard, then was picked up by the neck.

Alisa winced in sympathy of the pained expression on his face and slid her hand into her pocket to wrap it around his broken pendant.

The pirates hoisted Mica and Alejandro over their shoulders and toted them out of the rec room. Alisa lifted her hand, about to stop the playback, but paused when the last two pirates stopped before exiting. They spun toward the corner with the speaker, pointed at it, jabbered something to each other, then charged out of the room. A moment later, all of the pirates appeared in the cargo hold. They still carried their prisoners over their shoulders, and several had stolen duffel bags from the passenger and crew cabins, but that was all they had taken. They hustled quickly off the ship.

"We better leave too," Leonidas said. "With luck, we can—"

"No, we don't need to," Alisa said as the computer spoke again, announcing that they were down to six minutes.

She strode past Leonidas, into the corridor, and through the mess hall to the rec room. If she hadn't played the game before, she might have been fooled, too, but now that she had seen Mica tinkering with the panel, she realized what she had done.

Leonidas followed her and watched as she hit the power on the table, turning off the game.

"If I'm right," Alisa said, "that'll be the end of the announcements."

His gaze shifted from the table to the speaker, then he grunted with understanding. "She fooled them into thinking the ship would blow up."

Alisa nodded. "A good thing for us—we would have been stranded if the pirates had left in both vessels—but that doesn't help them at all."

She closed her eyes. How were they going to get Mica and Alejandro back? If these were the same pirates that had chased them in the mining ship, there could be hundreds, if not thousands, of crew in there, with dozens of smaller ships they could launch at any time. And those pirates would be holding a grudge after she and Leonidas had caused their two bombers to blow up. They might be taking that grudge out on Mica and Alejandro right now.

"We're going after them," she said, opening her eyes.

Thankfully, Leonidas did not object or point out that it would be a suicide mission. After all, he had already said he would get them back.

"You have a plan?" he asked.

"Going after them *is* my plan."

"It could use refinement."

"Are all cyborgs so critical?"

"The ones that survive more than five years in the service, yes. We don't—didn't—get chosen for the moonpuff missions."

"No, I suppose you wouldn't." Alisa slipped past him and headed for NavCom again. Yumi and Beck were in the mess and watched her go by. "I'm going to get us out of this asteroid before they're too far away for us to catch on our sensors. Anyone who wants to help me brainstorm a plan is welcome to join me."

Leonidas followed on her heels.

"What about the countdown?" Beck asked.

"What's the last number you heard?" Alisa called back as she reached the pilot's seat. Her fingers flew over the controls as she closed their airlock hatch and maneuvered the ship away.

"Six," he said.

"How long ago was that?"

"It *has* been a couple of minutes since the computer made an announcement," Yumi said.

"That's because it was a ruse, nothing more," Alisa said. "And we're going to need another ruse if we want to get our people back. A big one. I wonder what the odds are that the mining ship is still out at the edge of the asteroid field and that the small attack craft we saw is what they're flying the prisoners away in. If we could catch it before the pirates reunited with their mother ship…"

"We would still be outgunned," Leonidas said.

Outgunned, right. A polite way of saying the freighter did not have weapons at all. What she had was two men in combat armor.

"We'll have to catch them and board their ship," Alisa said.

Leonidas grunted. "It's more likely that they'll see us, catch us, and board *our* ship."

"Well," Alisa said, thinking as she turned the *Nomad* so it could fly through the tunnel, "that could work too. Maybe certain well-armed and armored people could lie in hiding near the airlock and rush aboard their ship to take it over while their search party is in our ship looking for us."

The pirates might have superior numbers and superior ships, but Alisa had one advantage, a well-trained cyborg in top-of-the-line combat armor. Unfortunately, her well-trained cyborg was making a sour face at her words.

"How did they get in through the security trap?" Yumi asked, pointing toward the place where the *Nomad* had been held on the way in.

"Uh, that's a good question." With everything else going on, Alisa had forgotten about that. She turned in her seat. "Leonidas? That scan that searched our ship—it let us in because you were on board, right? It was programmed to let cyborgs—or cyborg parts—through? It assumed that whatever imperial ship brought cyborgs in would be delivering them to the scientists to work on?"

He hesitated, as if ingrained instincts told him not to give any information to Alliance pilots, but eventually he nodded. "Delivering them to Dr. Bartosz for upgrades, repairs, or initial installs, yes."

"But you had never been here before today?"

"No, Dr. Bartosz usually came to the Corps headquarters to do the work. But I'd heard of men being sent here if he was busy with research."

"Is he the one who initially…made you?"

Leonidas's lips twisted, and she thought he would object to the term. Instead, he said, "Like Victor Frankenstein himself."

"Ah." Alisa remembered him objecting to being called anything other than human, but here he was, making a connection to an Old Earth legend, Frankenstein's monster. There was a dark expression in his eyes. It was not sorrow, not exactly, but it made her regret calling him a mech earlier when she had been angry. "Is he the one who was dead on the floor in the lab?"

"Yes. I saw the name tag on his lab coat."

"I'm sorry," she said quietly.

Surprise flickered across his face, but he sublimated the emotion quickly. "We weren't close."

"He was just someone you thought would have answers?"

Leonidas ticked his fingernail on the control panel in front of her seat. "Pay attention to your flying, Marchenko."

"You're not the captain here, Cyborg," she said, crossing her second and third finger in the classic screw-you gesture. It didn't matter that he was right—she *should* be watching the tunnel ahead. She didn't take orders from him.

Surprisingly, he smiled slightly.

"Uhh, so," Beck said—Alisa had forgotten that he and Yumi were hovering in the corridor, that she had invited them to help come up with a plan. "What did we decide after that little exchange?"

Leonidas's expression grew grim. "That they might have a cyborg too. Or more than one."

Just when she had been thinking that Leonidas would be her singular advantage...

"Cyborg pirates? Those exist?" Beck asked.

"With the empire gone, there's nobody left to pay the salaries of career soldiers," Leonidas said. "People do what they have to do to survive."

Alisa thought about asking what had brought him to that junkyard on Dustor, but they had navigated more than halfway through the tunnel. Soon, the distant stars of the galaxy would come into view, and she would have a pirate ship to hunt down. She glanced at the sensor display, wondering if anything would show up yet. She did not see any blips, but the denseness of the ore packed into the asteroid around them might be dulling the sensors' effectiveness. She would have to wait until they were out in open space.

The stars soon came into sight, along with the body of another asteroid tumbling slowly in the distance. Alisa accelerated toward the opening, eager to have room to maneuver again, the freedom to fly.

A bleep came from the sensor display. She glanced back as they soared out of the asteroid, then cursed. A ship was waiting for them, a *huge* ship.

She reversed the thrusters to brake, having some notion of flying back into the tunnel, but it was too late. Alarms clamored, and the control panel lit up with warnings as a grab beam clamped onto them.

This time, it wasn't a trap placed by the security station. The hulking mass of the miles-long mining ship hovered right over the tunnel exit. And it had them in its clutches.

CHAPTER FOURTEEN

Bangs and thumps sounded on the other side of the airlock hatch. Alisa stood by herself in the cargo hold, the weapons belt hanging at her waist the only sign that she might put up a fight. She would be foolish to do so, however. It had crossed her mind to station all of her people behind cover and open fire when the pirates charged in, but they would be in combat armor, and would far outnumber her forces.

Besides, a firefight wouldn't do anything to free Mica and Alejandro. Better for her to stand here, as she was, and be the distraction. She had stuffed Beck, Yumi, and Leonidas into one of the hidden nooks in the cargo hold—the entrance looked like nothing more than a bulkhead to an observer. She hoped that the pirates would take her and not search too hard for others. She had considered climbing into that nook herself, leaving an empty ship for them to find, but the pirates would surely search until they found crew. They would know the ship hadn't been flying itself.

She smiled, remembering Beck and Leonidas both arguing to have the honor of being the decoy, both saying that being captured might be even worse for a woman. She wouldn't argue that, but they were the most likely to be able to sneak onto the ship after she was taken and free everyone. As much as she hated the idea of needing to be saved—and in putting her fate in someone else's hands—this seemed most logical. She just hoped she wouldn't regret it.

The hatch banged open.

Alisa could have locked it, but then they would have torched their way in, and the ship might not have been spaceworthy afterward. The odds were stacked against her, but she still had the vain hope that she might collect her people and fly away from this.

The boarding party appeared to be the same group of pirates that she had seen on the camera, men wearing a mishmash of combat armor and weapons. Her gut tightened when she spotted something she hadn't noticed in the footage, tufts of hair adorning several of their belts. Human hair. Scalps.

The pirates charged onto the ship, surrounding her, six blazer rifles and pistols pointed at her.

Alisa stood with her arms spread, struggling to keep from panicking. Maybe she should have asked Yumi about that breathing thing she did. She reasoned that if the men started pummeling her—or worse—right here in the cargo hold that Leonidas and the others would come out to stop it. They couldn't see what was happening from their hidden niche, but they would hear if she started screaming. She gulped, hoping she was not given a reason to start screaming.

Four more men in armor jogged into the cargo hold. They diverted immediately toward the stairs, charging up to search the rest of the ship. Even if their suits had sensor units, they shouldn't be able to see the life forms hidden in the walls—that nook was shielded. Alisa's mother had hidden her meager valuables inside of it. It was likely that some past owner of the *Nomad* had installed the space for smuggling cargo.

One of the pirates came forward and unclasped her weapons belt, taking her guns and multitool. Then he stepped back, lifting his rifle and aiming at her chest again, as the others were still doing.

Alisa waited for someone to talk, to ask her for the story she had rehearsed, the story that explained that yes, she *was* the only one left on this ship. No, of *course* she did not have any allies…The pirates had already taken her people.

Heavy boots clanged in the distance, someone walking across the landing bay that the *Nomad* had been sucked into by that grab beam. The even tread had an ominous ring to it. As did the way the pirates stood utterly still, waiting for the owner of the tread to arrive.

Alisa's breath caught when a man in crimson combat armor strode through the hatchway, a rifle cradled in his arms. There weren't any scalps dangling from the utility belt, but she doubted that meant she would be safe with him.

The owner of the armor wore his helmet, and was not close enough for her to see through the faceplate, but she could not help but think that it was Leonidas, that he had somehow gotten outside of the ship. But no, she had locked him into the cubby not five minutes ago. This was someone else. Someone else in Cyborg Corps armor. She hoped it was just some scruffy pirate who had managed to steal the suit, not someone that could equal—or best—Leonidas in a fight. But she recalled the discussion they'd had about the security trap on the station, about the possibility that the pirates, too, had a cyborg.

The red suit stopped in front of her, the pirates shifting to the side to make room.

"One girl?" a hollow voice rang out from inside the helmet. "I put on all of this for one girl?" The gauntleted hand flicked, gesturing toward the owner's torso.

"The rest of the men are searching for more, Sublime Commander," a nervous-sounding pirate said.

Sublime Commander? Alisa almost choked on the ostentatious title. Only a pirate…

The figure lowered his rifle, letting it dangle on its shoulder harness, and lifted his hands, thumbing the buttons that released the helmet. The man—or the cyborg?—lifted it free. He gazed down at her. With short black hair, dark eyes, and bronze skin, nothing about his features reminded Alisa of Leonidas, but that didn't mean he wasn't a cyborg. It wasn't as if those people were genetically related. As far as she knew, they were just men who fit the physical criteria and volunteered for the procedure and the life in the military. This fellow *did* have a thickly muscled neck, and he would have been tall and brawny even without the armor adding mass.

He quirked a smile at her and stepped forward, lifting a hand. Alisa tried to skitter back, but the muzzle of a rifle poked her between the shoulders. Even if she'd had more room, it would not have mattered. That hand darted in with a viper's speed—maybe *more* than a viper's speed—and grabbed her by the front of her shirt and jacket. He lifted her from her feet, nearly ripping the material of her shirt and half-choking her in the process.

A cruel glint entered his eyes. Apparently, he enjoyed half-choking women.

"You don't look like an imperial officer," he observed.

"Nothing gets by those cyborg eyes, does it?" she gasped out, struggling to breathe. Being lippy with this thug was probably even more ill-advised than being lippy with Leonidas, but she had more in mind than annoying him. She wanted to see his reaction, to find out if he *was* a cyborg. The servos in the combat armor could have given a regular man the strength to lift her—she wasn't exactly a behemoth.

"Nothing," he breathed, leaning his face close to hers. "Where is he?"

"Who?"

"The imperial officer who had the command codes to lower the shields on my bombers."

Oh, shit. If her feet hadn't been dangling above the ground, Alisa would have kicked herself for her mistake. Why hadn't she claimed to be an imperial officer? There had been hundreds of thousands of soldiers in the empire's armies. It wasn't as if he could have known if she had lied.

"You think other people haven't gotten those codes?" Alisa tried for a laugh—it came out like more of a strangled cough. What were the odds that this brute would put her down someday soon?

"You couldn't use them even if you had them, little girl."

She sneered at him. "I can use a lot of things I'm not supposed to."

Damn it, that had sounded more clever in her head. Obviously, there was a shortage of oxygen reaching her brain.

More boots clanged on the metal of her walkways.

"Haven't found anything, Sublime Commander," one of the pirates reported, the scalps on his belt swaying as he trotted down the steps. "Might be she's the only one here. We got the engineer and the doctor. Could be her whole crew."

"She's not alone. The bears would have gotten her if she had been wandering around that station alone."

The pirate who had reported touched a scar on his cheek. "That's the truth. Glad you're here to go in with us next time, sir. Lost three men last month when we tried. Don't know how them bastards got on that asteroid, but they're not looking to let the station go easy." He looked at

Alisa. "Reckon we can go in soon, seeing as this ship hasn't blowed itself up yet."

The cyborg—Alisa refused to think of him as the sublime commander—lowered her to the deck. Unfortunately, he did not let her go. Instead, he yanked her close, and her shoulder clunked hard against his torso protector. His hand wrapped around her throat before she could attempt to squirm away. Three suns, she hated feeling helpless, but it was as if his hands were ahridium vises clamped around her.

Elbowing him in the gut or the crotch was out of the question—aside from his head, every inch of him was covered in that armor. And she was too short to thunk her skull into his nose.

"Imperial officer," the cyborg called, his voice echoing in the empty cargo hold. "If you want this woman to live, show yourself."

Several of the pirates shifted, pointing their weapons toward the walls of the hold instead of at her. Alisa tried to swallow, but the hand wrapped around her neck prevented it. This wasn't at all how she had imagined this exchange going. She was supposed to be a diversion that would allow her team to sneak in and strike, not a pawn to be used against them. Why couldn't the pirates have just dragged her off and thrown her in a cell with the others?

"So slow to respond," the cyborg said. "Hm, where shall we start?" He pushed Alisa out to arm's length.

"We could take her, sir," one of the men offered, leering at her chest. "That ought to flush anyone out. And if there's nobody to flush, then we'd still have a good time."

"Take her where?" the cyborg asked.

Alisa stared at him. He couldn't possibly have missed the man's meaning.

"You know, screw her, sir."

"Oh." The cyborg's nose wrinkled, as if he was too good for such base actions. "I doubt you want your cock hanging out if a bunch of armed men jump out of hiding."

"I'd risk it. She's got a nice ass."

Alisa gritted her teeth, more annoyed with her helplessness than the conversation—she'd heard worse in the army.

"What are you doing here, Cyborg?" she asked to buy time while she groped for inspiration. What could she do to get herself out of this situation? "It's lowly working for pirates after being a soldier in the empire, isn't it?"

Not that she considered the empire any better than a bunch of pirates, but he doubtlessly would.

His lip quirked up in what seemed a regular gesture for him, half smile, half sneer. "You think I'm *working* for them? I *lead* this outfit now."

Alisa looked to the ring of pirates and got a few nods of confirmation.

"Imperial officer," the cyborg called again. "You've had your warning."

Before Alisa had a chance to brace herself, his thumb dug into the tender flesh under the edge of her jaw. Her body went rigid, her spine stiffening, and a gasp slipped out. His other hand went down to the side of her stomach, digging in like a knife, finding an excruciating pressure point. She couldn't keep from crying out, especially since the iron bar from that grid had dug a gouge near that spot earlier. She started bleeding again, warmth trickling down her side. She barely noticed, as he switched to other carefully selected points, knowing better than she what would create pain so intense that she couldn't keep from crying out. And feeling utterly useless. A failure. How had she even ended up in this mess? She just wanted to find her daughter and make a new home, start over with the only family she had left.

Metal clanged.

With the pain hazing her mind, it took Alisa a moment to realize what it signified. The cover on the hidden hatch being kicked out.

The pain lessened as the cyborg loosened his grip on her, letting his fingers merely rest on the pressure points rather than digging in. Warm tears trickled down her cheeks. She hated herself for it, but she was relieved that the others had given themselves up.

The cyborg's grip tightened again, and she cringed, anticipating more pain. But he wasn't attacking her. He had stiffened himself, his head turned to the side, toward Leonidas. He was walking toward them slowly, his helmet off, his hands empty at his sides, though he still wore his armor, armor that appeared identical to that which the pirate leader wore.

"*You*," the pirate cyborg breathed. He sounded stunned.

Though Alisa didn't want to look at Leonidas, didn't want him to see the tears in her eyes or how weak she had been, curiosity made her turn her head. This new cyborg recognized him.

"Me," Leonidas agreed, his voice cool, his face a mask. His eyes were locked upon the pirate leader; he did not acknowledge Alisa whatsoever.

"Never thought I'd see you hide behind a woman's skirts, Colonel."

Colonel? No wonder he had been so comfortable flinging commands around. So much for her initial guess that he was a sergeant. The revelation did not matter much now, though, not unless he had outranked this would-be pirate king and could cow him.

"That wasn't the original plan," Leonidas said.

"No shit." The pirate cyborg laughed. The men stirred, exchanging uncertain glances with each other. "So *you're* the one who killed my bombers. Damn, sir, one of those was my own craft that I flew out here. You know, back before I had an enormous ship." He spread a hand toward the ceiling and walls to encompass the lumbering mining vessel.

Alisa held her breath, finding that "sir" that had slipped out worthy of hope.

"You're working with pirates now?" Leonidas asked, his tone neutral, not as condemning as Alisa would have expected.

"As I was telling your girl, they're *my* pirates." The cyborg clenched a fist and smiled.

None of the ten men watching said anything to deny the statement.

"I took the ship, made the current leader my lieutenant," the cyborg continued. "We're going to start a whole fleet out here. I even thought I might get more of our old battalion to join. You interested, Colonel?"

Alisa nearly choked on his audacity. After Leonidas's talk of honor and after he had balked at her scavenging that station, she sincerely doubted he would be interested in joining up with people who fired on unarmed freighters and wore scalps on their belts.

"You want me to work under you, Malik?" Leonidas arched an eyebrow.

"I *did* commandeer the ship and do the hard work whipping these men into shape. I wouldn't be looking to lord it over you, Colonel. You were always fair. Not like those human officers, all stiff from having their pricks shoved up their asses."

"We're human too," Leonidas said in that familiar dry tone of his. Alisa could read the disapproval in there. She wasn't sure if the pirate cyborg—Malik—could.

"We're *better* than human."

"I see."

"Join us, Colonel. Join my team. If you don't...well, I'm sure you can understand. I'd rather not get in a fight with you, but I can't have you competing with me, either." Malik's dark eyes narrowed, a warning in them.

Alisa lost some of her hope that he might stand down if Leonidas gave an order.

Leonidas tilted his head. "I'd have to consider it. Let's talk."

Malik hesitated, his eyes still slitted. "And your people?" He flicked his fingers casually toward Alisa, but she sensed a trap being laid. If Leonidas demanded that she and the others be left alone, would this Malik find it suspicious? How far did he trust what sounded like his old commander?

"My people?" Leonidas grunted. "I needed a ride out here. She's the pilot of this barge. I've known her for a week."

"So you don't care about her fate? You rushed out here quickly enough when she started crying."

Alisa glared at the cyborg. If not for that armor, she would have kicked him. She was tempted to do it, anyway, but she would only end up breaking her toes.

"I'm not an animal, Malik," Leonidas said, that dryness in his tone again, as if none of this particularly bothered or concerned him. "I don't want to see a woman tortured."

"Who cares about human women? You're too damned noble, Colonel. You think any of them care worm suck about us?"

For the first time, Leonidas looked over at Alisa, meeting her eyes. She held his gaze, but she couldn't help but think of the way she had called him "cyborg" for most of the week. And "mech," Beck's favorite slur, when she had been pissed at him.

"No, likely not," Leonidas agreed.

"Well, we don't have to torture them. These craven bastards used to kill people, scalp 'em and make jewelry from their bones before I came along. They were trying to make themselves seem scary, or so they say. I figure let's make some money. Sell them into slavery. The trade's picking up nicely without anyone out here policing the Dark Reaches. We can make a lot of money. Carve out an empire of our own. There'd be nobody telling us what to do anymore. Say, were you in the station? Did you find the doctor? I figure the same thing brought us both out here."

"Oh?"

"The latest parts he was working on—to make us stronger, faster." Malik clenched his fist again, his eyes lighting up.

Alisa shifted uneasily. Leonidas was hard to read right now. Was that what had brought him to the station? A desire for improvement parts? A little upgrade to the operating system?

"I did come out to see him," Leonidas said. "He's dead."

"Damn. I was afraid of that when I heard from my new men that they'd found the place but half of them had gotten themselves eaten by animals while investigating it." Malik thumped his fist against his torso, the gauntlets clanging hollowly off the chest plate. "I plan to deal with those animals later, but let's go talk in private without the goons listening, eh?" He pointed at one of his "goons." "Take the woman and whoever else is in that bolt hole and dump them in the pens with the others." He extended a hand toward the open hatchway, an invitation. "Colonel?"

Leonidas inclined his head once and walked toward the hatch with Malik. He did not look back as the pirates closed on Alisa, grabbing her and hoisting her from her feet.

CHAPTER FIFTEEN

Beck put up a fight, but he was too vastly outnumbered. Already disarmed, Alisa could not help at all. The pirates searched them, removed their weapons and valuables, hoisted them all over their broad armored shoulders, and took them out of the *Nomad* and into a bay the size of a hangar in the air yard back on Perun. Four dirigibles could have fit in it with room to spare.

Alisa found herself twisting to give the freighter a long look as they traveled away from it. When she had first decided to find it and refurbish it for the trip to Perun, she hadn't liked the idea. She hadn't wanted anything to do with the *Nomad*. But flying it this last week had stirred up old memories, memories of more than learning of her mother's death. There had been memories of the past and of good times growing up in the ship, of going on adventures with her mother and of meeting interesting people and seeing interesting places.

As her captors passed another ship and the *Nomad* disappeared from sight, Alisa felt a twinge of distress that had nothing to do with her injuries. She was afraid she wouldn't see the freighter again, and that disturbed her more than she would have expected.

As they traveled through the vast mining vessel, Alisa tried to note their route so she could find her way back later. Unfortunately, she did not have the best view as she flopped about on her captor's shoulder, her pain renewed as the armor banged against her injuries. But she had a sense of massive rows of mining equipment, of an indoor smelter with robots processing metals, and of huge storage rooms of unprocessed ore. Now and then, flying robots zipped overhead on some errand or another.

They seemed to walk a half a mile before they reached corridors filled with what she assumed were crew quarters and the main living areas. All she saw were pirates and more pirates wearing all manner of scruffy clothing with all manner of weapons hanging from their belts. Many of them had scalps dangling from those belts, even boys who could not have been more than thirteen or fourteen. Alisa wondered if Malik truly meant to spare her people's lives long enough for them to reach some slave auction. And how insane was it that such a fate sounded like an improvement over their current situation? Slaves. What a crazy notion. Slavery had always been outlawed in the empire. She couldn't even imagine life toiling for someone else with no freedom to be found.

But it was life, and if she was kept alive long enough to be sold, she could find a way to escape. One way or another, she would make it back to her daughter. Of course, she would prefer to do it with her ship and to escape sooner rather than later.

Her captors turned into a narrow corridor with old-fashioned iron bars lining the fronts of a dozen cells. Still dangling from a man's shoulder, Alisa glimpsed unfamiliar people packed into almost all of them. Most had contusions, scrapes, and other signs of injury. Some of the women were naked. Her gut twisted with unease as she remembered how the one pirate had shown an undue interest in her ass.

A pirate stopped in front of one cell and leaned a garishly beaded earstar toward a reader while others moved to cover him with rifles. The chip in the wall chatted with the chip in his personal device, and the iron bars slid up into the ceiling. Alisa found herself dumped inside, her wounds protesting anew and eliciting a gasp of pain. She rolled to a stop in front of a familiar gray robe as the bars slid back shut. The pirates left without a word.

Alejandro helped her to sit up.

"I'm afraid I can't say I'm happy to see you here, Captain," Mica said—she sat against the wall, her knees drawn up and her arms hugged around them.

"Not happy to see you two here, either." Alisa started to scoot toward a wall as Beck and Yumi were ushered in behind her—she needed something to lean against for support.

Alejandro stopped her with a hand on her shoulder. "Captain, I must ask." He glanced toward the bars, but the pirates had already shuffled away.

He also glanced toward a corner of the ceiling where a dark round smudge might have been a camera. Or a squashed spider. "I must ask," he whispered, "did they loot the ship?"

"Mica's ruse fooled them," Alisa said. "They left in a hurry."

He slumped back against the wall.

"None of our equipment was scrounged as far as I saw," she said, "but the *Nomad* is stuck in their docking bay, I'm afraid. Oh, and I watched the video footage when I was trying to figure out where you all went. They did steal our duffel bags, probably stuffed in whatever looked valuable in our rooms. Which wasn't much in my…" She trailed off, the horrified expression on Alejandro's face making her stop.

He lurched to his feet, almost tumbling over her in his agitation. "Shit, shit, *shit.*"

He paced to the wall, slapped it, and pushed off and paced in the other direction. There was only room in the tight space for four steps. A handful of gaunt, bearded men in the cell opposite from them watched him with hollow eyes.

"Is he allowed to swear when he's wearing that robe?" Mica asked.

"I don't fully know the rules," Alisa said, watching his agitated pacing. She supposed this was not the time to ask him to look at her punctures and gashes. They didn't have a first-aid kit, anyway.

Alejandro gripped his hair, then shoved his fingers through it with both hands as he turned again. He muttered furiously to himself, and Alisa only caught snatches, "…get caught up in this…a fool…shouldn't have trusted… fail. Failure. Can't fail."

Alisa did not know what to say, or if she should say anything. She already felt guilty for getting everyone involved in this. Oh, Leonidas was truly the one to blame, but she had known they would be taking a detour when she invited her passengers on. And she hadn't been up front with them. She had waited until they were underway to announce that the *Nomad* would be heading out to the T-Belt. And now this. If they didn't find a way off this ship, the time lost for the detour would be the least of their problems.

"Where's our cyborg?" Mica asked as Alejandro continued to pace.

"Communing with his own kind," Alisa said. She looked at Yumi, half expecting her to lose her composure the way Alejandro was. At the least,

Alisa expected one of her passengers to curse at her and make accusations. She surely deserved them.

But Yumi had found a corner of the cell and was sitting cross-legged, her eyes closed as she practiced some breathing exercise. Interesting time to meditate.

Alejandro stopped in front of one of the walls, placed his palms on the drab gray metal, and thumped his forehead against it. Maybe Yumi could teach *him* to meditate.

"What's that mean?" Mica asked.

"Turns out the pirate leader is someone in matching red armor," Alisa said, scooting over to sit against the wall beside her. "Oh, and they know each other. Malik is the leader's name, but he calls himself Sublime Commander. He called Leonidas *Colonel.*"

Alejandro was still leaning his hands against the wall, his head down, but he rotated his neck to look at them.

"But I figure the doctor already knew that," Alisa said. "That Leonidas was an officer high up in the Cyborg Corps."

Alejandro dropped his head again. If he knew, he didn't care. Not right now. What had he been carrying in that bag that was so important? Some secret plans that would magically bring the empire back to full power? That was an appalling thought, but probably a silly one. One man couldn't undo what had happened, not when it had taken tens of thousands if not hundreds of thousands of people and fifty years of planning and four years of all out combat to bring down the empire.

"What does that mean *exactly?*" Mica said. "He's not going to help us?"

"I don't know," Alisa said, "but he and Malik walked off practically arm in arm, and he didn't look back at me. He seemed fine with the idea that we'd be sold into slavery."

"Slavery?" Mica pointed a finger at Alisa's nose. "Captain, *this* is why I'm always pessimistic. Bad things happen *all* the time. Good things are an oddity."

"They certainly have been this week." Alisa let her head clunk back against the wall. It hurt, but not any more than the rest of her body. "Alejandro?" she asked carefully, worried that he would snap at her and blame her for all this. "If you know something about Leonidas that could help us…I mean, should he deign to visit us or if our paths should cross before we leave this ship, if there was something we could say to persuade him—"

"You mean to blackmail him," Mica interrupted.

"*Persuade* him," Alisa emphasized. "If there is something, I'd sure like to know so I could try to use it."

"I would be open to blackmailing him," Beck said. The pirates had removed his armor, and he almost looked small without it. It did not help that he wore a sad, defeated expression as he slumped against the wall.

"I only know him by reputation," Alejandro said, looking at the wall instead of her. "He was around the capital from time to time, getting orders for his troops."

"The Cyborg Corps?"

"The Cyborg Corps."

"Was he in charge of them? All of them?"

Alejandro lowered his hands. "Do you have any thoughts as to how to get out of here?"

"Not yet," Alisa said, surprised he was looking at her. "Why, did you expect some genius ideas to pop out of my head?"

"You've done satisfactorily so far. And you seem determined."

"I've got a reason to be determined." Alisa pictured her daughter's face in her mind, wishing it hadn't been so long since she had seen it in more than a photograph.

"Good. As do I."

"Not just taking the tour of the system and spreading your religiosity then?" Mica asked.

"Not exactly. Though I can prepare a lecture or sermon for you later, if you feel the need."

"I vote you lecture the pirates, Doc," Beck said.

"Seconded," Alisa said.

Yumi pressed her hands together in front of her chest and inhaled noisily through the back of her throat. Alisa wasn't sure if that counted as a third or not.

Alejandro crouched in front of Alisa, looking her in the eyes. "I have to get my bag back, and we have to escape. There's something in there—the pirates can't have it. It cannot be permitted. Our escape *has* to happen."

"I'm amenable to that," Alisa said, though she questioned whether they would truly be able to find the pirates' booty room in this giant ship. If she got out of this cell, she intended to beeline for the *Nomad* and pilot it out. Unfortunately, with that grab beam of theirs, it would not be easy. She did not want to escape the bay, only to be sucked back in again. No, they would have to distract the pirates and find a way to disable the grab beam generator. She already had a daunting task without promising to hunt for the pirates' loot. She didn't even know yet how they were going to get out of this cell.

"I'll tell you what I know about Leonidas if you swear to help me get that bag. Swear it." Alejandro sounded like a boy on the playground rather than a man in his fifties, but it was clear from his eyes that he was utterly serious.

Alisa licked her lips. Hadn't she just been listing all the reasons why looking for a few duffel bags would be suicidal? Was satisfying her curiosity about Leonidas worth making this deal? She might never even see him again. Even though she would like to think he would not take up with a pirate, he had taken up with *her*, hadn't he? Someone he clearly disapproved of, someone he had caught stealing cyborg implants to sell...This Malik had a lot more power and resources to get him to wherever he needed to go for whatever the next step in his quest was.

Aware of Alejandro looking at her, his dark eyes earnest and determined, Alisa took a deep breath. She hated to make false promises, but maybe she could somehow pull this off. With as many other things as had to go right for them to escape, what would adding one more detour to the list matter? Besides, if one of her people found the loot room and threatened to blow it up, maybe it would distract the pirates while the rest got to the ship. The brutes probably had a huge vault of goodies they had stolen from the miners and anyone else who had flown into their web.

Alisa looked through the bars toward their cellmates across the way, wondering if they might be a resource. Eight men were packed in there, and she had seen numerous people in the other cells too.

"If we can get out of here," Alisa told Alejandro, "I'll make sure we look for your bag on the way out. I promise."

Alejandro frowned slightly, no doubt noticing that she had not exactly given a promise to get the bag back, but what could she do? She wasn't in a position of power here. She wasn't even sure why he thought she would be more likely to come up with a plan and lead an escape than he. He had to be twenty years older than she was, more experienced in life. But, she reasoned, perhaps not more experienced with getting out of jams.

"As long as we're making promises," Beck said, "can we promise to get my combat armor on the way out too? That's the most valuable thing I've ever had in my life, and until my sauce line gets going, I reckon I'm going to have to fight for my tindarks. Can't fight without a good suit."

Alisa patted his shoulder. "Maybe they'll be stored in the same place."

"Just so long as some slimy pirate hasn't claimed it for his own. I don't like another man's sweat in my suit."

"I have nothing I need in my trunk," Yumi said, "but if we can get it, I would also be pleased. After all, half of my fare is inside of it."

"Can I say," Alisa said, looking around at her little group, pleased that nobody was curled in a ball on the floor and moaning that the end was near, "that I'm glad that everyone is so certain that we *are* going to get out."

"Not everyone," Mica grumbled. "I expect we'll be raped and tortured and made to watch, and that half of us will get killed before we get thrown into this slavery ring. And then the other half will wish they had been killed too."

"Sounds like a good reason to expedite our escape then." Alisa pushed herself to her feet.

Alejandro stood up next to her.

"About Leonidas," she said, "should I work him into my plans or not?"

"I probably know less about him than you wish, but he's known to be an honorable man."

Alisa lifted her brows. She had already guessed that. The problem was that she didn't know if Leonidas considered *her* honorable and worthy of helping out.

"His name is Colonel Hieronymus Adler," Alejandro said. "I would guess Leonidas is a call sign, though he could have made it up on the spot. He *was* the commander of the Cyborg Corps for the first couple of years of the war. I'm not sure what he did after that—you have to understand that I wasn't a military doctor, and I rarely interacted with soldiers—but I believe he may have done some special assignments for the emperor."

"Oh." Alisa didn't know what else to say. If Leonidas had been the emperor's special man, that meant he was even more of an enemy to her and the Alliance than she had realized. She definitely shouldn't factor him into her plans or expect him to risk himself for people that he, too, would consider enemies. "Do you know what his mission is? Why he was so determined to go out to that research station? And if he was one of the emperor's favorites, why was he stranded on Dustor?"

"He hasn't confided in me. I don't think he recognized me when we met or considered me someone who might be a confidant."

Might be a confidant? Was Alejandro saying that he would help Leonidas if he could? Or just that they were both from the empire and could have stuck together?

"Do you think his mission is personal or that someone sent him out here? Is it like Malik said, that the cyborgs were drawn to the research station because they wanted upgraded parts?"

Alejandro hesitated. "After the emperor was killed, I don't think there was anyone left back home who could have sent him on a special assignment."

Alisa held back a frown, though she noted that hesitation. Did that mean he was lying?

"So, you think his mission is personal?" she asked.

"I have no way of knowing."

"All right." Alisa walked the three steps to the bars, not sure she had gotten any useful information in exchange for her promise. Just Leonidas's name and confirmation that he was someone she should go on hating, or at least thinking of as an enemy. If he had truly been that high up in the fleet chain of command and that close to the emperor, having him roaming around free out here was a dangerous thing for the Alliance.

She nodded toward one of the men across the way who looked over at her movement. She tapped a bar to make sure it wasn't charged with electricity, then draped her arms around them. "Any chance you fellows would like to chat?"

"Not unless one of you girls wants to come over and keep us company," one of the scruffier men said. He was missing an eye. The wound looked recent. "Those bastards didn't see fit to supply our cell with any women."

Alisa had seen the women in another cell, and they hadn't looked like they wanted to be molested by fellow prisoners. They had looked like they had already been molested enough. She shuddered, thinking of Mica's pessimistic predictions. She needed information, so she forced herself to continue the chat, to be friendly.

"Any preferences as to which one?" she asked.

"You'll do. They haven't even uglied you up yet. Come on over."

Alisa ticked the bar. "It seems the pirates don't want us commingling." She pressed the side of her face into the gap between the bars, peering as far up and down the hall as she could see. She spotted someone's sleeve next to the exit. They had at least one guard.

"I don't care what those mother-forsaken thugs want," one of the other men grumbled. "I just want to get out of here."

"How long have you been in that cell?"

"Months. Sparky and Phan are the only ones who get to go for walks now and then." The speaker waved toward two men lying on one side of the cell.

"Why are they special?"

"Engineer and mechanic. The pirates aren't a real educated lot. They've got no use for those of us who were just miners, but if something goes wrong with the ship, they come and collect someone who knows how to fix it."

Alisa moved along the bars so she stood in front of the specialists. Aware of the guard and the cameras, she made a *psst* sound and waved, hoping one would come closer. One man did not acknowledge her at all. The other one glowered.

"You want them to move, you'll have to show Sparky some tits," the man she had been speaking with said, giving her a lurid wink.

"Actually," someone else said, "I've heard Sparky would rather see the tits of her muscleman back there."

Beck's eyebrows flew up, and he touched his chest in a self-conscious gesture.

"I'll arrange that if we all get out of here," Alisa said.

"Really, Captain. That *wasn't* in the job description."

"I'm positive I asked for open-mindedness and versatility down in the fine print of my recruiting flyer."

"Which of those things was supposed to imply I'd disrobe for other men?" Beck asked.

"The first, I think." Alisa nodded to the glowering engineer. "Sparky, how often do they come get you?"

"Every few days. This ship is fifty years old. Things go wrong often, especially since they're not caring for her like they should." He sighed and ran the palm of his hand along the wall of his cell in a sad caress.

"And you fix the problems for them?"

"Don't have much choice."

"Have you ever thought of—" Alisa lowered her voice, "—*creating* a problem? Sabotaging something and using the diversion to escape?" She ticked the bars again. Unfortunately, they wouldn't go away if the power went out. It was too bad the cells did not use typical forcefields.

"The *last* engineer had thoughts like that," Sparky said. "They scalped him, then dumped his body into a vat of molten ore."

"Did the last engineer have a pilot with a freighter in the bay, ready to give you a ride out?"

"Kiss that ship goodbye, girl. They've probably already scrapped it."

Alisa forced herself not to shudder or be daunted by that idea. "So, you wouldn't be willing to sabotage something the next time you're out? Even if Beck took off his shirt and danced for you?"

"*Captain*," Beck said in a pained voice.

Sparky shook his head.

One of the other miners said, "You're not going to escape. You think everyone who gets shoved in here doesn't think about it? Forget it. We've tried everything. Chances got even slimmer after the cyborg took over. The guards pay more attention, and you better believe they're recording you right now. If you make trouble, they'll kill you. Best to go along with things and hope for a good owner or a chance to escape once you're sold on the auction block."

The guard walked into view, as if to emphasize the miner's point. He banged the muzzle of his blazer rifle against the bars in front of Alisa.

"Too much socializing down here."

The miners turned away from him, their shoulders hunched. A few of them had holes in their shirts, revealing whip scars on their backs.

"You're welcome to join in if you like," Alisa told the guard. She doubted she could establish a rapport with him, but maybe she could get a few drops of information.

"With what?" the man asked. "Looking at your brute's tits?"

"I'm amazed at how much interest there is in that."

"Me too," Beck muttered.

"Options are limited here." The guard smirked.

"Say, Sparky, what kind of engine runs a ship this big?" Alisa asked.

Sparky looked at the guard, then gave her an incredulous look, as if he couldn't believe she wanted to continue chatting with the man right there.

"A Molbydam 850," Sparky muttered.

"Mica," Alisa said, "that's a smallish engine for a ship this big, isn't it?"

Mica gave her a flat why-are-you-including-me-in-your-troublemaking look, but answered. "It's the factory original for a Tolican Ore Driver. Nobody designed these ships to go fast. They just have to get their load from place to place."

"This ship is fast enough," Sparky said, sitting up. "Me and Hemm made plenty of modifications over the years, back when the company paid us well and didn't make us sleep in cells with a bunch of sweaty men."

"What kinds of modifications?" Mica stood up and joined Alisa at the bars. "I've seen a few ships blow up because some uneducated mechanics thought they were being clever."

The guard seemed bored with the discussion and walked farther down the corridor, checking on the other cells.

"Keep talking to him," Alisa whispered. "Make it sound like you know more about engines and this ship."

"I *do* know more," Mica said. "I grew up on a mining moon. I've seen every ship and configuration in the business."

"Then it should be easy."

"What should be?"

"Proving you're the one the guards should select the next time they need something fixed."

Mica's eyes narrowed.

The guard ambled back toward them. Mica hesitated, but then launched into a lecture for the engineer, calling him a self-taught muck-for-brains who would likely get this ship blown up. Alisa gave her a surreptitious bright sun gesture, hand to chest, fingers splayed.

A door clanged open. Alisa hoped that meant a senior-ranking guard was coming, someone who might pass along word of Mica's expertise if he heard about it. Instead, a familiar figure strolled into view. Malik.

The so-called *Sublime Commander* had removed his red armor and wore a sleeveless shirt that revealed thick arms and chiseled muscle, exactly what Alisa expected from a cyborg. He still wore the mottled black and gray uniform trousers of an imperial soldier, along with a flat ID chip on a neck chain. A rifle was slung on a strap across his back, and a long knife hung from a sheath on his belt.

Seeing him up close made Alisa want to step back as adrenaline surged through her veins. She couldn't help it. After the war, she feared someone like this far more than she ever would one of the grubby pirates. It didn't matter that both could kill her in exactly the same way.

A second man walked beside Malik. Alisa wished it had been Leonidas. Even if she didn't think he would be a savior, she had a notion of what to expect from him by now. But it was one of the pirates from the cargo hold. He had also changed out of his combat armor, but she recognized the voice when he exchanged a few words with the guard. It was the one who had wanted to have some fun with her. Great.

She hoped that Malik and his buddy had come down to hand out lunch and had nothing more inimical in mind. Unfortunately, neither one was holding a box of ration bars.

"You." Malik pointed at Alisa, barely glancing at the others in the cell.

"Me?"

Alisa made herself step back up to the bars, not wanting him to see her fear and also wanting a glimpse down the corridor. Had Leonidas come on this visit? Did he *know* about this visit? Where was he, anyway? When the two cyborgs had met, she hadn't gotten the impression that Malik would do anything to make him disappear, but what did she know? Maybe what he had offered Leonidas had been a lie, and he had shot his old commander in the back as soon as he had a chance.

"Got a few questions for you," Malik said, giving her that discomfiting half smile.

"I expect I know a lot less than you think." Alisa couldn't imagine what he thought she knew. Unless he had a question about the *Star Nomad*—and why would they?—she wouldn't be the person to ask.

"We'll find out," his subordinate said, leering at Alisa's breasts.

Malik thumped him in the chest. On the surface, it looked like a friendly thump, almost something done between buddies, but the force of it made the pirate stumble back and bump his shoulder blades on the bars across the way. Too bad none of the miners were poised to take advantage. One might have jumped forward, wrapped an arm around his throat, and broken his neck. Not that they would win an uprising with Malik there, but everyone here seemed so complacent, so accepting of their fate. Alisa wished they would fight, if only with words and spirit.

"Not until later for that, Bruiser," Malik told his subordinate.

Bruiser. What a name.

"Sooner might help get her talking," Bruiser said, leering again. "I can be forceful."

The guard smirked. Malik just looked at him like he was an imbecile.

"Open it," Malik told another guard that Alisa couldn't see, someone near the door at the head of the corridor.

That meant there were three men and a cyborg out there. Unfortunately, Alisa did not see how her people could come out on top, even if they got a chance to charge out. If Malik hadn't been there, maybe.

A clank sounded in the ceiling, and the grid of bars disappeared into holes up there. Malik reached for Alisa. Beck pulled her back and tried to step in the way. The guard stepped forward, pointing his rifle at him. Beck lifted his hands, as if to show he was only interested in putting himself between Alisa and Malik, then kicked out before that muzzle fully pointed at him. The rifle flew upward, and Beck flung himself at the man.

Malik lunged forward, moving too quickly to track. He caught Beck by the throat, halting his charge before it got far.

"Don't," Alisa yelled, reaching for Malik's arm, knowing he could snap Beck's neck easily. "Please."

Malik paused and looked at her, his fingers wrapped around Beck's neck but not squeezing all the way. Beck bared his teeth and grabbed his assailant's forearm with both hands. The cyborg barely seemed to notice.

"He is your lover?" Malik asked Alisa.

"My security officer. I pay him to protect me from thugs. Whatever he does is my fault, so you should blame me, not him. Not his neck."

Malik snorted. "Whatever you pay him, it's too much."

Beck grabbed his forearm and tried to kick him in the balls, but the cyborg lifted one thickly muscled thigh, blocking the attack easily. Alisa made a cutting motion, hoping Beck would pay attention. The odds were too ridiculously against them as long as Malik was there. Besides, she might be able to learn something if they took her someplace for questioning. Assuming she could avoid Bruiser's attention.

"Did you hire the colonel too?" Malik tilted his head, watching her as he avoided everything Beck attempted.

"No." Alisa figured she shouldn't imply any relationship between her and Leonidas. She wasn't sure if there *was* one, but just in case, she would not thwart whatever plans he might have. "I didn't even want him on my ship."

Malik snorted again. "Because he's a cyborg."

"Mostly because he's imperial and I'm not. Fire and water, you understand."

"Nobody's imperial anymore. The war's over." Malik flung Beck away from him with no more effort than if he were tossing a wadded up ball of paper into a trash bin. Beck was hurled through the air, knocking Alejandro over before landing hard in the corner. His head struck the wall, and he slid down.

Alisa started toward him, worried that might have broken his neck after all, but Malik grabbed her before she could take more than a step. He yanked her into the corridor with enough force to take her from her feet. Fresh pain came from all the day's injuries, and she clenched her teeth to keep from gasping. She tumbled against his chest, loathing that he could pull her around like a doll.

"Shut it," Malik said.

The bars clanged back into place, separating Alisa from her people. Bruiser looked her up and down with a contented smile.

"Where are we going?" Alisa asked, focusing on the cyborg instead of the lusty creep. She feared Malik, there was no doubt about that, but at least he did not act like a sexual predator.

"Bruiser and I are going to have a chat with you." A gleam of pleasure entered his dark eyes, and she wondered if she'd been too quick to judge his subordinate as the more vile person. "This way."

Malik shoved her down the corridor with the gentleness of a jackhammer.

CHAPTER SIXTEEN

Alisa stood in the center of a space that looked like a cross between a break room and a gym, with a table and chairs surrounded by weight-lifting equipment that had been creatively made from chains, cables, and spare parts that looked like they had come out of the smelter. The two doors leading to the room were shut, leaving her alone with Malik, Bruiser, and a simple wooden box resting on the table. Malik had searched her again, apparently not trusting that his pirates had done a good enough job, then handcuffed her wrists in front of her. She was not sure why he had bothered since he could thwart any attacks she might have come up with, but then the thought came to her that he might intend to leave her alone with Bruiser eventually. She dreaded that, but tried to tell herself that her odds of escaping would be better then.

"The colonel said he thought this was yours," Malik said, walking to the table and putting a finger on the box.

"I've never seen it before," Alisa said before it occurred to her to wonder why Leonidas had said that. Was it something out of *his* room? Something he did not want Malik knowing was his? If so, she did not appreciate him putting the onus on Alisa to explain it.

"No?" Malik asked. "It was in one of the cabins on your ship."

Alisa almost said that one of the passengers had probably brought it on because the *Nomad* hadn't had any personal effects left on it when she had gotten it, but she caught herself. If the box had been in someone's bag, she did not want to get that person interrogated. Maybe this was Yumi's stash of whatever it was she had intended to trade for her passage. Or maybe it was Alejandro's missing item that meant so much to him.

"Was it?" Alisa asked. "What is it?"

Malik rested a hand on her shoulder, his fingers digging in slightly. It was more of a warning than an attack, but she had no doubt that he could crush her bones with those fingers. It made her appreciate that Leonidas, even if he had been grumpy on occasion, had never threatened her, physically or otherwise. She found herself wishing he was here, standing at her side, though that was silly. Like she had said, imperials and Alliance did not mix. Malik was wrong. For some people, the war would never be over.

"I believe you may be feigning ignorance," Malik said softly.

Bruiser was watching from the doorway, and he bit his lip, his eyes gleaming as he leaned forward. Was the sick bastard getting excited at the notion that the cyborg might hurt her?

"Not me," Alisa said. "I really am this ignorant. All I know how to do is fly. But maybe I can help you figure out whose box it is if you send your thug away." Feeling audacious, she lifted her cuffs so she could pat Malik on one of his prodigious pecs. It was amazing his shirt did not rip from the strain of holding all those muscles in. She also wriggled her eyebrows at him. She had never been good at flirting her way out of trouble, but since she did not have a weapon or a ship to throw at him, she had to try what she could, so she thrust her chest toward him.

Her friendly pat and waggling eyebrows did not move him noticeably. He did not even give her chest a glance.

"Bruiser has been one of my loyal pirates since I took over," Malik said. "He helped me overthrow his boss when he saw what I was."

What he was? A megalomaniacal asshole?

"He knew that someone with my strength deserved to lead here," Malik continued.

Yes, megalomaniacal asshole was the appropriate term.

"You have to reward your men once in a while to keep them loyal, and he's taken a fancy to you." Malik shrugged and stepped toward the table. "But first, I want to know what this is."

He flicked the lid open, and a golden light filled the room. Alisa stared at it, forgetting thoughts of flirting. A sphere rested on a velvet cushion inside the box, the luminescent material alive with all the colors of the rainbow along with a few more. Within the surface of the orb, clouds and shapes swirled, morphing and changing in front of their eyes. It was beautiful, but Alisa had no idea what it was.

"Is it just a bauble?" Malik asked. "Or does it have some function?"

He picked it up with both hands, though the orb would have fit in one. He twisted it, and it came apart into four pieces, which he laid on the table. They glowed from their inner edges as much as they did on the curved surface, and Alisa had to squint to make out the shapes of those inner edges. They were jagged, with matching pins and holes, the whole thing designed to fit together like a puzzle, but with only four pieces, it was not a very complicated puzzle. It definitely arrested her attention, though, and she found herself wanting to reach out and touch those pieces, to hold them and not let them go. She struggled to focus, to come up with something to say that might improve her situation.

"Pretty, pretty," came a whisper from the wall. Bruiser. He was staring at the pieces, transfixed.

"I've noticed it has some glamour that attracts the weak-minded," Malik said dryly.

Alisa flushed. It had certainly pulled at her.

Still staring, Bruiser did not seem to notice that he had been insulted. Maybe he would want to sit and play with it all day and forget his interest in her.

Malik put the pieces back together—despite the simplicity, it took some effort for him to align them correctly to make the orb again. He set it back on its velvet cushion and shut the lid on the box.

The beautiful illumination ceased, and a pang of loss came over Alisa. Her fingers twitched toward the box as an urge to open the lid again filled her. She shook her head, trying to rid herself of the spots it had left in her vision and also of the strange longing it had stamped into her mind. Three suns, what *was* that thing?

"You've never seen it before," Malik said, disappointment tingeing his voice. Whatever her reaction had been, it must have convinced him of what her words alone had not. "But surely you know which one of your crew brought it on board."

Alisa said nothing, though she was ninety-nine percent certain this had to be the object Alejandro had been so desperate to get back. It must have some religious significance. Maybe it was even tied to whatever had made him decide to retire from his last career and put on that monk's robe.

"She knows," Bruiser said, the leer back on his face. "I'm sure she does. Let me find out for you, Sublime Commander."

"I'd be more likely to tell *you*," Alisa said, meeting Malik's eyes and giving him another suggestive smile, trying to look alluring. "Why don't you get rid of your friend there, and we'll talk."

She could not believe she was thinking of seducing a cyborg, but maybe she could get him to take her to his cabin where he might eventually leave her alone. Escaping from a cabin would be easier than escaping from a guarded jail cell.

Malik's earstar must have beeped for him, because he touched it and walked away from her, his lips moving as he answered subvocally. Alisa sighed. Even if he hadn't been interrupted, she doubted her ruse would have worked. He had not appeared noticeably interested in her allure.

With his boss distracted, Bruiser sidled away from the wall.

Alisa appraised him warily. He struck her as an idiot, but he was a big and strong idiot. He wore twin-barreled Chargers on his hips. Fighting him off when her hands were cuffed would not be easy. That knowledge did not keep her from scheming. If she could get one of those guns when he was distracted by his lust, she could shoot him and get out of here, especially if Malik left the room.

She just hoped she could find her opportunity before Bruiser attained his goal. She had never been captured during the war, and she had avoided the realities of what happened to those women who had been. The idea that it might catch up with her here, when she had been on her way home, horrified her. Fear clutched her for a moment, keeping her from reacting as Bruiser slid close enough to wrap an arm around her. Only when his hand came up to mash her breast did a jolt of reason burst through her, reminding her that she had to act if she wanted to stop him and get one of those weapons.

She was about to stomp on his instep, or at least try, when Malik cleared his throat.

Bruiser froze, his hand still on her breast, and looked at the cyborg. His arm tightened possessively around Alisa. "You said I could have her,

Sublime Commander." It sounded like a whine. "I'm not doing anything you didn't say I could."

Malik flicked a dismissive hand. "Have her. Just don't forget to find out whose rock this is."

He picked up the box and walked out the door. It closed, a beep sounding. The electronic lock being thrown.

"Yes," Bruiser hissed, shoving her back against the wall and smothering her with his body so quickly that the terror almost overwhelmed her again, keeping her from acting, from doing anything useful. She tripped over a weight that had been left on the floor, and it further flustered her.

No, she growled to herself as he rammed against her, his oversexed cock already hard in his pants. With his body shoved against hers, her arms pinned in front of her as he groped her, she could not reach his guns. His belt mashed against her knuckles, but the butts of the weapons were six inches away. It might as well have been a mile.

She shifted, trying to get a knee up, to put some space between them. The horny bastard was all over her, grabbing and squeezing. He yanked her shirt open, buttons popping off, then bit her on the neck, breaking the skin.

The pain sent a bucket of cold water over her mind, clearing her brain. Just struggling wouldn't do much—he was too strong. She had to be smarter than he was.

"Hold on there, big fellow," Alisa said, forcing her voice to come out sultry and interested, rather than pissed and terrified. "Let me help you."

"Unh?" He lifted his mouth, blood on his lips, and looked her in the face, his own face puzzled.

Yeah, she had a feeling women didn't have much interest in helping him very often. Still, he appeared intrigued by the idea.

"You're still wearing all of your clothes," she said, smiling, hoping he did not see the calculation in her eyes. "Let me help, eh?"

She shifted her fingers, forcing herself to hold that smile and to keep looking into his eyes as she grabbed the fastener of his belt. It wasn't easy with her wrists bound awkwardly, nor did it help that her fingers were shaking. Any second, he would realize she was planning something. But that befuddled look on his face turned to excitement, probably because she was doing something he had planned to do anyway. She unclasped the fastener and moved her hands to his hip, as if to help push his pants down.

A hint of wariness entered his eyes as her fingers slid closer to one of his guns. It wasn't going to work. She would only get one chance. If it wasn't perfect, he would have time to react, to toss his guns across the room where she could not reach them again.

Alisa licked her lips. "Bite me again, big fellow."

He watched her tongue, then grinned. "Yeah."

He leaned into her, finding her ear with his teeth, groaning as he ground against her. But this time, her right arm wasn't completely pinned. She pretended that she was excited and that his bite didn't hurt like touching a burning pan. She moaned into his ear as she eased her fingers around the butt of the gun. He grabbed the front of her trousers to yank them down. She grabbed his gun and yanked it free.

She got it all the way out, but he noticed. Damn it. She tried to twist it to point at his chest, tugging her other bound wrist along with her right one.

"Bitch," he growled and leaned back so he could clobber her in the face.

Before his blow landed, she rammed upward with her knee, now having the space to do so. She skittered to the side along the wall, turning so she could finally aim the gun at him. He lunged for it, but his foot caught on the weight on the ground. It only distracted him for a split second, but it was enough. She fired.

She leaped back as he lunged toward her, firing again. He screamed in pain, smoke wafting from his chest. She fired one more time, taking him square in the face, terrified that someone would hear his yells and come to check. The energy bolt hollowed out his eye, and his features froze in a rictus of pain.

He tumbled to the ground, and she backed farther until she ran into a rack of weight equipment. She kept the gun pointed toward him, half expecting him to rise again and come after her. But he wasn't moving.

Alisa wanted to take a moment to calm herself, to find her equilibrium—and a way to close her shirt—but there wasn't time. The Charger wasn't a noisy weapon, but someone could have heard his cries of pain. She could have company at any moment.

She dropped to her knees and made herself touch him, patting him down and hoping to find whatever electronic key opened the handcuffs. If Malik had it, things would be more difficult. But she found a jumble of devices on a ring in his jacket pocket. She tugged it out and started pressing buttons. Most of them did not do anything, not here anyway. She imagined the hangar bay doors lifting on the other side of the ship.

Finally, her cuffs clicked, and she could shake her hands free. She almost left the cuffs on the floor, but grabbed them and stuffed them into her jacket pocket along with the fob that opened them. Maybe she would get a chance to return the favor to one of the pirates.

With her body aching and blood dripping from her ear to spatter the shirt she managed to partially close—a few of the buttons remained—she walked toward the door. Malik had locked it, so she was not surprised when it did not open for her. There wasn't a control panel on the inside, either. She stepped back, debating if randomly shooting at it would do anything.

A beep sounded, the lock opening, and the door slid aside.

CHAPTER SEVENTEEN

Alisa jerked the gun up, pointing it at the door as it slid aside. Leonidas stood there. Alone.

Not certain what their relationship was now, she did not lower the weapon. He had removed his combat armor and wore the clothes he'd worn on the *Nomad*, the partial uniform with the jacket that proclaimed him a member of the Cyborg Corps. The *leader* of them, she reminded herself. Or at least he had been at one point during the war.

Leonidas glanced at the gun, but then looked to her neck and her torn shirt, the blood spattered on it. His gaze shifted toward Bruiser, then back to her.

"Good." He nodded. "I thought I would once again be too late to protect you—I don't have free rein here."

Leonidas glanced up and down the corridor before taking a step inside. He arched an eyebrow at the gun. He was close enough that he could have used his enhanced speed to rip it from her hand before she could fire, but he didn't move anything except the eyebrow.

Alisa lowered the weapon. "You weren't too late last time."

"Just unforgivably tardy?"

"Not unforgivably so." She managed a wan smile, though her whole body hurt. She might not know if they had a relationship or not, but she knew she was glad he was the one standing here, rather than Malik. "Besides, I didn't think that promise of protection extended past our excursion to the research station."

"You're always supposed to protect people when you're in combat armor and they're not."

"You're not in combat armor now."

He grunted softly. "Yeah, I am." He lifted a hand toward her, as if to check her injuries or offer support, but lowered it without touching her. "Are you all right?"

No, she wanted to curl up in her bunk on her ship far, far away from any pirates. And for the first time in a long time, she wished her mother would be there to take care of her, as she had been when Alisa had been a child. She would have also been pleased to have Jonah there to take care of her. Why had all of the people who could take care of her left her?

"I'm fine," was all she said, swallowing the lump in her throat. "Why did you tell them I had a clue about the orb?"

"I needed a chance to talk to you."

"Been pining away in the absence of my company, eh?" Alisa backed up to the table. Relaxing probably was not a good idea, but she needed a second to gather her wits and recover her strength, so she laid the gun down and sat in a chair.

"Your humor is still intact," Leonidas said.

"You're supposed to sound more approving when you make observations like that."

"Ah."

Leonidas walked to the table and paused, again lifting his hand like he meant to pat her shoulder or maybe say something reassuring. She must look awful to elicit such feelings from him. He didn't seem to know if she wanted to be touched, though, because he ended up lowering his hand once more. He pulled over another chair, sitting on the edge and turning it so he faced her and also the door.

"Is the orb the doctor's?" he asked.

Alisa shot him a wary look. It crossed her mind that Malik might have sent him in to pretend to be a friend and get the answers from her that way. Maybe Malik had known Bruiser would fail.

"I really don't know," she said.

"Ah," he repeated, a hint of sadness in his blue eyes. Sadness that she didn't trust him? Well, could he blame her? When he sat there in that uniform and when he had, as far as she could tell, joined forces with Sublime Commander Malik? "Let's get to what I wanted to talk to you about then." He leaned forward, draping his forearms across his thighs. They were just as meaty as Malik's. There must be a rule against scrawny cyborgs. "If I can arrange for the gates to open on the cells in the brig, do you think you can make your way to your ship? And will you take the other prisoners with you? Drop them off someplace safe along your way?"

He looked in her eyes, and she sensed that the request meant a lot to him. For some reason, it stung that he was more concerned about getting people he had never met to safety than her. It wasn't as if she had ever given him a reason to care, but she wished he wanted first and foremost for her and her crew to get out safely.

"If I can get out of here, I will absolutely take everyone I can with me," Alisa said, pushing aside her silly feelings. She might have to steal some food and water to sustain those people until they got to civilization, but Alejandro already wanted her to go on a trek to find his orb—which Malik was apparently carting around with him—so what was one more stop?

"Good."

"What about you? You're staying here?"

"I'm going back to the station with Malik to do a more thorough search. He also seems excited about hunting a few bears."

"So, you're buddies now, eh?"

"He was in the Cyborg Corps," Leonidas said, as if that made everything fine.

"He's a creep." Alisa pointed at the dead pirate. "He set *that* up to happen."

Leonidas frowned as he looked at the body.

"Not the killing part," she said, realizing she might not have been clear. "The raping part."

He flinched at the word. Good. She thought of Alejandro's claim that Leonidas was an honorable man. Honorable men shouldn't work with creeps.

"I'm sure it's not any consolation, but I doubt he cares one way or another about that."

"Oh, he cares. He likes seeing people hurt. You can see it in his eyes. He enjoys the hells out of being *better* than human." Alisa couldn't keep herself from scowling at him. She did not want to alienate her only ally on this station, but she could not help it. She had to make sure he knew. Maybe Malik and Leonidas hadn't worked together that much in the past, and he truly didn't know. Or maybe he had just never seen it because he had been the commander and not the victim.

"You may be right," Leonidas said slowly, his gaze still toward Bruiser's corpse. "But we have a common purpose at the moment. Besides—" his eyes shifted back toward her, "—I'm not welcome on your ship. There's nowhere else for me to go."

Was *that* why he had agreed to work with Malik? He didn't think she would willingly take him with her to Perun? Yes, she might have been think-ing of leaving him on that station, but that had been before he'd saved her life from an overgrown bear with bad breath, and before she had come to realize the same thing that Alejandro had said, that even if he had been the enemy, he was an honorable man.

"Shit, Leo, I'll gladly welcome you back onto my ship if it means you're not going to combine forces with Malik and set yourself up as some pirate overlord. I'll even grab Beck and go help you kill the bears on that station so you can root around for whatever you want to find. You know he wants a chance at taking down another left rear haunch."

He snorted.

"Go ahead," she said.

"What?"

"Remark on the inappropriateness of my humor."

"Actually, I was thinking that it's impressive that you've managed to retain it after all this." He glanced at her torn shirt, then sighed and stood up. "You have my word that I will not become a pirate overlord. But he wants me to be his guide down there—he doesn't know what he's looking for. Besides, if I take him down there, he won't be here." He spread his hand toward her.

"Meaning we'll only have to deal with normal human pirate obstacles during our escape?"

Leonidas inclined his head once. For some reason, she had the sense that he was sacrificing himself for her crew—and to get those people out of here. Maybe *sacrifice* was an overstatement. It wasn't as if he was helpless. Still, if all of the future slaves escaped imprisonment while Malik was down on the station, and if Malik found out that Leonidas had been responsible…

Alisa frowned deeply. Maybe he *was* sacrificing himself for them.

Someone banged on the door, and she leaped from her seat. She cursed under her breath. Bruiser's body was off to the side, but it definitely was not hidden.

"Bruiser?" a man called from the other side of the door. "You done yet? Commander said to take the prisoner back to her cell."

"Stand there," Leonidas whispered, pointing to a spot that might block the view of the body from the doorway, then he headed over to answer the call.

"Leonidas?" Alisa asked.

He paused in front of the door and looked at her. She wanted to thank him or to apologize for calling him a mech. Or both. There didn't seem to be time to express what she wanted to say, though, especially since she would no doubt trip over her tongue doing it.

"Malik was wrong about what he said in my cargo hold. You *could* get a human woman to care about you. If you wanted to."

He inclined his head once more, then opened the door.

The pirate outside saw him and jerked back in surprise.

"It's *Sublime* Commander," Leonidas corrected, his voice cold, so different from what Alisa had just heard from him.

"Ye—yes, sir. Is the, uhh, prisoner here?" The pirate glanced past his shoulder and toward Alisa.

She hoped he would not think to ask where Bruiser had gone.

"Take her." Leonidas waved Alisa forward as he shifted his position to take over blocking the view of the body.

"This way, woman," the pirate said, making his voice gruff. As if he hadn't just been knocking his knees together at Leonidas's unexpected appearance.

Alisa walked into the corridor without making trouble. She looked back at Leonidas, noting the grimness of his face and wishing she had found a way to apologize and thank him, after all. Then the door slid shut, and she lost her opportunity.

Wondering if she would ever see him again, Alisa let the pirate push her through the corridors. There were other men about, perhaps getting ready for the trip down to the station, or she might have tried to get away from her guard. But she was injured, and he kept his rifle pointed squarely between her shoulder blades, not giving her any opportunities to take advantage. He was far more professional than Bruiser and did not leer at her, nor did he look like a leer from her would do anything for him.

Soon, she was pushed back into the short corridor that held the jail cells. She counted all of the faces she passed—their numbers mattered more now that she had agreed to take them all with her.

She was still counting when her cell came into sight, and she frowned when the count came up short. Beck lay on the floor in the back, sleeping or unconscious, and Alejandro sat near him, a hand on his chest. Mica and Yumi were gone.

CHAPTER EIGHTEEN

Alisa rushed into the cell, barely aware of the bars clanking into place behind her. She dropped to her knees beside Beck.

"What happened?" she asked Alejandro.

"Several thugs came to take Yumi away. Beck flung himself at them, almost overpowered them too. One of them hit him with a stun gun. He's lucky they didn't kill him. Slaves are worth money, apparently, so it's a shame to lose them. But mauling them beforehand is fine." Alejandro clenched his jaw. "My attempt to steal a gun was not successful, nor did they have an interest in my attempts to sway them into doing the right thing so that they could stand tall and be proud when their Reckoning Day came."

"If the pirates had scalps on their belt, I suspect they've already given up on the notion of their reckoning going well."

"I fear that's so." Alejandro's eyebrows drew together, as if he couldn't imagine the concept. "They must be praying that there is no afterlife where they will be held accountable."

"Can you pray for a lack of religion? Is that how that works?" Alisa rubbed the back of her neck. If Leonidas were there, he would point out that this was an inappropriate time for humor. And he would be right. She couldn't deal with the idea of Yumi being mauled by pirates. Not just one. *Several*, Alejandro said. How would she survive that? How could Alisa have brought her into this situation where such an atrocity could happen? "Did they take Mica too?"

"No, she was taken earlier, according to your plan."

"My plan?" Alisa gave him a bleak look. Nothing here was a part of her plan. None of this. It was all a mistake. They never should have been out here.

Maybe Leonidas felt guilty for having inadvertently caused this, and that was why he was going to risk getting himself killed to free them and the other prisoners. She only hoped he could arrange for the gates to open soon. She should have gotten more specific details from him. What was the timeline they were working with? Had he meant that he would take Malik down to the station later this day? Later this week?

"She argued engineering with that miner in front of the guard and sounded like she knew what she was talking about." Alejandro spread his hand and shrugged. "I wouldn't know. But when some pirates showed up down here, needing something fixed, she finagled herself onto the team. They took Sparky too. Told him he'd better watch and make sure she didn't sabotage anything, and he agreed. He seemed happy to tattle on her if she *did* do something wrong. But she didn't appear deterred. She wore a very determined look."

Alisa rubbed her neck harder, as if that could help with anything. She wished now that she hadn't come up with that plan. Now, Mica was off who knew where, and Leonidas might arrange for the security failing at any time. How could Alisa lead these miners to her ship when she had to run off and find Yumi and Mica? At least she had an idea as to where Mica would be, but those pirates might have taken poor Yumi anywhere.

"I'm sorry about Ms. Moon," Alejandro said quietly.

Alisa lifted her head. "It's not *your* fault that we're here."

"Perhaps, but I always envisioned myself as…someone capable. I ran an emergency room for several years. I was good at my job, so good that I attracted the notice of influential people. I—That's not important. What I mean is that I always thought that if I had to take care of myself in some less than civilized setting…" He sneered at the old rusty walls of the cell. "I imagined myself being able to handle myself. To be flung aside so easily has been humbling."

"Don't be humble, Doc. Be pissed. And then when you get a chance to pay them back, use it."

"Not entirely injudicious advice, I suppose."

"Given the source?"

"Given the source." He gave her a half-hearted smile, one that faded quickly.

Alisa was tempted to tell him that they needn't give up yet, that if Leonidas acted quickly, there might be time to get Yumi before it was too late, if they could just find her. But she remembered her suspicion that there were cameras monitoring the cells and kept her mouth shut. Instead, she laid a hand on Beck's cheek, hoping it would rouse him. If the gate opened, she did not want to have to figure out a way to carry Beck. Even without his combat armor, he had to be close to two hundred pounds.

She turned the touch into a poke, then a prod. "Tommy? Wake up, will you?"

"Old Earth fairy tales tell of a princess waking a prince with a kiss," Alejandro observed.

"Yeah? What do they say about pilots and security officers?"

"I'm not sure working career men and women were mentioned."

"No? So, you were out of luck if you weren't a prince or a princess?"

"I believe so." Alejandro patted Beck's chest. "He should wake soon. It's been almost a half an hour."

A half hour. Already? Alisa worried that Yumi could have already been raped in that time, especially if the pirates had just dragged her to the nearest empty room.

She pushed herself to her feet. There was nowhere to go, but she paced anyway.

Beck groaned.

"It seems you're the one with the power to rouse him." Alisa grabbed one of the bars, as if she could push them up into the ceiling with her strength. "And you didn't even have to kiss him."

"I have experienced hands."

Beck rolled over, nearly putting his face in Alejandro's lap. "Wassit?"

A comm panel beeped at the end of the corridor. Alisa pressed her face to the bars, glimpsing a guard's sleeve as he answered. She couldn't hear the conversation, but it was short. A moment later, the door opened, and the guard walked outside, leaving the prisoners alone in their cells.

Alisa rubbed the bars. This might be it. She willed them to retract.

But it was the door that opened again, not the gate. She slumped. The guard had probably just gone to the lav.

A slight form scurried into view, glancing over her shoulder several times.

"Yumi," Alisa blurted, shocked. She was alone. "You got away?"

The miners across the way, men who had heretofore ignored the goings on in Alisa's cell, now perked up. A few peered up the corridor, perhaps noticing the missing guard.

"Captain Alisa," Yumi said, spreading her arms, as if they could hug through the bars.

Since they hadn't hugged at all before, Alisa found the gesture a tad odd, but she was so glad to see Yumi again that she would have returned it if she could. Yumi did not even appear hurt. *Her* dress wasn't torn and dotted with bloodstains. Her eyes, however, were dilated and her cheeks had a flush to them. The pirates hadn't drugged her with something, had they? Why would they bother?

"Yumi, it's good to see you. How did you get away from your captors, and is there any chance you can find a button on that control panel over there to let us out?"

Yumi grinned broadly. "I convinced them that sex is far more stimulating when under the influence of rifters. I'm not sure they believed that, but they were intrigued when I promised I could get them some. They just had to take me to my trunk. Which they were happy enough to do. There's an entire room full of things they've stolen from people, did you know?"

Alejandro jumped forward, joining Alisa in gripping the bars. "Did you see my duffel bag?"

"I don't know. I saw lots of bags. I was only looking for my belongings, and they were getting quite grabby, so I had to act quickly. When they saw the various herbs and mushrooms I keep with me, the pirates were quite excited. And overeager. They overdosed themselves. I may have helped them." She grinned again. "I had to help myself, too, or they wouldn't have relaxed enough."

"Did you kill them?" Alisa asked, patting Alejandro on the shoulder. He looked like he wanted to reach through the gate and shake Yumi by the shoulders until she gave him more information on his bag.

"Not at all. I left them having a very exciting time, all within their own heads. Only one of them noticed that I was leaving."

"What did he do?" Alisa glanced toward the door.

"He waved and said to enjoy my trip." Yumi chuckled. "Adolescent humor in grown men. Always a strange thing." She gripped her chin and walked up the corridor to the guard station. "I don't see any buttons. There's nothing up here but a chair and a half-eaten bar of some mysterious and dubious substance. Those words are quite mellifluous, aren't they? Mysterious and dubious."

Alejandro thunked his head against the bars. "I'm relieved she's safe, but this will wear off soon, won't it?"

"You're the medical doctor, aren't you? Don't you know?"

"My clientele rarely came into the hospital because of overdoses on street drugs. I'm not even sure what *rifters* are."

Alisa imagined him presiding over the emergency room of a hospital in a wealthy neighborhood where the presence of the imperial authorities was so strong that a drug dealer wouldn't dare wander the streets.

"They're mushrooms," Yumi called from the guard station. "Most exquisite psychedelic mushrooms." She giggled, and a cabinet or drawer thumped shut.

"Try the control panel, Yumi," Alisa suggested again. Had she even noticed it?

Alejandro sighed.

"She'll find it," Alisa said. "She not only escaped from a group of pirates but also managed to finagle herself a tour of the loot room. All while drugged. I'm going to make that position of science officer official and offer her a job. When she's sober."

"Yes, I'm sure a knowledge of psychedelics will be useful on a long freight-hauling mission."

"I've pressed everything," Yumi said. "Nothing's working."

Alisa peered down the corridor again—Yumi was wandering about near the door. "You're sure?"

She glanced toward the smudge on the wall that she had worried was a camera. Maybe she had been wrong and the cells *weren't* being monitored.

"You can't open the gates from in here unless you have one of the remotes," a miner said. "You—"

The door opened.

"There she is," someone immediately said. "How'd she get out?"

Alisa groaned.

"Hello, pirates," Yumi said cheerfully, spreading her arms, now offering *them* a hug.

There were two of them, and they strode through the doorway, pointing their guns at her.

"Get back, Yumi," Alisa whispered, though it was useless advice. There was only so far she could go before running into a wall.

"I...yes." Yumi frowned at the fearsome faces of the pirates. They didn't look pleased that someone was on the *outside* of the bars. "I'll just go back here."

She scooted back until she was even with Alisa and Alejandro. Alisa gripped the bars, as if she could do something. Beck growled and rose to his feet, joining Alisa on her other side.

"How did you get out, girl?" one of the men asked, advancing.

Yumi backed farther, until there was nowhere for her to go. When the guards drew even with the cell, Alisa was tempted to reach and try to grab one of their guns, but her arms weren't that long. She—

A clang sounded as the gates on all of the doors rolled open.

The guards spun. "What the—"

Beck was the first one out. He bowled into the lead guard, knocking him against a wall with a roar. The second guard aimed at him, but the previously apathetic miners came to life and leaped from their cells. The guard shifted his aim, his gaze jerking from threat to threat.

Alisa kicked the bottom of his hand. His blazer rifle flew out of it and clanged off the ceiling. As she kicked him again, this time in the side of the knee, the weapon hit the ground in front of her cell. The guard tried to spin toward her, but his knee gave out. She snatched up the weapon as he reached for a dagger at his belt. She shot him in the chest.

Beck and the other man were grappling, and Alisa turned the blazer toward them. She needn't have bothered. Beck had gained the advantage, wrapping his hands around the pirate's neck and bashing his head into the floor. He finished the abuse with a palm strike to the nose. The pirate's head clunked against the hard floor, and he did not move again. Beck knelt back, his chest heaving.

"My way seemed easier," Alisa said, waving the blazer when he looked in her direction.

"I'm a tactile fellow. I like to use my hands."

"Is that why you took up grilling?"

"That was because the closest thing to a cook we had on my first ship was the private who handed us our ration bars." Beck stood up, frowning at what was quickly becoming a crowd in the hallway.

There had to be at least forty prisoners. Several were already heading for the door.

"Wait," Alisa called.

"The hells with that," several of them growled, their backs to her.

"I have a ship."

Everyone stopped and turned.

"And I'm a pilot," she added. "I'm getting off this barge, and I plan to take you with me."

They cheered. She bit back a grimace, not sure making noise was the best way to go. Leonidas might have gotten Malik off the ship by now, but there would still be plenty of pirates between here and the landing bay. Even though she had been hanging off a man's shoulder on the way in, that hadn't kept her from noticing what a long walk it was.

"We like that plan," someone said. It was the one who had wanted to see Beck's tits earlier. Lovely.

"Arm yourselves as much as you can. If we run into pirates, we don't want to leave them free to warn others."

Another ragged cheer went up, the miners excited at the idea of being armed, or perhaps about pummeling pirates. They turned and headed out the door. Alisa realized they probably had a better idea on how to get to the landing bay than she did. This had been their mining vessel once, after all.

"Alejandro, Yumi, Beck," Alisa said, waving them over as miners pushed past her. They were going to have to act quickly if they wanted to find Mica *and* find Alejandro's orb before their mob was caught and detained again.

"We going to engineering?" Beck asked, having armed himself with a rifle.

"I need my bag," Alejandro said as they walked after the mob. "Yumi knows where the loot room is."

"I do," Yumi said brightly.

"I don't know if the orb is back with the other loot," Alisa said.

Alejandro looked at her sharply. "How did you—"

"Malik brought it out to question me about it. He thought it was mine."

Alejandro's face closed down, and she had the distinct impression that he was upset that she had seen it. As if having it in Malik's hands wasn't worse than her knowing about it. She didn't even know what it *was*.

"The last I saw of it," she said, "Malik was walking out with it in a box."

Following the mob of prisoners, they came out of a corridor and into a wide four-way intersection with robot ore carts floating past.

"Let's check the loot room first," Alejandro said. "Yumi?"

"It's that way," Yumi said, pointing to the right.

The miners were all going to the left. To the landing bay, presumably.

"I'm looking to get my underwear and deck of nudie cards back as much as the next person," Beck said, "but shouldn't we head to engineering to find Mica first?" He pointed straight ahead—a faded plaque on the wall said that engineering and mining operations lay that way.

Alisa appreciated that he was more worried about her crew than material items, and she almost split them up, but they only had two guns between four people. They might find more weapons in the loot room.

"What about your combat armor?" she asked him.

Beck cursed. "You're right. I could mow down pirates a lot more easily that way."

Especially if they ran into pirates who were in combat armor. It wouldn't take long for them to realize their prisoners had escaped and to gear up.

"Yumi?" Alisa prompted.

"This way." Yumi took the lead, and Alejandro puffed out a relieved breath.

Beck hurried to catch up with Yumi, walking at her side and watching for trouble. Alisa and Alejandro followed, and she glanced back often, certain pirates would catch up with them any second.

Trouble was waiting in the room Yumi led them to, rather than in the corridor behind them. Voices came from behind the door where she stopped, a pockmarked old metal door with a plaque reading *Refining* next to it.

"There were four of them when I left," Yumi whispered.

Her eyes did not seem as dilated now, and some of her effervescence had faded. That meant the pirates should be coming down from their drug highs too.

"We'll take 'em by surprise," Beck said, waving his rifle at the door.

Alisa nodded, stepping up to join him, ready to charge in.

He waved a hand at the door sensor on the side. A red light flashed. The door didn't open.

"Probably need clearance," he grumbled.

Seeing no better option, Alisa knocked on the door with the butt of her purloined blazer.

"Are we still taking them by surprise?" Alejandro asked.

"Absolutely," Alisa said. "Perhaps you can give them a surprise lecture."

A thump came from the other side, followed by curses.

"I'll give them a surprise crack on the head," Beck said.

The door opened with a puff of smoke. Unless mushrooms could be smoked, the thugs had sampled some of Yumi's other wares.

As soon as a man appeared in the haze, Beck leaped inside, firing. Someone cried out. Alisa went in after him, wanting to choose targets more carefully, but a pirate bowled into her in his haste to escape. She stumbled back and stuck her leg out to trip him. He stumbled but didn't fall, grabbing a gun holstered at his waist and twisting toward her.

Alisa shot him in the chest. He fell on his back in the corridor between Yumi and Alejandro, their eyes wide as they gaped down at him.

"Wait," someone blurted. "They're not—"

Gunfire drowned out the rest of his words. Beck moved in a frenzy, shooting and punching and kicking, occasionally stumbling because there was junk all over the floor, bags, boxes, clothes, books, papers, and all manner of personal belongings. Alisa stepped on a hairbrush as she moved farther into the room. She searched for a target, but Beck knocked out the third man as she watched. He spun slowly, his rifle at the ready, making sure nobody rose.

"Good work, Beck," Alisa said.

"Thanks. I would feel slightly prouder about my abilities if they hadn't all been spaced out of their minds."

"I'm sure we can find some sober pirates for you to shoot later."

Alisa felt uncomfortable about killing addled people, even murdering and raping pirates, but leaving them alive to sound an alarm would not have been acceptable, either.

A clang came from somewhere down the corridor.

"Help me drag that one in," Alisa told Alejandro. Her team did not need pirates stumbling across dead cohorts while they searched.

His face paler than usual, Alejandro bent to comply.

"They were smoking my *jashash*," Yumi said, sniffing as she entered the room. "I did *not* offer to share that with them."

"Clearly, they should have come to the brig and asked for your permission before digging in."

"I'd say so. Look at this mess." Yumi clambered up a pile of trunks and bags that was scattered with needles, patches, and hand-rolled cigarettes, along with numerous bags and canisters of dried herbs, mushrooms, and who knew what else.

"It looks like a pharmacy exploded," Alisa said.

"I may struggle to come up with enough product that hasn't been tampered with to pay the other half of my fare," Yumi said, snatching up bags.

"Believe it or not, getting paid isn't my primary concern right now." Alisa spotted her own duffel slumped near the metal legs of a machine and picked her way toward it. She did not have many valuables left, but she at least had a couple of changes of clothes.

Alejandro was digging furiously through another bag, sending undergarments and shirts flying. Alisa found her gun belt and strapped her Etcher on, then tossed her duffel onto her back, keeping both hands free for fighting.

"Yes," Beck said, slapping a hand down on his hover case of armor. "It's here."

"Get dressed," Alisa said. "We need to get to engineering."

"Yes, ma'am."

Alisa itched to get going, but it would take Beck a few minutes to get his gear on. She prayed that the miners would reach the landing bay without being recaptured, especially since Leonidas had specifically asked her to see them out. She felt responsible for them.

"Can I help you search?" she asked Alejandro.

He looked up, a lost expression in his eyes. "It's not here."

"Are you sure?" Alisa looked at the messy piles.

"You said Malik had it? He must have recognized its value and decided to keep it on him." Alejandro surged to his feet. "Or maybe it's in his quarters."

Alisa wanted to tell him that they could not go tramping all over the ship, that they would end up captured that way, but she had given her word that she would help him find it.

"Captain," Alejandro said, touching her forearm. He looked like he wanted to grab it and shake her. "This is more important than you and I or any of this." He waved his arm toward the ship as a whole. "I was given a task. I can't fail."

"Yumi," Alisa said, "help Beck with his armor and keep the door locked. Alejandro and I are going to find the Sublime Commander's quarters."

Beck had been clasping his leg greaves on, but he halted to stare at her. "Wait, you can't go off alone. This will only take me a few minutes. I—"

"When you finish, head to engineering, and find Mica," Alisa said. "We'll meet you there. If you're not there, we'll head to the landing bay."

"Captain, you hired me to—"

"Protect my crew," she said. "That's an order, Beck."

He let out a frustrated huff, but went back to donning his armor.

Yumi joined him and picked up pieces to hand him.

"Alejandro," Alisa said, waving toward the door.

There was no need. He was already charging for it, not bothering to grab his personal belongings.

"Stuff those in your armor case, will you?" Alisa asked Beck as she headed out, knowing the case had hover capabilities and that he could easily bring the doctor's gear along.

"Yes, ma'am," Beck said, his voice hollow as he stuffed his helmet on.

He would be ready soon, and he and Yumi could head to engineering. Alisa just hoped this side errand would not delay her and Alejandro for long. Or get them shot.

As they stepped into the corridor again, an alarm started wailing, and she feared her hopes were in vain.

CHAPTER NINETEEN

None of the plaques at the intersections mentioned crew quarters, nor did Alisa see anything so handy as a map anywhere. With little to go on, she headed back to the break room where she had been questioned, figuring it might be near the personal areas. She and Alejandro had to duck into cabins and hide behind machinery several times to avoid pirates stomping through intersections, some wearing combat armor, some not, but all armed. A siren continued to wail, and she could only assume it had to do with the escapees. She grimaced, imagining a bunch of unarmed and malnourished men and women trying to defend the *Star Nomad* from murdering pirates while they waited for the pilot to show up.

"I think we're close," Alejandro whispered as they headed down one of a dozen narrow door-filled corridors that looked the same.

"How can you know?" Alisa felt like they were going in circles, visiting the same passages over and over.

"Some of them are up here," came an authoritative voice from an intersection ahead.

Alisa cursed and waved at door sensors along the way until one opened. She and Alejandro slipped into a tight lav, a light flickering weakly overhead. Heavy footfalls pounded past in the corridor outside.

"Can you sense it?" Alejandro whispered, a distant look in his eyes. Had he gotten some big whiffs of what those pirates had been smoking?

"The stench of this lav? Absolutely. I don't think these people have ever heard of disinfectant."

Alejandro shook his head. "The map."

"Map? You mean the orb?"

He blinked and focused on her. "The orb. Yes."

Someday, Alisa was going to ask him what exactly that map led to, but for now, she said, "I don't feel anything."

She pressed her ear to the door.

"I do. I've grown attuned to it over the last few weeks."

Alisa almost accused him of spending too much time with Yumi, but she *did* remember that the orb had some kind of presence. An effect on weak minds, as Malik had said.

"I think it's clear," she whispered, not hearing any more footfalls, though it was hard to be certain with the alarm blaring.

"I'll lead," Alejandro said, but she held up her hand and went out first. He didn't have a weapon and had not asked for one. She did not know if he knew how to shoot.

She eased into the corridor, checking both ways and almost jumping. There weren't any pirates, but a hover robot floated toward them. It had four sets of arms, a boxy body, and a head with sensor plates that reflected the overhead lights. Two of its claw-like gripper hands held laser tools for melting ore, and the others grasped cutting tools. She had seen several of the robots working in the smelter area when they had first been brought on board. Her first thought was that it would float past, harmless to people as it went about its job, but it stopped, its head rotating toward them.

"Intruder," it announced from a speaker where a mouth would have been on a person.

Alisa might have ducked back into the lav, but Alejandro had already crept out behind her and was jogging down the corridor in the opposite direction. The robot raised one of its cutting tools, a tiny metal circle with serrated teeth spinning ominously. Sparks leaped from another tool, and an energy bolt streaked out of it. Alisa couldn't leap out of the way quickly enough, and it bit into the sleeve of her jacket, searing flesh beneath the material.

She yelped and scrambled backward as she fired at it, choosing the pirate's blazer rifle that she had grabbed since it would be quieter than her Etcher. An orange bolt slammed into the robot's blocky torso, and it wobbled backward a few feet, but it recovered and started after her again.

Two more similar robots floated around the corner of the nearest intersection and turned in her direction.

Alisa sent a barrage of fire at them, then sprinted after Alejandro. He was disappearing around the corner of another intersection up ahead.

A hum from behind Alisa was her only warning. The hairs on the back of her neck rose, and she dove to the deck, sliding several feet on her belly. She almost felt silly—she was running from smelter robots, after all—but then a huge beam of energy shot over her head, slamming into the wall on the other side of the intersection. It left a smoking crater.

Cursing, Alisa scrambled around the corner on her hands and knees before springing to her feet. Just ahead, Alejandro stood with his back to a door, his hands raised. A long-haired pirate held a pistol to his chest, a knife raised in his other hand.

With adrenaline surging through her veins, Alisa reacted on instinct, firing as the pirate spotted her and shifted his gun in her direction. The man never got a shot off. Her bolt slammed into his forehead, and he toppled back, hands and boots twitching.

Aware of the robots trailing after her, Alisa sprinted for Alejandro, stopping only long enough to grab the pirate's gun.

"We have to run," she said, giving Alejandro a shove. "Here, take this. You need to be armed."

"No. I'm a doctor, not a killer." He turned back to the door, resisting Alisa's attempts to move him down the corridor. "It's in here." He waved at the door sensor, but nothing happened.

"Are you joking? We can't stop here." Alisa flung her hand toward the dead pirate and another toward the intersection as the first robot floated around the corner. Without hesitating, it swung toward them, pointing those tool-filled arms at them.

Alejandro wouldn't move.

Alisa thought about running and trying to lead the robots astray, but what if they simply stopped and shot him? Alejandro was jabbing at buttons on the sensor panel, but nothing happened. Alisa leaned past him and fired at the panel, sending shards of metal spraying.

A hum of electricity ran along her nerves again, and she shouted, "Down."

This time, Alejandro listened, dropping into a low squat. The door opened as the robot hurled a red beam of energy down the hall. At first, it cut over their heads, but the construct's arm lowered, adjusting the aim.

Alejandro dove into the cabin, and Alisa scrambled after him even as she worried that this was a horrible plan. They were going to be trapped, and she had no idea if one could surrender to a robot. Would it simply blast down the door and annihilate anything moving inside?

She glimpsed a second one rounding the corner before making it into the cabin. Despite her tampering, the door slid shut behind them. That was good, but she did not know if she could lock it, not after blasting the panel.

Alejandro helped her to her feet and took the recently acquired pistol from her hand. "On second thought, that does seem useful."

He sprang for an armoire and a chest on one side of the cabin. Besides a bed and a table, they were the only places where someone might have hidden something, unless one counted the empty combat armor case, its crimson sides neither scuffed nor dented. They gleamed as if they had been recently polished. Malik's cabin. Alejandro had guessed right. Amazing.

Alejandro flung open the chest. More worried about the approaching robots than finding the orb, Alisa tried to find the door lock, but the panel on this side of the wall beeped angrily at her, the surface hot from her attack on the other side.

She shot it, blasting the face in some vague hope that she might melt the lock. Not trusting that to happen, she jumped for the armoire. Alejandro had it open and was tearing through clothes, but she rammed her shoulder against it and shoved it in front of the door.

"Let's pretend that will keep out a robot capable of smelting tons of ore." Alisa looked around the cabin for more obstacles she could add to the roadblock or a way out, but there were no other exits in the room. "Suppose hiding under the bed wouldn't fool them."

Alejandro didn't answer. He was too busy flinging clothing out left and right, enough items that Alisa suspected Malik might have taken over the old commander's quarters without moving the original contents out.

Clanks sounded at the door, demanding clanks.

Imagining all three robots and maybe some pirates out there, Alisa headed for the armor case, hoping Malik might have left some weapons behind that were more powerful than her handguns. A snap sounded, and she was almost brained in the head with a shelf that went flying over Alejandro's shoulder.

"I know it's in here," he snarled. "I can feel it."

Alisa's senses crawled, too, as they had in the break room when she'd been looking at the orb, but she did not take the time to debate it. A hiss and a grinding noise came from the door.

"They're cutting their way in," Alisa said. "You might want to finish there quickly, so we can, ah…" She had no idea. Get caught?

Another shelf flew across the cabin, knocking over a display device on the bedside table rotating through holo photos.

Alisa rooted into pockets and sleeves in the sides of the armor case, patting around the indentations built to fit the specific pieces. "Come on, Malik," she whispered. "You're a soldier. You must have some—" Her fingers brushed over some hard lumps in a pouch. "Yes, what's this?"

A screech sounded as metal warped. Stronger light from the corridor flowed in around the armoire. Alisa pulled out two compact canisters. Rust bangs. And not the homemade version Mica had made, but legitimate ordnance from an imperial armory.

"This'll do," she said at the same time as Alejandro jumped back, a familiar box in his hands. He flicked open the lid, and golden light shone out.

"Got it."

"Great. Now get back here, because we're about to be invaded."

Alisa had no sooner finished the words than something slammed into the armoire. It skidded forward a foot, wobbling precariously. Using her teeth, Alisa tugged free the tab that armed one of the rust bangs. She forced herself to hold it, recalling that the imperial ones had a five-second delay. The armoire tipped forward, revealing three robots and at least ten pirates crowding around the doorway.

Alisa threw the rust bang as they started to charge inside. The men's eyes widened, and they stumbled back. One reached out, as if to grab it, but he must have recognized it, because he yanked his hand back and disappeared around the doorjamb. The robots did not sense their impending doom.

"Get down," Alisa barked, shoving Alejandro toward the corner of the room behind the bed.

An explosion boomed, drowning out the warnings and imprecations of the pirates. Alisa and Alejandro tumbled into the corner, throwing their arms over their heads as corrosive ichor flew out in the corridor and also into the cabin.

The photo display toppled off the bedside table, landing on the floor in front of Alisa. She watched it out of the corner of her eye as shouts and cries of pain came from the corridor, and smoke wafted in through the doorway. The pictures continued to cycle, and she had glimpses of burly men in T-shirts lounging around a table and sharing drinks. Leonidas and Malik were both in the picture, glasses raised. The next photograph was a formal one, rows of men lined up in their army dress garb. She spotted Leonidas in that one, too, standing at the top left and wearing a crisp black imperial uniform bedecked with medals and ribbons, his face cool as he gazed at the photographer from beneath a black hat gilded with gold braids and insignia. Even though she knew what he was, what he had been, seeing that made her insides clench with discomfort.

Or maybe that was the damned orb. She and Alejandro were tangled on the floor, and it had ended up pressed against Alisa's shoulders. A strange, numbing power coursed through her. Even through the box, it seemed to vibrate with energy.

"What *is* that thing?" She shifted away from it, half wondering if it was some super weapon despite Alejandro's earlier slip when he had called it a map.

A spatter of corrosive goo dropped off the ceiling and landed on the picture displayer. The case sizzled, smoke wafting up, then hissed and died. The photos disappeared.

"Something very old," Alejandro said, lifting his head and looking warily toward the doorway.

"If I were you, I wouldn't hold it close to my balls, not if you ever want to have kids."

"I already have children—they're grown."

"Ah, then maybe you're safe, so long as your wife no longer expects you to perform husbandly duties."

"We're divorced—she didn't understand my dedication to my work. Or my pathological obsession, as she called it."

Alisa crawled out of the corner, the second rust bang in her hand. "Then by all means, cuddle that orb in your lap. Just don't touch me with it."

It had grown quiet in the corridor, and she risked peeking around the doorjamb—most of the door was gone, a giant hole torn out of the middle. The remains lay in the corridor along with the three robots. They weren't floating anymore. The goo that was designed to eat through combat armor had corroded holes in their carapaces, revealing smoking wiring and gears. The decking also smoked, the acidic substance eating into it too.

Most of the pirates, their skin not as vulnerable as metal in this case, had made it to safety, though a couple lay stunned from the shockwave. She spotted several faces peering in her direction from the intersection. Someone poked a gun around the corner, and she jerked her head back into the cabin. She grabbed her own gun and, using her teeth, armed the second rust bang.

Without risking her head, Alisa hurled it into the corridor, bouncing it off the wall in the hope that it would angle toward the shooters. Blazer rifles squealed and red bolts streaked past the doorway, but the attack was short-lived.

"Move, move," someone shouted.

"Now's our chance," Alisa whispered, waving for Alejandro to join her. He crouched behind her, ready to spring out.

As soon as the corrosive goo stopped flying, she peeked into the corridor. Nobody had a head around the corner now.

"This way," she whispered and clambered out over the fallen armoire, trying not to make any noise. One of the robots twitched feebly, but none of them looked like they would be smelting ore—or intruders—again.

Alisa waited for Alejandro before turning to run. Unfortunately, they could not head back the way they'd come, not if she wanted to avoid angry pirates. At the first intersection, she let Alejandro choose the way. She had lost all sense of direction and hoped they would come to a sign that proclaimed the way to engineering.

The sounds of a firefight came from somewhere ahead of them, perhaps pointing the way better than a sign. It might be something to do with the escaped miners—some of them could have acquired weapons by now—but she did not think they were close to the landing bay yet.

"You know we're running toward trouble, right?" Alejandro asked, his pace slowing. He had lost some of his intensity since recovering the orb. He carried the box tucked under his arm, his fingers curled possessively around it.

Alisa did not slow down, well aware that pursuers were after them. "I hate to tell you this, but on this ship, we *are* the trouble."

"Maybe that's part of our problem."

"Just part?"

She paused before running into an intersection to make sure nobody was coming, robot, human, or otherwise. The way was empty, only the peals of the alarm filling the passage. A plaque pointed the way to engineering. That would have been excellent, except that the sounds of gunfire and ricocheting bullets were coming from that direction. She feared that was Beck, Mica, and Yumi, and that they were at the heart of more trouble.

Alisa picked up the pace. Up ahead, the corridor opened into a larger chamber. A red beam burst past the doorway. A second later, something was hurled from the other direction, a long cylinder, twirling end over end. As Alisa and Alejandro neared the chamber, an explosion ripped through the air.

The decking shuddered under their feet, and Alisa thought of the inadvisability of hurling bombs within a spaceship. Even though this behemoth of a vessel seemed too large to be vulnerable to anything, she knew that was an illusion. A hull breach was a hull breach, no matter what the size of the ship.

At the end of the corridor, Alisa paused to scan the large chamber. A sign said engineering was to the left, but an open space lay in the way. Running out there with people shooting and blowing things up would not be healthy. To her right, she could make out a tangle of mining equipment, towering pumps and holding tanks, some warped and bullet ridden. Smoke hung in the air, and a couple of unmoving men sprawled on the deck. Voices came from her left, familiar voices.

"Now?"

"*Now.*"

Beck, Yumi, Mica, and Sparky, the engineering miner from the other cell, raced out from behind one of several piles of dirt and rock that appeared to have been freshly acquired from an asteroid. They sprinted for the corridor where Alisa and Alejandro waited. She stepped out and started to wave them in, but a pirate rolled out from behind the smoking equipment to fire at them.

Alisa fired first, shooting him in the shoulder. An instant later, Beck's blazer bolt hammered the man in the chest. The pirate flew backward, his weapon falling from his fingers.

Sparky reached the corridor first, nearly crashing into Alejandro. Alisa covered the rest of her comrades as they ran over. Beck fired again, a half second before a blue blazer beam streaked out from behind an equipment stack. It struck him in the side, and he grunted and staggered, but kept running, his armor protecting him. He returned fire as he ran, then threw something from his other hand. Another cylinder—was that a pipe?—flew across the chamber.

People shouted and ran away from the equipment stack. Another explosion poured smoke into the air and launched shrapnel in a thousand directions. Some of it pelted Beck in the back as he ran into the corridor, waving for them to hurry ahead of him. It clanged off his armor and the back of his helmet.

"Good to see you, Captain," he said brightly, ignoring the shrapnel. "I found Mica. She made me *bombs*."

"I saw. She's very useful." Alisa patted Mica on the back.

"I don't suppose there's a ship waiting for my useful backside?" she asked.

"We're heading there now. Anything we need to know about?" Alisa pointed back the way they had come. Beck was jogging backward, guarding their rear.

"That it would be wise to leave sooner rather than later."

"You have a diversion coming?" Alisa asked as they ran toward the nearest intersection.

"This ship is going to have some trouble in about fifteen minutes." Mica glanced at Sparky. "I talked our new friend here into helping instead of reporting that I was arranging a small explosion. Unfortunately, one of the pirates watching over us had a few brain cells and figured out what I was doing. We had an exchange. Beck had good timing in showing up to help."

While continuing to watch behind them, Beck tossed a salute toward her, revealing a scorched armpit from where that bolt had struck him. It didn't seem to bother him.

"Landing bay this way," Alejandro said, pointing at a sign.

For the first time since the day had started, Alisa felt excitement instead of dread and apprehension. Might they actually reach the ship and get out of this?

"Any chance you destroyed the grab beam?" she asked.

Mica shook her head. "The generator isn't in engineering. But I looked at a map, and it's accessible from the landing bay."

"Good, good. Things are going our way." Alisa thumped Mica on the back. "This is excellent."

Mica made a dour face. "Don't get prematurely excited, Captain Optimism."

"Who, me?"

They turned a corner, following another sign pointing the way. Eventually, the cavernous landing bay appeared at the end of their corridor. Alisa listened for sounds of gunfire or miners being captured, but she did not hear anything other than a few bangs and clunks. Only automated equipment being operated, she hoped.

Alisa picked up her pace, taking the lead, but before she reached the entrance, a tiny light flashed on a wall panel to its left. Three quick beeps sounded, and the thick door swung shut with an ominous thump.

"No," she blurted, sprinting forward to stop it.

Had someone on the bridge figured out where their prisoners were going? Were they being tracked right now? Halted just before they could reach their destination?

Alisa peeked through a tiny rectangular window, the surface so scratched she could barely see through it. There was the *Nomad*, right where she had left it, except someone had raised the ramp, and red light throbbed in the bay, reflecting off her hull.

It took her a moment to realize what that light and the closed door signified. Feeling numb, she looked at the panel on the wall.

"Landing bay depressurizing," a computer voice warned. Coming from inside the bay, the sound was muted.

A row of blue lights that ringed the large rectangular exit at the end of the bay flashed, the stars of open space visible through the forcefield. The *Nomad* lifted from the deck, thrusters flaring orange. Alisa banged on the door, as if that would help.

"They're taking my ship," she groaned. "Those ungrateful bastard miners."

"Uh," Mica said. "That's inconvenient timing."

"Inconvenient timing?" Alisa whirled toward her. "When is it *good* timing to steal someone's ship?"

"When there's not a bomb ticking down in engineering that could take out life support and several other systems on the ship one's currently on."

"Might blow up the whole ship with what you did," Sparky said, poking Mica in the shoulder.

Alisa's head thunked back against the wall. "We're screwed, aren't we?"

"Sorry, Captain," Mica said.

"Got some more bad news," Beck said from the back of their little group. "I hear pirates coming."

CHAPTER TWENTY

Alisa spun back toward the door and looked through the window. The *Nomad* was gliding toward the hangar exit, but there were other ships in there, including a couple that the Alliance had used and that she was familiar with. They were not long-range craft, but if she could use one of them to catch up to the *Nomad* before it escaped the asteroid field, and if whoever was piloting her freighter wasn't an asshole, she could connect to the airlock and go aboard. She could not run out there until the landing bay pressurized again and she could open the door, but that should happen as soon as the *Nomad* was gone.

"New plan," Alisa announced.

Beck fired his blazer. Alisa spun in time to see two men leaping back around the corner of the closest intersection.

"Does it involve opening that door?" Beck asked. "Because you may have noticed this is a dead end with nothing to hide behind."

"Eventually," Alisa said. "Keep them off us, please."

"Stay behind me." Beck took a wide stance in the middle of the corridor, using his armored body to provide shelter.

Alisa grimaced. She appreciated the gesture, but even armor would not hold up indefinitely under fire. She thumped on the "open" button on the control panel, even though she knew it would not do anything, that the door would remained locked until there was air and gravity in the landing bay. As she drew her Etcher to help Beck, she looked through the window again, now wishing her ship would fly away more quickly.

As the *Nomad* closed on the exit, another vessel flew into view, angling in from outside. A four-man craft with a bubble top zipped toward the landing bay. It had to bank sharply to avoid the unexpected freighter ambling toward the exit.

Alisa groaned. "Tell me that isn't Malik returning already."

The four-man craft zoomed into the bay, and the flashing lights rimming the exit turned from blue to red.

"Landing bay exit is secured," the computerized voice announced.

"Don't ram my ship into that forcefield, you fools," Alisa grumbled.

But they did, the freighter hitting the invisible barrier with a jolt. The idiotic pilot bumped against it several more times before accepting that he wasn't going to get out.

Beck fired toward the intersection, and Alisa yanked her attention back to the knot of men trying to kill them. Heads and guns popped around the corner, energy bolts spraying the corridor. Yumi squeaked as one nearly grazed her, and she scooted closer to Beck's broad back.

"I knew we weren't going to escape this hell," Mica growled, pulling a blazer pistol from Beck's belt and using him as a shield as she joined in the exchange of fire.

Alisa did not have any optimistic words to counter her pessimism, not this time. She also leaned around Beck, firing at the first head that came into view. Her bullets skipped uselessly off the bulkheads. She was distracted, checking the controls and hoping the door would unlock, and they could escape into the landing bay. At least there would be more hiding places in there.

Another of her bullets ricocheted off the corner, not hurting anyone. Beck was more focused and caught a shooter in the forehead as the man leaned out. The pirate flopped to the floor, one arm extended.

The shooting paused after that. Alisa checked the control panel again. The red light flashed to blue.

"It's unlocking," she blurted.

She peered through the window, hoping they could run out and get to the grab beam generator, hopefully while the pirates in the other ship were busy trying to apprehend their escaped prisoners. Alisa did not want anyone apprehended, but the distraction could be helpful for her team.

"Look out," Beck said, shooting at an object hurtling down the corridor.

A bomb? Cursing, Alisa yanked open the door.

Beck struck the spherical object flying toward them. It exploded in yellowish smoke.

"Hold your breath," he ordered.

"This way," Alisa whispered before obeying him.

She eased through the doorway, an eye on the two ships near the exit. The *Nomad* had settled down—she had no choice. The clear bubble in the top of the second ship was opening.

"This way," Alisa repeated, hustling her people along the wall, hoping the pilot and passengers in the bubbletop craft were too busy glowering at the *Nomad* to notice them.

"How do I lock this?" Beck growled, as he closed the door.

Mica fired at the locking mechanism, melting metal with a stench that made them all step back.

"Guess that works," Beck said.

Alisa led them behind a row of mismatched fighters along the back wall. The parked ships could hide them from view from the rest of the landing bay if they hadn't already been seen. She crouched so she could see under the belly of one of the craft. Crimson boots came into view as someone jumped down from the cockpit of the newly landed ship. She recognized those boots—and the rest of the red combat armor as well.

"Malik is back," she whispered as her people joined her. "And he's armored."

Killing a cyborg would not have been easy under any circumstances, but if he wore his helmet in addition to the rest of the armor, it would take a ship's e-cannon to bring him down. Alisa's gaze drifted to the cockpit of the vessel they were hiding behind. As she had thought, it would only hold two.

"Not big enough," she mumbled.

If she could get her people into a ship, it would be safer for them there. As she had told Leonidas, a ship was her armor. Whether she could start any of them without a positive identity scan was another story. She did know some of the starter codes for Alliance ships...

"How about that one?" Yumi whispered, squatting close to her.

She pointed toward a corner of the landing bay where a six-man Mantis ship crouched like a giant bug. The old combat transports were ugly, but they had armor like a tank and two e-cannons under the cockpit.

"Good choice," Alisa said.

"I like insects," Yumi said.

"Who doesn't?"

Alisa led her group toward the ugly craft, using the other parked vessels for cover. The Mantis had a hatch on the side, but it did not open when she waved her hand at the sensor. She scooted farther along the hull, waving for the others to follow, aware that their feet would be visible if Malik crouched and peered in their direction. She could hear him through his helmet, shouting into his comm and asking what was going on.

Alisa reached a set of rungs built into the hull of the Mantis below the cockpit and climbed up, careful not to poke her head above the translucent bubble. Two pilots could sit inside, and a low hatchway led to the interior of the ship, where four more people could sit. She slid her hand along the back of the bubble, finding the button for it. It might also be locked, but most people went in and out through the side hatch and never opened this. It was possible the pirates did not know about it.

She peeked through the bubble, afraid Malik would hear when it popped open, *if* it opened. He had removed his helmet and run over to the hatch of the *Nomad*. He banged on it with his rifle, ordering the escapees to come out. If they did so, he promised he would spare their lives, only sending them back to the brig for a ride to a slaver's market. What a treat.

Alisa depressed the button, hoping he would not hear the noise over his own yelling, and the bubble popped open with a soft hiss. It was not that loud, but Malik's head swiveled around, his gaze locking onto her.

She leaped into the cockpit and hit the unlock button for the hatch on the side of the craft. "Get in," she barked, even as she knew it would be too late.

Malik dropped his helmet and sprinted toward the Mantis, his legs moving so quickly they blurred. A clank sounded over by the transport he had taken to the research station, and Leonidas jumped out, also in his combat armor. Alisa felt a glimmer of hope, that he might be coming to help her, but Malik was too fast. He was already springing into the air, leaping as high as the cockpit with no need for a ladder.

Familiar with the console, Alisa did not hesitate to hit the button that would close the bubble. It started down, but not quickly enough.

Malik landed on the side of the craft, holding on easily even though there was no ladder on that side, no ledge to support him. He caught the bottom of the bubble as it lowered and shoved it upward. Alisa hit the starter, having a notion of lifting off and flying crazily to buck him off. But it was a delusion. She barely touched the button before his hand landed on her shoulder.

It was like being hit by a tornado. She reached up, trying to push him away or at least deflect the oncoming attack, but he yanked her from the seat before she knew what was happening. Her shoulder thudded against the bottom of the bubble, and then she was flying through the air.

She envisioned smashing into the hull of some ship as she arced across the bay, but all that lay beneath her was empty decking. She twisted, trying to land in such a way that she could roll and absorb some of the force. Her feet struck down first. She did not break anything, but a painful jolt slammed her body, and her momentum carried her into a much faster roll than she could control. She went head over heels at least three times before skidding to a stop at the base of the *Nomad*.

Alisa groaned, every part of her abused body hurting. Why couldn't the people inside of her ship have lowered the ramp so that she could crawl up it to safety? Instead, the craft was locked up like a clam.

Malik jumped down from the cockpit and raced toward her, rage in his dark eyes. Alisa scrambled to her feet, but knew she could not do anything, that he would pin her—or kill her—before she could move.

A blur of red arrowed in from the side. Leonidas.

He slammed into Malik so hard that they flew twenty feet through the air, a jumble of twisting limbs, the men grappling with each other before they struck down. Neither wore his helmet, so they focused on each other's vulnerable heads.

Alisa had no idea which man was superior in a fight, but Leonidas was older. Malik might have the edge of youth.

A part of her wanted to watch, to find a way to help Leonidas, but she had no way of damaging Malik through his combat armor unless she could shoot him in the head. A difficult proposition when he and Leonidas were intertwined, wrestling and changing positions faster than cats in a back alley. Besides, if she got a chance to fire, she would prefer it to be with a real weapon, with something that could take Malik down even if it struck his armor.

Her eyes shifted toward the e-cannons on the front of the Mantis.

"Those might work," she muttered.

Clangs and thuds sounded as the men grappled, occasionally separating for a second to punch or kick or even get off a blazer blast with the weapons built into their armor, and then joining again. It was mesmerizing, their speed amazing, but Alisa made herself run. Giving the combatants a wide berth, she raced toward the Mantis. Her battered body felt like it had been through a blender.

Shots fired from the entrance to the landing bay. The men who had been after them earlier had gotten the door open. They weren't shooting at Alisa—not yet—but blazer bolts streaked toward the Mantis, toward the side near the wall. Beck must have drawn their fire.

Alisa reached the cockpit, coming at it from the side opposite the firefight. She climbed up and found Mica already buckled into the co-pilot's seat.

"Ready to leave, huh?" Alisa slithered over her to reach the pilot's seat.

"The others are in, and Beck is hanging out the airlock door, trying to protect us." Mica pointed over her shoulder to the passenger area, where Yumi and Alejandro were buckling themselves in. Did they expect Alisa to fly them home in this insectoid bucket? They would be lucky to make it out of the asteroid belt in the short-range ship. No, Alisa only intended to escape Malik and find a way to get the *Nomad* back from the people she was supposedly rescuing.

A boom came from outside of the ship as Alisa sealed the cockpit. Beck? Or the pirates attacking him? Either way, smoke flowed in through the side hatchway, making her cough. She started the engine. A light flashed on the control panel, alerting her to the open hatch.

"Beck, get in," Alisa ordered, flicking on the exterior cameras so she could see what was going on beside and behind them. No less than six men leaned out into the landing bay, firing at Beck, half of their shots blasting against the hull of the Mantis. The blows did not harm the thick armor of the transport ship, even with the shields down, but she saw Beck take a blazer bolt to his chest plate, the force knocking him against the hatchway. "Someone grab him," she added, her hand over the button that would close the hatch.

She craned her neck, looking for Leonidas and Malik. They had rolled out into the middle of the landing bay and were on their feet now, trading punches and energy bolts. Blood ran from Leonidas's nose, and he looked like he was favoring one leg. His armor was dented in several spots. Three suns, had Malik's *punches* done that?

Malik had taken some damage, too, and bled from one ear, and his nose was smashed into his face. Alisa could not believe their powerful punches had not broken each other's skulls like star melons dropped from skyscrapers, but she remembered that their bones were as enhanced as the rest of them. They probably knew their heads were vulnerable, too, and were protecting them.

Malik rushed in, his armored fists punching at Leonidas's chest plate in a rapid series of attacks. Leonidas blocked, but was pushed back. The expression of rage on Malik's face made Alisa shudder. Had this attack come as a betrayal to him?

The hatch on the Mantis's passenger compartment clanged shut. The light on the control panel stopped flashing, and Alisa activated the thrusters, taking them into the air.

The red lights were still flashing around the forcefield, denying anyone an exit, so she would only have the limited space of the landing bay for maneuvering. That landing bay was cluttered with several other ships, including the *Nomad*, which took up a quarter of the space, nearly blocking the exit completely. She shook her head. She did not need to exit, not yet. She just needed to stop Malik.

Blazer fire splashed against the clear cockpit bubble. Alisa snarled at a warning that beeped from the control panel and threw up the shields. She needed to deal with the pirates too. Leonidas and Malik were on the ground, grappling again, so she focused on the pirates first. Firing an e-cannon from inside the ship one was on was never a good idea, but she wasn't overly concerned about the mining vessel surviving this encounter.

"I'm trying to find an override for the exit door," Mica said, poking at the controls in front of her.

"We're not going anywhere yet." Alisa rotated them toward the pirates, flipping the switch to charge the cannons.

"We *have* to go. That diversion I set up? We've got less than five minutes until it goes off. We don't want to be onboard when it does."

Alisa clenched her jaw, wishing she had not requested that diversion. They still had to find a way to get onto the *Nomad*.

"We'll go soon, but instead of doing that, comm my ship, will you? Tell them—" Alisa almost said that there would be a serious ass-kicking if they did not open the hatch, but rewards might work better than threats. "Tell them we would appreciate it if they'd let us in before they take off, that we'll take them someplace safe, and that Beck will make them some fancy barbecue on the way."

"They're not going to wait. They're probably doing exactly what I'm doing." Mica waved at the controls and then at the exit. "They're not going to be happy about the idea of being recaptured."

"We'll take care of our enemies, and then they won't have to worry about being recaptured."

Alisa lined up her cannons with the doorway to the interior of the ship. The pirates must have realized what she was doing, because they scurried back into the corridor. She fired anyway. The weapon released with a soft *suck-thump*, a ball of white energy slamming into the bulkhead next to the door. Metal flew everywhere, the walls inside and around the mouth of the corridor warping, smoke flooding the air as some interior circuitry melted and went up in flames. She did not know if she had hit any of the pirates, but they would think twice about coming out that way again.

She rotated the ship, careful not to knock the back end against the wall or to fly too high and bump against the ceiling. Time to figure out how to help Leonidas.

He came into view just as Malik hurled him across the bay. He struck one of the parked ships ten feet above the deck, and Alisa caught her breath, not sure if he'd hit his bare head. Why hadn't these fools agreed to take the time to don their helmets before starting this? She could see Leonidas's on the floor where he must have dropped it when he had charged over to help her.

Malik looked like he would sprint after Leonidas, to continue the attack before Leonidas could recover, but Alisa hit the accelerator on the Mantis. She could not fire without risking hitting the *Nomad*, but maybe she could scare the piss out of him.

As fast as he was, he could not outrun a ship, and when she roared up behind him, he paused, looking back. She kept going, intending to plow right over him if she could. He sprang away, and she thought he would elude her, but the shoulder of the Mantis's bulbous body caught him. It knocked him away, and he spun through the air.

Alisa threw on the brakes and pulled her nose up, the bulky body of the *Nomad* filling her vision.

"Found it," Mica said. "I think I can override the bay door now."

"Well, don't touch it yet," Alisa said, banking, almost skipping off the hull of the *Nomad* as she brought them about. "Leonidas is down there."

"I'm not touching it yet, but you need to hurry. I commed your ship, and nobody answered."

She needed to hurry? She was already doing everything she could. She touched a finger to the cannon controls as she spun back toward the open part of the bay. With the *Nomad* behind her, she could risk a shot now.

But Malik had taken cover behind one of the parked ships. He leaned out and fired at her with a blazer imbedded in the arm of his suit. Between the shields and armor of the *Mantis*, Alisa did not worry about the bolts striking them, but she couldn't get a clear shot with her cannons, not with him wedged between two ships.

She was on the verge of firing anyway, and not worrying about destroying those craft, but she spotted Leonidas ahead and to the side. He had recovered from being flung against a hull and was creeping toward the wall on a route that would let him circle behind Malik.

Leonidas looked toward her as she flew across the bay, and an idea sprang into her mind. She pointed at him, patted the top of her head, and then pointed toward where he had left his helmet on the deck.

"Get ready to press that button," Alisa told Mica, then fired at the ships where Malik hid.

Another burst of fiery white energy blasted across the hangar. It clipped the nose of the ship that Malik had been crouching behind, blowing it off and hurling the ship several feet into the air. With shields, it could have withstood such an attack, but not while it stood empty and unprotected in the bay. She had the satisfaction of glimpsing red armor flying backward as she banked the Mantis, keeping them from crashing into a bulkhead.

An alarm sounded in the bay, the same alarm that had gone off a few minutes earlier.

"Did you press the button?" Alisa glared over at Mica.

She lifted her hands. "It wasn't me."

"Then who?" Alisa demanded as red lights flashed in the bay, warning of decompression and that the exit forcefield would open soon.

"Whoever's piloting your ship, probably."

Alisa glimpsed red armor as one of the cyborgs ran out from behind the parked ships and toward a control pedestal near the door she had partially destroyed. Malik. And she finally had a clear shot at him as he streaked across the bay. But where was Leonidas?

"He's got his helmet on," Mica said, pointing.

Alisa rose up in her seat, believing her but wanting to make sure. Yes, there he was. He finished locking it, and gave them a ready sign.

Alisa dove down, lining up her sights with Malik's back. He arrived at the control pedestal and reached for a button. She did not hesitate to fire. A fiery ball of energy sprang out of her cannon and slammed into his back. She could not tell if he had hit the button or not, but it did not matter. The lights around the exit turned from red to blue, and she felt the pull against her ship as the forcefield dropped, opening the bay to the vacuum of space.

Broken shards of metal flew past the Mantis, bouncing off the cockpit bubble and the hull as Alisa compensated for the pull. To her horror, Leonidas flew past too. He had not been near anything he could grab, and now he was blown out into space. The combat suit should give him air if it hadn't been too damaged in the fight, but there would be nothing to keep him from tumbling into the empty void.

Snarling with frustration, she looked for Malik. If she had not blown him to pieces already, she would do so now.

He was still by the control pedestal, hanging on to it as his legs flew free. She couldn't believe he was still alive after she had landed a direct hit with the cannon. He *must* be close to death. But even as she watched, he lowered one leg, activating the magnetic sole of his boot. Leonidas must have been caught by surprise before he could do the same, or maybe some of the debris had hit him, knocking him free before he fully secured himself. Alisa wished she'd had a chance to warn him about more than the helmet.

"Shoot that bastard," Mica ordered, thumping her fist on the console.

Alisa had exactly that in mind. She soared down, lining up her cannons again. As his second foot came down, he looked back. Almost on top of him, Alisa fired.

The cannon's blast slammed into his face, tearing his head from his body, which flew free from the annihilated pedestal and tumbled toward the exit.

Feeling grim satisfaction, Alisa turned the Mantis in the same direction. If Leonidas had not been hurt, just blown out into space, she could go get him. This ship had an airlock, so he could be brought on board.

But the bay exit was blocked—with *her* ship. No longer trapped, the *Nomad* ambled out into space.

"I thought you commed them," Alisa blurted.

"I did. Apparently, the promise of barbecue wasn't enough to make them stick around. Or maybe they'd rather claim your ship for themselves. That's usually easier if the captain isn't onboard."

"Damn them. We *saved* them."

CHAPTER TWENTY-ONE

As Alisa flew out into space, the *Nomad* flew ahead of them. The freighter had already cleared the mining ship.

"You better hurry if you want to catch them," Mica said. "You know this thing doesn't have much range."

"I know." But Alisa looked toward the small sensor display between them on the control panel. She tapped a button, asking it to look for life-forms outside of the ship.

Wreckage pinged off the back of their hull. Leonidas had to be somewhere out here, too, floating along like the debris. No, there he was, clinging to the hull of the mining ship, not far from the bay door. He had caught one of the crane-like protrusions on the side of the craft.

Mica looked at the sensor panel. "If you go after him, we're not going to catch your ship."

"Comm them again, will you? Tell them to wait."

Alisa turned the Mantis to follow the hull of the mining ship toward Leonidas's position, trying not to wince because the *Nomad* was heading in the other direction. Even if Leonidas had been less than forthright with her from the beginning, and he had gotten them into this mess, she could not contemplate leaving him behind. He had saved her life. More than once.

"What am I bribing them with this time that's going to be more valuable than a Nebula Rambler 880?" Mica asked.

"Given that the ship is nearly seventy years old, it shouldn't take much. You'd think the barbecue alone would have been a fair trade."

"Not if they found out they would be eating a giant bear that tried to kill us."

"Tell them there will be side dishes too," Beck called from the back. "I saw that there was some cabbage and some ready-bread in the kitchen. I can make some galaxy slaw. And don't forget the eggs, assuming the chickens haven't fainted from all of this excitement."

"If they steal my chickens, I'll be most peeved," Yumi said.

"Yes, the chickens were my primary concern too," Alisa said.

Leonidas was pulling himself down the crane and toward the hull, probably intending to crawl along it and back to the landing bay door. That might work if the pirates hadn't gotten in there yet to close everything down, but then he would be stuck there on a ship that—

A flash of orange erupted from the top of the vast mining ship. An explosion? Leonidas must have felt the reverberations through the hull, because he looked up. More smaller explosions followed the first, a chain reaction destroying parts of the ship.

"That was supposed to go off a minute ago," Mica said.

"Given that we've only been out here for about a minute, I'm glad it didn't."

Leonidas looked back as Alisa adjusted the thrusters so that they could come in slowly. His eyes, just visible through the faceplate of his helmet, grew concerned, his features tense. He must have been alarmed to see the ugly Mantis bearing down on him, its cannons pointed at him. Alisa thought they had been through enough that he would trust her not to shoot him, but who knew what went through the minds of career cyborg soldiers?

She nudged the thrusters so the Mantis turned to display the side hatch for him and fiddled with the controls to prepare the airlock chamber. More explosions ripped along the top of the mining craft. They seemed small in comparison to the vastness of the giant ship, but Alisa had no idea what Mica had done and what the final result would be.

Perhaps thinking the same thing, Leonidas pushed off the hull and toward the Mantis. She heard the soft clink of his magnetic boots clamping onto the side. She flicked the outer hatch open as she slowly maneuvered away from the mining craft.

"Make room back there," Alisa said over her shoulder. "You're about to have company." More quietly, she added to Mica, "The whole mining ship isn't going to blow up, is it?"

"It shouldn't. I was just trying to make a distraction, not earn the wrath of whatever corporation originally owned that ship. But I thought that if we could disable it, we might get a reward for reporting its location. It shouldn't be difficult for the original owners to find it."

"Has anyone ever successfully gotten a reward from a corporation?" Alisa asked.

"Am I being overly optimistic?"

"If so, it will be a first." Alisa sighed. "Since we may not have a way back to the core of the system now, I'm hoping it doesn't blow up. We may need you to fix whatever you did so it can take us to a space station."

More clinks sounded as Leonidas moved into the airlock. Alisa closed the outer hatch and ramped up their speed in what was likely a vain hope that the *Nomad* would still be around and they could catch her.

"You didn't mention creating a *fixable* diversion when you originally brought it up," Mica said.

"I was planning on riding home in the *Nomad* then."

Dented crimson armor came into view as Leonidas crouched to look through the low hatchway and into the cockpit. He had already removed his helmet. Alisa wondered if he'd heard them talking about the fact that they were stranded.

"Afternoon," she said over her shoulder, though she had lost all track of the hours and did not know what time of day it was aboard the *Nomad* now. "For a minute there, I thought you were going to think yourself too good to accept a ride with us."

"For a minute there, I thought you were going to shoot me," Leonidas said. His left eye was swollen shut, and blood caked the side of his face.

"Nah, I already got one cyborg today. I didn't feel the need to take out another."

"I saw Malik fly past. Without his head." Despite the fierce fight he and Malik had engaged in, Leonidas's face was far more grim—almost remorseful—than jubilant.

Alisa, remembering the picture of Leonidas's unit in Malik's quarters, wiped the smirk off her own face. She might never have known Malik as anything but an enemy, but that wasn't the case for Leonidas. Maybe he would even come to regret the choice he had made today, to save her in a way that ultimately led to his former colleague's death.

"I'm sorry," Alisa said quietly.

Leonidas's gaze shifted to her face, but Mica spoke before he could say anything—maybe he hadn't intended to say anything anyway.

"Look," Mica blurted, pointing.

They had flown around the blocky body of the mining vessel and out into open space. Alisa might have fallen out of her seat if she hadn't been strapped in. The *Nomad* was floating there, not moving at all. An equipment malfunction? Or were those people waiting for them?

"Mica, the comm. Can you see if they're open to talking to us?"

Before she tried anything, the comm light flashed, and a male voice filled the cockpit. "Mantis ship, this is the Rambler. If your work there is done, you're welcome to latch on and join us."

A tentative giddiness swept over Alisa. Was something finally going their way? She could scarcely believe it.

"We would love to latch onto you, *Nomad*," she said. "Appreciate you stopping to wait."

"The promise of a real dinner instead of ration bars was too good to miss. Most of us haven't had anything but dehydrated takka for months."

"You hear that, Beck?" Alisa asked over her shoulder. "If you can grill up something better than takka, we've got a ship to come home to."

"I would let the mech here chew my leg off with his enhanced teeth before I made something that didn't taste wonderful."

Leonidas's eyebrows twitched, but he did not otherwise comment.

Alisa took the controls and guided them toward the *Nomad*.

"Home," she whispered and was surprised she meant it.

Mica arched her eyebrows. "You might not be thinking that after spending a week packed on it with fifty escaped prisoners. I noticed from working with Sparky that hygiene wasn't encouraged while they were in those cells."

"I'm sure they can bathe along the way."

"There's only one lav. It's going to be a rough week."

"We've just defied impossible odds to escape with our lives, and you're worried about a line when you have to tinkle?"

"I'm pragmatic."

"You're a pessimist."

"Yes." Mica smiled, as if this were a great compliment. "And as a pragmatic pessimist, I'm going to give you a tip: when you're seeking to establish your authority over your crew and your new passengers, don't use words like tinkle. Nobody will take you seriously."

"What if I have a fierce cyborg looming behind my shoulder as I do it?" Alisa wondered what Leonidas would think if she tried to hire him. He hadn't completed his mission, whatever it was, but maybe once he had, he would consider coming back to work security on the *Nomad*. Would that be too lowly a position for a former colonel? If she had him on her team, she would feel a lot safer the next time she had to deal with pirates.

"It depends," Mica said. "While he's looming, will he be laughing at you for using words like tinkle?"

"I really should fire you."

"That would be more of a threat if you were paying me."

Despite her engineer's pessimism, Alisa smiled as the *Nomad's* airlock came into view. Soon, she would be back on her own ship. Soon, she would be home.

EPILOGUE

"You going to try my barbecue, mech?" Beck asked, waving a spatula as Leonidas made his way through the crowded mess room, the single table packed with scruffy miners who were, as Mica had predicted, in need of baths and fresh clothes. Alisa had nearly been overwhelmed by their collective aroma when she had finished piloting them out of the asteroid belt and left NavCom. Fortunately, the scent of roasting meat and spices was proving predominant as Beck's grill heated up. And, to Alisa's surprise, the bear smelled appealing.

Still, it was going to be a long trip to Saranth Three, the space station where Alisa had agreed to drop the miners off. Very few of them wanted anything to do with Perun or the remnants of the empire. Alisa couldn't blame them. Even though Leonidas was the reason they had been freed, they eyed him warily and made room as he passed.

"It's almost ready," Beck added when Leonidas paused. "Sweet spiced ginger marinade. I bet you've never had Octavian bear like this."

"I would be alarmed if he'd had it at all," Alisa said, leaning against the wall to stay out of the way as she watched Beck work his portable grill at the end of the table.

"I've had it before," Leonidas said. "I told you about our training exercises where I encountered them. We didn't have any ration bars, so we had to survive on what we could catch. I remember eating the liver raw and not finding it particularly delicious."

Alisa couldn't keep from wrinkling her nose in disgust. "You shouldn't say such things around women, Leonidas," she said, waving at Yumi, Mica, and a couple of female miners who had found seats at the table.

"Why?"

"You'll never get one of them to kiss you if they're imagining your mouth chomping into raw organs."

"Ah." He did not appear overly concerned. He continued on his path through the mess and into the crew quarters area.

Going back to his reclusive ways, Alisa supposed. He had been scarce since they had left the mining ship, staying in his cabin for the most part. As far as she knew, he had not mentioned to any of the miners that he had been the one to arrange for their cell doors to open in a timely manner. Maybe it was shallow, but Alisa would want credit if she had saved a passel of people. She was pleased that a few of the miners had come up to her after her team had re-boarded the *Nomad* and thanked her for ridding the universe of Malik. Apparently, some of them had been watching that final fight on the view screen while their pilot worked on overriding control for the forcefield.

Alisa moved away from the wall and joined Beck by the grill. "Going to have enough for everyone?"

"Enough for a little taste. I removed a fairly substantial cut of meat from that beast, but I wasn't thinking of feeding fifty at the time."

"Only forty-seven, including us. I took a census. From what I've heard, we didn't leave anyone behind except pirates, and they got what they deserved."

"Yes, they did." Beck grinned at her. "Am I going to get a combat bonus for my help?"

"Bonus? It's not enough that I'm letting you have the honor of cooking for everyone?"

He snorted. "The honor is all yours. You'll see. I've got some slaw and bread to go with this. You'll love it."

"Maybe someone here will taste your brilliance and turn out to have connections back in civilization, know someone who can help you in putting together that sauce line you mentioned."

"Someone here?" Beck perused the scruffy crowd. "Really, Captain, if you don't want to pay me a combat bonus, all you have to do is say so." He slathered some more sauce on his steaks and flipped them.

"You deserve a bonus. I may just have to owe it to you. The cyborg bits I agonized over taking got left behind on the mining ship, and we've got a lot of extra mouths to feed for the next few days, so I'm going to be gliding into Perun on fumes."

"Aw, I understand, Captain. Look, you keep saying you haven't seen me when the White Dragon people come around, and I can wait to get paid until you've finished your business on Perun and found some profitable cargo to run."

Alisa almost pointed out that running cargo was the last thing on her mind right now, but maybe it was time to start thinking about what she would do after she got her daughter. Beck seemed to think he would be working for her even after they reached Perun, and she had been thinking of giving Yumi a job and offering Leonidas one too. Didn't that imply that she intended to go on being captain and finding a way to make a living with this ship? There was no reason why she couldn't bring Jelena into the freight lanes and raise her out here, the way her mother had raised her.

"You're a good man, Beck," Alisa said and patted him on the back.

"And a good chef. Want to go tell the others that dinner is ready? I'd hate for the doctor to miss out. These miners look hungrier than Morakkan Glow Snakes coming out of their ten-year hibernation period."

"That they do. I'll tell them."

"Captain?" Mica asked, making Alisa pause before heading to the crew quarters.

"Yes?"

"I heard you're going to offer Yumi a job." Mica spread her hand toward Yumi who smiled from the other side of the table. "It sounds like she's interested."

"Ah, been talking to Alejandro, have you?" Alisa hadn't made that invitation official yet, since she was still figuring out her own plans for the future. But anyone who could escape from rapists by getting them high had creative initiative, and if Yumi spent time sampling her own wares, she always did it during the night cycle and in the privacy of her quarters. Alisa did not have a problem with that.

"Briefly," Mica said. "He disappeared into his cabin to cuddle with that box of his."

"Yes," Yumi said, "I would be curious to see the contents of that box someday."

"The contents are…unique." Alisa wondered if any of Yumi's interest in staying on had to do with Alejandro's orb. Could she feel its presence from across the ship? If anyone would be in tune with that kind of thing, she would. But Alejandro was getting off at Perun. She was sure of that.

Not that it wouldn't be handy to have a trained surgeon on board. Her hand strayed to the QuickSkin covering the gashes he had treated while she had been piloting them out of the asteroid belt.

"I have no idea what they, or *it* is though," Alisa added, since Yumi was looking at her in inquiry, as if she hoped for an in-depth explanation.

"I sense spiritual power emanating from his cabin," Yumi said.

"Are you sure that's not his body odor? We've all neglected the sanibox the last couple of days."

"You're amusing, Captain."

"I'm glad someone has finally realized that. Yumi, if I can scrounge up some cargo on Perun, I should be able to afford to hire you. Having a science officer might qualify us for more than simple freight hauling." Alisa had heard of live specimens for labs being shipped and needing someone who could oversee their care. That shouldn't be hard for a scientist who already tended chickens.

"Thank you, Captain," Yumi said.

Alisa waved and headed toward the crew quarters to find Alejandro. Surely, his life would be incomplete if he missed out on eating something that had tried to kill the crew.

As she reached the intersection and started around the corner toward the passenger cabins, she halted, spotting Leonidas standing outside the hatchway, talking to Alejandro. He shut his mouth when she appeared. Alejandro leaned out and looked at her. Maybe it was her imagination, but they looked like they'd been caught talking about something illicit. Or at least something that they couldn't speak of openly.

"Just came to let you two know that Grillmaster Beck's food is ready," she said.

"Thank you, Captain," Alejandro said.

Leonidas nodded once.

They looked at her like they expected her to leave so they could resume talking. She turned and headed toward her cabin, as if she needed to grab something. She didn't, but maybe she would catch a couple of snatches of their conversation. Leonidas stepped into Alejandro's cabin, and the hatch shut with a thud.

Alisa frowned down the empty corridor, telling herself that what they chatted about was none of her business. She had come to trust Leonidas, and Alejandro...Well, she didn't *not* trust him. He seemed a decent man. But he was on some mission for someone, something that revolved around that orb, and who knew what he might do in order to succeed? She ought to dump him on Perun and forget she had seen anything, but what if some trouble awaited him there, and what if it came his way before he was off her ship? Shouldn't she know about it ahead of time?

"You're a snoop, and there's no justifying it," she whispered to herself as she headed to NavCom.

Once inside, she shut the hatch, slid into the co-pilot's seat, and flicked one of a handful of intercom switches, one that connected with Alejandro's cabin. She muted her end and leaned close to the speaker, hoping to catch what they were saying. Even with the NavCom hatch shut, the noise from the enthusiastic conversations and occasional claps from the mess made it hard for her to hear.

"I have no experience working with biomechatronics," Alejandro was saying.

"I have his files," Leonidas said. "You could learn."

"Not easily, and if you'll forgive my self-absorption, that's not where my interests lie right now."

"It could be studied on the side. It need not interfere with your mission."

His mission. What mission?

Alisa leaned closer to the speaker, feeling like a dirty eavesdropper, but she couldn't help herself. She was curious, both about the orb and about Leonidas and what he wanted from the galaxy.

"Mastering bioengineering isn't a hobby, my friend," Alejandro said. "You need someone like Dr. Bartosz, someone who has advanced degrees in medicine and also in engineering. And who has experience working with cyborgs."

"Dr. Bartosz is dead," Leonidas said bluntly.

Bartosz, that was the man whose remains had been on the floor in that lab, wasn't it? Leonidas had mentioned him before.

"He's the only one I knew of who had those qualifications," Leonidas added.

"I'm afraid I can't help you in this manner. Even if the tenets of the sun gods didn't proclaim it an abomination to manipulate men so, it's not as if you're dying. I would try if that were the case, but this is…"

"Important to me," Leonidas said.

Alisa could hear the quiet plea in his usually stolid voice, and she winced, feeling guilty once again about eavesdropping. As curious as she was, this wasn't meant for her to hear. She moved her hand toward the switch to turn off the intercom, but froze at Alejandro's next words.

"It's not paramount to the revival of the empire," he said.

Alisa's breath caught. She had been right. That orb had to do with something huge. Something so huge it could reunite the empire and give them the boost they needed to fight the Alliance again? The emperor's fall had been the death knell for the empire, but there were rumors that the ten-year-old prince might not have been in the palace when it was destroyed. Alisa did not know if there was any truth to them, but there was always the possibility that loyalists would rally around the boy if he were found.

"Help me," Leonidas said, "and I'll help you with your quest."

"You won't help me anyway?" Alejandro asked. "To return the empire to power?"

"We'll see. Maybe I'll follow Malik's example and go build a pirate fleet of my own."

"I highly doubt that."

"You don't know me, Doctor. Do not presume."

"Very well, but—"

A knock sounded on the NavCom hatch. Alisa flicked off the switch, spinning to face her visitor. Beck stood outside and held up a platter of food to the circular window in the hatch.

Alisa almost waved him away so she could continue eavesdropping in private, but her stomach whined at the sight of that food. She couldn't remember the last time she had eaten. Besides, that conversation had sounded like it was winding up. She was glad Leonidas had not outright agreed to help the doctor. Whatever Alejandro was up to, it couldn't be good for the Alliance. As a former soldier and a current citizen, she ought to report everything she knew about him and his orb to the government. But that would take a trip to Arkadius, and she wasn't going to plan any more stops until she had Jelena. Maybe later, she could try to find cargo that needed to head in that direction.

Alisa opened the hatch to let Beck in. "They let you leave the grill?"

"Just for a delivery." He strolled in and set the platter on the console. There was food enough for three or four, and she thought he might want to join her, but he lifted a hand in parting. "Got the next round of steaks on. Just wanted to make sure you ate. When I sent you to round up the others, I meant for you to come *back* afterward."

"Thank you, Beck."

Leonidas appeared in the corridor behind Beck, and he jumped. "Damn it, mech. How can someone so big be so stealthy?"

Leonidas's eyes narrowed. Alisa remembered the way Alejandro had implied the gods thought cyborgs were an abomination and wished Beck would stop calling Leonidas a mech. Not that she had been any better a few days ago. But since then, they had been through a lot together.

"Cybernetically enhanced sensors on the soles of my feet," Leonidas said.

"Really?"

"No."

"Oh."

"You want something to eat, Leonidas?" Alisa asked, waving at the platter.

"Hm."

"It's not poisoned, I swear," Beck said. "Since I had the captain in mind when I made that plate. And since poisons are expensive."

"I would detect them anyway," Leonidas said. "I *do* have enhanced taste buds."

"To detect poisons?"

"Yes."

"Huh. Bet you'd win a spice contest."

"A what?" Leonidas looked at Alisa.

She shrugged at him. It sounded like something Yumi might do to her crops or batches or whatever they were called.

"A blind spice tasting," Beck explained. "You have to identify everything by taste alone, and they always have some exotic stuff."

Leonidas regarded him like something sticky one might find on the bottom of one's shoe.

"I'll get back to my grill," Beck said, waving to Alisa and easing past Leonidas while being careful not to touch him.

Alisa wondered what Beck would think if she made that job offer to Leonidas and he accepted it. She had originally only been thinking of her own needs in considering it, but if Leonidas was working for her, he wouldn't go off with Alejandro to help with a quest that might not be good for the Alliance. But would Leonidas be interested in the gig? And how would she pay all of these people if she managed to hire them?

"You're wearing a pensive expression," Leonidas observed, as he reached over to pick up a piece of meat from the platter and gave it a sniff.

"I was contemplating deep thoughts," Alisa said, picking up a piece of meat.

"Not inappropriate humor? Odd."

"Well, we're relaxing over food. Humor wouldn't be inappropriate now, would it?" While she debated on how to raise the subject of employment, or perhaps on how to gauge his interest first, she pointed to the food in his hand. "Are you going to try some? It's not a raw liver, but it's tasty."

He took an experimental bite.

"I haven't had a chance to say it yet," Alisa said, "but I appreciate that you hauled Malik off me and that you were willing to fight him so that we could escape."

"There was never a question."

"That you would choose to save an Alliance pilot and a bunch of scruffy miners over someone you used to command?"

His eyebrows rose, and she remembered that he had never spoken of his command.

"While Alejandro and I were dodging the fire of irate pirates and over-zealous attack robots, I saw some pictures on display in Malik's quarters," Alisa said. "You were all drinking beer in some bar."

"Ah."

"You know," she said, watching as he took another bite, "the stories all say that cyborgs don't need food or drink. Or alcohol." There hadn't been any mentions of colleagues sharing a beer either. Belatedly, it occurred to her that the words might offend him—he wasn't as obviously proud of being super human as Malik had been.

"Yes, we're supposed to get by on engine oil," he said, giving her a dry look. "We're human, Marchenko. Until I was twenty, I was just like you. I played sports, ran around the neighborhood with friends, studied engineering at the university. We're human. Fewer weaknesses perhaps, but all of the failings."

"I'm beginning to see that."

"That I have failings?"

"That you're human."

She expected him to snort, but all he said was a soft, "Good."

"So…engineering at the university, huh? I guess that explains one of Mica's mysteries."

He lifted his eyebrows.

"We were wondering who had been fixing the ship before we got on board," Alisa said. "I expected that we would have to do a lot more repairs before we could get the *Nomad* in the air."

"It was the most promising vessel in the junkyard."

"Were you also going to pilot it if I hadn't shown up?"

"It crossed my mind. I've flown helicopters and air hammers."

"But not spaceships?"

"No, but I was optimistic about my capabilities. And the effectiveness of the autopilot."

"The autopilot doesn't know how to handle pirates," Alisa said. "And it would have beeped incessantly at you if you tried to order it into an asteroid field."

"You're saying I should consider myself lucky that you came along?"

"Oh, that's a given." She grinned at him.

He didn't exactly grin back, but the corners of his mouth *did* twitch slightly.

"Leonidas...do you want a job?"

"A what?"

Perhaps that hadn't been the best segue. "It's like what you were already doing this week, except with payment. You beat up pirates, smugglers, mafia, gangsters, and anyone else who gives my ship the squinty eye, and I'll pay you for it."

He looked into her eyes as if trying to decide if she had been inhaling something from Yumi's trunk. "Will you be paying me with stolen cyborg implants?"

"No, those got left behind unfortunately. I would pay you a legitimate split from carrying cargo and passengers."

Leonidas clasped his hands behind his back and gazed at the starry blackness displayed on the view screen.

"Even though you're the sole reason my ship and my people were attacked again and again this week," Alisa said, "I've come to realize that you're more appealing as an ally than as an enemy."

"Not the sole reason," he said. "I had nothing to do with the White Dragon ship."

"That's true. You're only mostly the sole reason." She spread her palm upward. "Are you interested? I could perhaps be talked into taking you wherever you're heading next for your quest." Alejandro hadn't been willing to help him, but *she* would. Maybe that would make a difference to him.

"I'm heading to Perun next."

"That's perfect, since *I'm* heading to Perun next."

He snorted.

"And after you finish your mission there?" she asked. "You're too young to retire, and clearly if you fly around with us, you'll get lots of opportunities to flex your muscles and shoot things. On account of my mouth."

"Of that I have no doubt."

Alisa raised her eyebrows and smiled. She wouldn't push further, but hoped he would consider it even as she decided it was crazy that she wanted a former commander of the Cyborg Corps to join her crew.

"Do I get to outrank Beck?" Leonidas asked.

Her smile turned into a grin. "Probably. He may get laterally transferred to the position of chef. This bear is amazingly un-disgusting."

"An accolade like that on the side of his sauce bottles will make him a millionaire."

"Alas, I doubt he'll put me in charge of his marketing."

"I'll think about it," Leonidas said.

"Marketing slogans or the job?"

"The job."

That was more than Alisa had expected.

"Good," she said.

THE END

Made in the USA
Charleston, SC
11 November 2016